# THE BIG SNOOZE

*A*

Duffer McDermott

*Mystery*

## CORNELIUS PETER

*Highland Park Press*

*For Sue*

Once in a while, you get shown the light,
In the strangest of places if you look at it right.

—GRATEFUL DEAD

# 1

It was the opening night gala of the annual La Siesta Open golf tournament when the president of the La Siesta Country Club, Don Osborne, dropped dead on the dais during his welcome speech. Just seconds after he stood up in front of a ballroom full of people and raised a glass to deliver his toast, a bullet pierced his heart, silencing his speech forever.

"Is there a doctor in the house?!" a voice cried out.

Twenty-seven club members rushed forward, running the gamut from plastic surgeons to podiatrists, but none was able to save him. Initially, everyone assumed he'd had a stroke or a heart attack. At seventy-one years old, Don Osborne was not exactly in the prime of his life. Healthy enough to play eighteen holes, sure, if he used a golf cart, but natural causes were far from out of the question. However, when the pool of blood began to form on the crisp white linen tablecloth beneath him, it was clear this was no heart attack.

At first there was stunned silence, followed by an anguished cry. "He's been shot!" screamed a female voice from the crowd.

After that, the scene quickly descended into chaos as everyone in the clubhouse scrambled for cover, pushing each other out of the way in a panic. They didn't yet know that one shot was all that was coming, fired from the patio outside the ballroom, leaving a pane of shattered glass from the French doors scattered on the polished wooden floor. The one and only target had been hit. A bullseye, straight through the heart. The clamor and confusion lasted just long enough for the assassin to slip away into the night.

I didn't see it happen. At the time I heard the scream, I was fifty yards away in the sand trap of the eighteenth hole with Don Osborne's beautiful young wife, Kitty, struggling to pull up my pants. I didn't tell that to Chief Garrett, of course, when the police came around asking questions. Being caught half-naked with the wife of the deceased might be a solid alibi, but it was not one I wanted to cop to right away.

Besides, Chief Garrett already hated me. He and I had a long history dating back to my days as a detective in the La Siesta Police Department, and none of it was good. In fact, he was the reason I was no longer on the force. As it turned out, being fired from the police force had been a blessing in disguise, since it freed me up to pursue my lifelong dream of playing golf professionally. Unfortunately, up until now that's meant running the crummy Pitch N' Putt Family Entertainment Center out on the edge of town, while on the weekends I drive around the country from tournament to tournament in my old Crown Vic, playing for peanuts on one of golf's many minor league circuits.

I realize that the odds of a man like me, over forty years old with a slight paunch and a semipermanent hangover, could make it onto the PGA Tour are next to zero. But then, what are the odds of being shot dead at a country club gala? Tonight, Don and I had both beaten the odds. Now he was dead, and, improbable as it sounds, I was set to tee off in the morning, playing in my first ever PGA Tournament.

For me, winning a PGA Tournament was nothing less than a chance to start my life over. It was a chance Don Osborne would never get.

———————————•

By the time I appeared on the patio, straightening myself up and brushing sand from my clothes so it didn't look like I'd just been rolling around in the sand trap, I heard police sirens coming closer up the long driveway leading to the club. As the dark tree-tops lit up with pulsing blue and red lights, I slipped into the club-house, hoping to go unnoticed.

Moments before all hell had broken loose, Kitty had gone around the side of the clubhouse and in through the locker room entrance so we wouldn't be seen together and arouse suspicion that we were having an affair. The plan seemed to work, as Kitty was found twenty minutes later in the bathroom of the women's locker room by a group of "ladies-who-lunch," a passel of wealthy older women who spent most of their days playing mah-jongg on the patio and drinking gin and tonics disguised as seltzer water.

As I entered the clubhouse and took in the chaotic scene, my first instinct was to turn around and get the hell out of there, but I stopped myself, figuring that my best move was to stay put and blend in. After all, if I was in the room when the fatal shot was fired, there was no way I could be a suspect, just the same as all the others. However, if I was seen leaving the country club after the murder, I would have a lot of explaining to do. And then I'd have to explain that I was outside the clubhouse when the shot was fired, in a sand trap no less, with the wife of the victim. I decided to stay put and see how it all played out. I hadn't been invited to the gala, but in light of the circumstances I thought it was better to be found guilty of party-crashing than murder.

I rounded the corner to the grand ballroom, where everyone was still in a state of panic, some cowering on the ground, others huddled under the buffet tables and a scattered few hiding behind the drapes. Tonight, the room was set up for the opening night banquet of the La Siesta Open, with twenty or so tables arranged on the floor for dinner guests, and a raised platform supporting the head table for the PGA bigwigs, country club board members, and its president along the back wall. Nearly everything in the dining room was stiff and white: the tablecloths, the napkins, the waiters' jackets, even the club members. I was the only one standing upright, and I looked over to see Don Osborne's dead body slumped over the dais.

The La Siesta Country Club was a world of wealth and privilege above and beyond what the average paycheck-to-paycheck clock puncher like myself could ever envision in his wildest dreams. Suddenly the word *opulence* seemed to have far too few syllables. The grandeur of the space was overwhelming, the sheer scale slightly disorienting. The room was roughly the size of a small airplane hangar, and stepping into the ballroom felt like stepping inside an enormous wedding cake. Above my head, a vaulted three-story ceiling opened up like the sky, painted a pale blue and trimmed in ornate gold leaves and vines that curled toward the top of the dome, where a crystal chandelier the size of a planet hung over the room like a cloud of diamonds.

The piece de resistance was a mural painted across the length of the far wall, a panoramic view of the La Siesta Country Club golf course featuring detailed depictions of famous golfers throughout history playing its fair links. From Francis Ouimet to Tiger Woods, all the greats were there, playing a type of fantasy tournament, with Jack Nicklaus putting on the eighteenth green and Tom Watson hitting out of the sand trap on seven. I took a few steps closer to get a good look. I couldn't believe what I was seeing, but there, directly behind the dead body of Don Osborne, was a fresh bullet hole in the wall, right through the left eye of Bobby Jones.

*Sacrilege.*

The first thing the La Siesta Police Department did was lock down the clubhouse, nobody in or out, except for the EMTs who could do nothing for Don Osborne besides a fruitless attempt at CPR, which by now was merely for show.

Looking around the club, I quickly realized it was my worst nightmare come true: a locked room full of strangers, a cocktail party I couldn't leave. I decided to do what I usually did in these circumstances and headed for the bar. I'm not really a people person, never have been. I feel more comfortable alone than I do in a crowd. Especially a crowd like this: rich, beautiful, confident people, captains of industry and scions to multigenerational fortunes. I grew up around people like this on Long Island, caddied for them and played against their kids in the local tournaments, and even when I beat the pants off them on the golf course, I never felt like I was truly one of them.

I was different. When the golf was over, they got into a top-of-the-line Mercedes and were driven back to a mansion, while I rode my old Huffy ten-speed home and placed the trophy at the feet of my sleeping father, passed out in his Barcalounger after a sixteen-hour shift in the police department darkroom, golf highlights playing on ESPN with no sound as he slumbered.

I hate people like this, but fuck it, at least the bartender was still here.

---

Dr. Ira Levin was on his third wife and second martini when he buttonholed me at the bar. He was a balding cardiologist with a deep tan and a beautiful wife ten years his junior who was busy flirting with the bartender.

"Aren't you Duffer McDermott?" he inquired, a slight smirk on his face.

"My mother called me Francis," I replied, friendly but matter-of-fact.

"I saw you play the Korn Ferry Tour at La Quinta a few years back. You had a good showing. I think you were still a cop back then, if I'm not mistaken."

"You're not mistaken. I shot a five under par to tie for tenth that year. My best finish to date."

"And are you still solving crimes?"

"I've got my PI license, but I don't use it much. Only when the La Siesta PD screws things up royally."

"Sounds to me like that would keep you pretty busy." We shared a chuckle at that. "So what are you doing when you're not solving crimes?"

"After I left the force a few years back, I decided to focus on making the tour."

He looked at me skeptically over the oil-slicked surface of his martini. "Left the force, or forced out?"

"Technically, I left of my own accord," I said defensively, scanning the room for someone to save me from this interrogation. When it comes to questions, I prefer to be on the other side of the equation.

"And the real reason?"

"Let's just say the chief of police and I don't see eye to eye," I responded vaguely, taking a long pull on my beer.

He looked at me with a knowing twinkle. "I see." A pause, then, with an eye on my beer bottle, he said, "Drink yourself off the force?"

I put my beer down on the bar and squared my shoulders. "You know, that's what everybody thinks. Just because I'm Irish and enjoy a beverage now and again, I must have drank myself off the job. And it's bullshit. That's just a stereotype. It's not true."

"Hey, no offense intended. But if it wasn't that, what was it?"

"Truth is, I golfed my way out of a job."

"*Golfed* your way out of a job? How did you manage that?"

"The chief and I never really got along to begin with, mostly because he hated my golfing. Every time I came back from a weekend tournament and I'd done well, he'd place me on shit duty."

"Jealous?"

"A little, maybe. But I think he just hated the fact that I had something in my life that I cared about more than the force; he couldn't handle it. To him, being king shit in this sleepy little town was the end-all be-all, and he didn't like anyone trying to imagine a life outside La Siesta. Especially a life on the PGA Tour. I think the very idea that I might make something of myself gave the poor sap hives. But he couldn't get rid of me, because I was the best officer on the force and everyone knew it."

"So what happened?"

"What happened was fate stepped in."

"What do you mean?"

"I mean the universe saw my ball heading for the safety of the fairway and stuck a tree in the way. Changed my life forever."

"How's that?"

"I was on the bluffs above the inlet at La Siesta cove—you know where all the boats head out to sea?"

"Out on the point. I know it."

"I like to go up there sometimes with a bucket of balls and just crack a few off into the ocean. It's beautiful. You'll never see a ball fly so far as one you hit from the top of a cliff."

"So? Was that illegal?"

"It was. Littering, to be exact. But that wasn't what got me fired."

"So what got you fired?"

"Hitting Chief Garrett in the eye with one of my drives."

"You hit him in the eye?! How?" he exclaimed, almost choking on his olive.

"He was sailing past on a yacht, I still don't know whose, but it was a big one. Anyway, with my binoculars I spotted him standing on the deck, drinking a glass of champagne and looking like a smug little shit in his blue blazer and captain's hat. I decided now was my chance to take a shot at him, so I teed up a Titleist and let 'er rip."

"Ha! I guess you gotta take your shot when you see it," he said, sipping his drink.

"I never imagined my aim was good enough to hit a moving target from that far away, but I guess I underestimated myself."

"You really hit him?!" he gasped, gin dribbling down his chin.

I nodded. "Nailed him dead in the eye. Shattered his aviator shades and knocked him the hell out."

"Holy shit! What a drive!"

"Tell me about it. Unfortunately, someone on the boat saw me standing up on the bluffs and called the police. When the patrol car pulled up, I was still putting my clubs in the trunk."

"So that's why the ol' bastard only has one good eye?"

"That's why."

"But he claimed he was injured in the line of duty."

"Of course he did. He was far too embarrassed to admit what really happened. He gave me a clear choice: leave the force, or spend the next twenty years writing parking tickets to rich old ladies on Worthmore Ave. So I saw my opportunity to pursue golf full-time, and here I am."

"Well, good luck out there this weekend. You've got some stiff competition."

"So do you," I said, with a glance back at Mrs. Ira Levin, now fully invested in seducing the bartender.

I left him to sort out his marital issues himself while I ventured into the ballroom to get a glimpse of the police proceedings.

———•———

I was heading toward the ballroom when I was relieved to spot my old partner, Lopez, entering the club. *Thank God*, I thought. At least there was one decent cop in the building. Lopez was a good cop and a better friend, and I knew he'd be a good source of useful information. We had been partners for three years, the entire time I was on the force, in fact, after I'd come to La Siesta seeking solace from the chaos of the NYPD, and instead found the chaos of the world's worst-run police department. Lopez was the only one from my old life I stayed in touch with, until now. I caught his eye and summoned him over with a nod.

"Jesus, Duffer, what the hell are you doing here?" he greeted me, scanning the room to make sure nobody saw us talking.

"I came for the free cocktails, what do you think?" I replied with a friendly smile, raising my beer to him in a silent salute.

Lopez paused a moment, cocking his head to one side as if he were thinking.

"Yup. Story checks out. That definitely sounds like you," he said with a chuckle.

We exchanged a quick handshake, mindful not to make our

friendship too obvious, but we were both glad to see each other.

"What's Chief Garrett up to?"

"At the moment, old Elmer Garrett and his merry men are busy questioning everyone in the ballroom, grilling the one group of people who could almost certainly *not* have committed the crime. The shot came from outside."

I let out a knowing sigh. That was how the La Siesta Police Department worked, ass backwards and always missing the point, and that was why I was happy to be an innocent bystander and not in charge of this soon-to-be-fucked-up-beyond-belief investigation. My only hope was that I *remained* an innocent bystander in the eyes of the chief and all his little gaggle of Keystone Cops.

"Anything stand out?" I asked.

"Nothing. Everyone saw the same thing. Don Osborne stood up, was about to start his speech, then—pop—he went down like a puppet with his strings cut. He was shot from outside it appears, from the patio. There's a bullet hole through a pane of glass in one of the French doors. Looks like a sniper took him out."

I stopped dead in my tracks. "A sniper?" I squawked. "You're kidding me."

"Do I look like Dave Chappelle?"

I shook my head in disbelief. "I mean, shit. A sniper?" I said. "Lopez, what the fuck? Am I right?"

"I know. It seems a little crazy. A bullet through the heart is no joke."

"For an old guy like Don Osborne? Seems like overkill."

"Overkill or not, they got the job done."

"But a sniper? That's how you assassinate the president of a small Central American country, not the president of a country club."

"Whoever wanted him dead knew what they were doing. Looks like the killer holed up on that scaffold out on the patio by the first tee. They set it up just the other day for the coverage of the golf tournament this weekend. From there they had a clean shot into the ballroom. They could see everything through the glass doors."

As we entered the ballroom, I looked over and saw what he meant. The entire left wall of the dining room was made of French doors that opened onto a wide stone patio that ran the length of the building. It was there, on the patio just outside the glass doors, that the scaffolding had been set up to serve as head-quarters for the Golf Channel, a roped-off structure surrounded by large boxes of equipment for the television production. It was a perfect sniper's roost, three stories tall with a clear shot of the entire dining room. Tarps and boxes provided plenty of cover.

The first thing that struck me about the killer's choice of hiding place was that it was temporary. It had only been there a day or two, but whoever shot old Don Osborne had taken advantage of its perfect sight line. The scaffold wouldn't be there year-round, only during the tournament, so the killer must have not only known the layout of the club, but been here during the tour-nament on a previous year and seen the tower set up there.

It was a clever plan, I had to admit, and based on the clean kill, a single bullet directly through the heart, the killer picked his spot well. The tower also had one other thing going for it, its loca-tion at the far end of the clubhouse, making it easy for the killer to jump off the side and disappear into the acres of golf course that lay behind it.

*But why a sniper?* The oddness of the method struck me. A sniper is a difficult and messy way to kill a man. Weren't there easier ways to dispose of a seventy-one-year-old than with a bullet to the heart? And why kill him in such a public manner? Killing a man in front of a hundred guests sent some kind of message, but what? And to whom?

"Who would want Don Osborne dead?" I asked Lopez.

"Well, as it turns out, plenty of people. In fact half the people in the room used the same word to describe Don."

"What word was that?"

He checked his notebook. "Asshole."

I looked around the room at the assembled guests. The room that night was filled with the cream of the La Siesta crop, full to the brim with CEOs, CFOs, doctors, dignitaries, professional golfers, and professional hangers on. Everyone was impeccably dressed, the men in black tie and the women in elegant evening gowns. Everyone except me, that is. I looked down at my jeans, t-shirt, and sneakers and cringed.

I scanned the crowd, recognizing a few of the more prominent members of La Siesta society, some from the gossip rags and even a few from my days as a police officer. I'd learned a long time ago that rich doesn't always necessarily mean law-abiding. In fact it's often quite the opposite. You'd be surprised how far a sense of entitlement can drive some people.

"What would you say, there's a hundred-odd people in this room?" I wondered aloud.

"Come on Duffer, don't call these people odd, they're rich enough to be considered 'eccentric.'"

"What about the staff? There must be a hundred waiters, caterers, and valets running around here tonight. Anyone see anything?"

"The only thing we got was a security guard stationed by the locker-room door. Said he saw someone running down the eighteenth fairway, but it was dark and he couldn't see much beyond a running shadow."

"Couldn't he make out anything?"

"All he could see was a ponytail bouncing away."

"A ponytail?"

———•———

I was headed out of the ballroom when the person I'd been trying to avoid all night appeared. I ran straight into Chief Garrett. Or more specifically, he ran into me.

He was feeling his way through the building with his arms outstretched in front of him like Frankenstein's monster, running his hand along the wall wherever he went to guide him. Since I'd cracked off that tee shot from the bluff and blinded his left eye, the chief's depth perception had been blown to hell, and he was now constantly off-balance and befuddled. It was fun to watch, like a baby learning to walk, but the fact that I had done it to him was what made it so personally satisfying.

Police Chief Elmer Garrett looked like he'd been carved out of butter. A soft, slope-shouldered man with a sallow, yellowish complexion and jowls so slack and pendulous it appeared as if they were about to roll down his neck and disappear into his shirt. A short, squat, mean-looking man, he wore a permanent scowl and always smelled vaguely of French fries, a "secret" bag of which he kept in his bottom desk drawer.

Of all the things that bothered me about the chief, top of the list was that he was a tragically unskilled police officer. It takes a certain instinct to be a good cop, an eye for telling details, a nose for bullshit, a gift for pulling the facts out of a reluctant witness or suspect, a task that sometimes required a bit of charm and finesse. Garrett possessed none of these qualities. However, he was highly trained in the art of ass-kissery and had leveraged his wiles in this capacity to rise through the ranks of the La Siesta Police Department until somehow, improbably and unfortunately for us all, he ended up chief.

The only thing Chief Garrett was good at was hiring cops who were better than him, and he somehow managed to gather some really top-notch cops, Lopez for example, or myself for another, so it was La Siesta's good fortune that there was actually some competent law enforcement here. But he was also fond of sycophants and brownnosers like himself, and filled the rest of the ranks with drones who would do his bidding.

He wheeled around and fixed me with his one good eye. He was not happy to see me.

"Oh dear sweet Christmas Christ! What in holy hell are *you* doing here, McDermott?"

"I heard they had a beautiful buffet. Thought I'd come check it out for myself."

"Bullshit, numbnuts. They wouldn't let a loser like you into a place like this if you won the lottery."

"Well, they're going to have to let me into the clubhouse to collect my trophy when I win the La Siesta Open."

His face contorted into a look of surprise, which slowly turned into a smile as a laugh began to vibrate through his thin rubbery lips. "*You*, win the La Siesta Open?! Ha! That's a good one."

"I'm glad you find it so improbable. It'll make it all the sweeter when I win."

"Duffer, don't be an asshat. This tournament is for *professional* golfers! They'd never let you tee off!"

"Well, as much as I hate to contradict you, Chief . . . actually, scratch that, I *love* to contradict you. I *am* playing in this tournament."

He scoffed. "How is that even possible?"

Lopez looked interested now as well. "Yeah, how is that possible?" he asked, not helping me out one wit.

"It's an *open* tournament. That's what open means, open to all. All you have to do to qualify is win the Monday qualifier round, and well—"

"You won the Monday qualifier?! Shit, Duffer, that's awesome, man," said Lopez.

Garrett shot Lopez a look that could bore through a bank vault.

"Thanks, man. And if I win the tournament outright, I automatically get my tour card to play in the PGA next year."

Garrett would have none of it. "Duffer, you'll never be anything but a ball washer at the Pitch N' Putt. I'd bet good money you get nowhere."

At that moment an anguished cry erupted from behind me, and I turned to see Kitty standing in the doorway, her hand covering her mouth and tears streaming down her cheeks. She was looking across the ballroom at the body of her dead husband being hoisted onto a gurney by the paramedics.

"Kitty . . ." I said, without thinking, and when she turned and saw me she ran to me and collapsed in my arms, sobbing.

"Oh, Duffer, no. Please no. Tell me it isn't true."

I held her up, barely able to keep her from collapsing onto the floor, and did my best to soothe her. "Shh, Kitty. It's all right, just let it out."

"It's not all right!" she cried. "It'll never be all right!"

I glanced over at the chief, and the look on his face could have stopped a clock. I realized then that this did not look good. I didn't want the chief to know anything about my relationship with Kitty, and here she was collapsed in my arms. I signaled for Lopez to step in and take her off my hands.

"Officer Lopez is going to help you out, Kitty, okay? He'll take you and get you some water . . ." I said in what I hoped was a sympathetic but professional tone as Lopez scooped her from my arms and escorted her toward the bar.

"What the hell was that, Duffer?" asked the chief, his curiosity clearly piqued.

"That, Chief, was a woman in crisis," I replied. "I was only doing my job."

"Your job? I thought your job was polishing putters at the Pitch N' Putt."

"It is now, thanks to you. What's your point?"

"My point is you two seem to know each other pretty well."

"I've given her a few golf lessons. Is that a crime now?"

"Interesting," he said, tapping his chin as he tried to stimulate thought in the bucket of inanimate gray matter he called a head. "Very interesting."

I could tell he was suspicious, so I tried to get out ahead of it. "Wait a minute, Chief. You don't think I had something to do with this murder?"

"At this point, everyone's a suspect," he replied, noncommittal, but not ruling me out. I couldn't tell if he was simply hedging his bets or getting up his hopes.

"But me? Come on, Chief, I know you don't like me, but I'm no killer."

He pondered the idea for a moment, eyeballing me, and I could tell he liked the idea of putting me away in a dark, damp cell for eternity, but he had no proof, not that that's ever stopped him before. In the chief's rheumy eyes, revenge was just as good a reason as guilt to arrest a man and ruin his life.

"What are you even doing here tonight, Duffer? You don't look dressed for a ball," he said, peering at my rumpled clothes.

"I came to talk to the groundskeeper, Mr. Lo, about the course conditions. He's an old buddy of mine."

"Okay, so you say," he said, fixing me with his one good eye. "And just where were you when the shot was fired?"

*Shit*, I had to think fast. I was with Kitty in the sand trap, but obviously I wasn't going to tell him that.

"Me?" I stalled. "I was down by the greenskeeper hut looking for Mr. Lo."

"So you were on the grounds, but not in the clubhouse."

"That's right."

"And what did you and Mr. Lo talk about?

"Well . . . he wasn't there . . ."

"I see, so you were at the scene of the crime when the shot was fired, but the person you came to see didn't see you."

"I wasn't *at* the scene. I was . . . nearby."

"Right," was all he said.

I took a deep breath. "Well, I guess if you put it that way, it doesn't look so good."

*Shit, how did this get so off track?* I thought. Now I was in a hole. My only hope was to appeal to logic.

"But why would I kill him, Chief? I didn't even know the guy."

The chief thought about this for a moment and clearly couldn't come up with a good explanation. I pressed my case.

"Honestly, Chief, I had absolutely nothing to do with this. I'm just here to play golf."

I could tell he didn't believe me, or didn't want to believe me, but there wasn't much he could do.

"I don't like it, Duffer. I don't like it at all."

"You mean you don't like *me*, Chief. And I get that. But I swear on my father's grave I didn't have anything to do with Don Osborne's death."

He gave me the stink eye one last time. "Don't go anywhere for the next few days."

"Don't worry, Chief. I'll be right here, all weekend, playing golf."

## 2

As I drove back to the Pitch N' Putt, my temporary home after losing my police pension and being evicted from my last apartment for nonpayment of rent, I reviewed the events of the evening in my head to see if any clues would jump out at me. If I was going to be on Chief Garrett's suspect list, I figured I'd better have a list of my own going. Solving a murder was the last thing I wanted to do when I was about to play the biggest golf tournament of my life, but I knew two things: Chief Garret would never solve it himself, and he'd gladly pin it on me if he could.

I knew that I had nothing to do with Don Osborne's murder. Everyone else however, including, I'm sorry to say, Kitty, was a suspect. I didn't want it to be true, but a good cop has to consider all the possibilities. Even the ones that made me uncomfortable. Like Kitty. She was his wife after all, and, statistically speaking, most murders are committed by someone close to the victim. At the time of the murder she may have been close to me, but I still had to consider her a suspect if the chief was going to, and I knew he would.

I hadn't planned on attending the opening night gala. I had not, in fact, been invited to attend. What I'd told the chief was true: I had gone to the club to ask my buddy about the condition of the course. If I was going to have any chance of winning the La Siesta Open, I had to use every bit of information about the course I could get my hands on.

Mr. Lo was an old friend and a man that knew more about grass than Willie Nelson. Originally from Vietnam, he had been an award-winning botanist in his home country, but when he arrived in the states, he was downgraded to mowing the greens and fairways of golf courses. However, unwilling, or perhaps congenitally unable, to do anything in a half-assed manner, Mr. Lo had become such an expert on golf course maintenance, studying climate conditions, soil erosion, and grass phenotypes that it was rumored Jack Nicklaus himself consulted him on every golf course he designed.

Unfortunately for me, it wasn't Mr. Lo I found at the greenskeeper's shack, but Kitty Osborne, shivering in her evening gown as she sucked down the last of a cigarette, out of sight from the prying eyes in the clubhouse.

"You know those things will kill ya," I said, startling her and causing her to choke a bit on her last drag.

"Duffer, Jesus Christ, you almost gave me a heart attack!"

"Hey come on. I asked you not to call me Duffer. You know my real name." I don't mind when people call me Duffer, not too much anyway; I've gotten used to it. But I draw the line when it comes to the woman I'm sleeping with.

She smiled, a flash of white as bright as the strand of pearls around her neck, showing me she was just having a bit of fun. "I'm sorry, would you prefer I call you Mr. Sensitive?" She stubbed out her cigarette under the heel of her Jimmy Choo and turned to me.

"Francis will do just fine," I replied, softening.

The second I saw the mischievous look in her eye, I knew I was caught in her web once again.

"Kiss me, Francis."

"Come on, Kitty, not here," I said, making a feeble attempt to rebuff the advances of a beautiful woman for maybe the first time in my life. "What's gotten into you?"

But she wouldn't take no for an answer.

"You know I can't resist tall, drunk, and handsome."

She leaned in and gave me a deep, passionate kiss. She tasted like tobacco and top-shelf gin, but to me it was a little taste of heaven. Kitty Osborne was the kind of woman every guy dreams about but only a select few have the pleasure of actually experiencing in the flesh.

And what flesh it was.

Kitty Osborne was dangerously sexy. Standing six feet tall in heels, she had a track star's legs that drew your eyes upward to a perfectly toned body, the kind of body you can only achieve with the help of a personal trainer, a private chef, and the Pope putting in a good word for you with God. She had a pert little nose and a mischievous smile that lit up her face, which was framed by jet black hair that shimmered like the ocean on a moonlit night. Her emerald-green eyes were like a magnetic force I could not escape.

Even though she was a married woman and what we had was nothing more than a covert fling, I still had feelings for her. Deep feelings. Kitty was unlike any other woman I'd met in my life, and there'd been more than a few. For one, her preferred mode of transport was a Ducati Panigale, known to motorcycle enthusiasts to be the quickest bike ever built in Bologna, Italy. Getting stuck behind her in traffic as she rode to the club in one of her too-short tennis skirts made any man's day better. She was a phenomenal woman, somehow fundamentally different than the other women I had found myself shacked up with over the years. She was intelligent and funny, but she was also more human than most of the women parading around La Siesta. Kitty had a heart beating beneath her beautiful exterior. In a town full of fake smiles, fake friendships, and fake tits, Kitty Osborne was real.

"What are you doing out here?" she asked when we broke the embrace.

"I was looking for Mr. Lo. What about you? Shouldn't you be inside schmoozing and boozing?"

"Ugh, I can't stand these damn things. More stiffs in there than a morgue."

"Yeah, not exactly my crowd either."

"At least it keeps Don busy enough that I can sneak away and have a smoke," she said, lighting another from her clutch purse.

"Or two."

"Listen, don't give me shit. Not tonight. It's been a long night already, okay?"

"All right, all right, I was just messing around."

She exhaled deeply, a cloud of smoke billowing out over the rolling fairway in front of us. She looked troubled, stressed out even, which was unusual for Kitty, whose day-to-day life was so posh and pampered I couldn't imagine that anything in her world was stress inducing.

"You okay?" I inquired with genuine concern.

"I will be."

I didn't know what that meant, so I gently probed. "Trouble with Don?"

She looked startled by the question. "Why would you say that?"

"Well, the way you kissed me just now doesn't exactly point to marital bliss."

She sighed and exhaled another plume of smoke. "It's nothing I can't handle."

I could tell she wanted me to drop the matter, and I wasn't one to stick my nose in other people's business, other parts of my anatomy, maybe, but not my nose, so I let it drop. As I looked at her profile in the moonlight, my head was flooded with memories of our last night on the beach together, rolling in the dunes as the waves lapped at the shore of La Siesta cove. I could still smell the salt in her hair when she turned to me and flashed that mischievous smile.

"Remember our night at the cove?" she purred.

"You read my mind."

She looked at me, my longing reflected back at me in her green eyes.

"Oh Duffer, I wish I could go back in time and do it all over again."

She fell into my arms, her head against my chest as tears began to dampen my shirt. I realized then that maybe what she was feeling was more than just desire, which made me momentarily ashamed of my excitement, which was now clearly apparent against her thigh. I pulled her to me.

"Hey, hey, come on. Everything's going to be all right."

She looked up at me with tears brimming over her long dark lashes. "Oh, Duffer, I wish that were true. I wish everything could stay the same as it was that night. It was perfect, the moon, the sand, the stars. Just the two of us."

Her face brightened at the memory, and without thinking I leaned down and kissed her. I knew it was a bad idea even as I did it, but the way she kissed me back told me she was glad I did. When we finally broke the embrace, both of us were ravenous for each other.

"I wish we were on the beach," she panted, clutching at my shirt and grinding against me in a way that turned off my brain and left my body completely in charge of all decision making.

"We don't need the beach," I cooed, pulling her toward Mr. Lo's office, but she resisted.

"I know where we can find some sand," she said, grabbing my hand and leading me off into the night.

The next thing I knew we were in the sand trap on the eighteenth hole. When it was over we lay in the sand, cuddling like a couple on the beach, when she reached into her purse and pulled out her phone to check the time.

"Shit!" she exclaimed. "Duffer, I've got to go." She zipped up the side of her dress and scrambled to her feet.

"Just like that, huh? Love me and leave me?"

"I'm going to miss Don's speech," she said, brushing the sand off her dress.

"I'm afraid that makes two of us. My invite got lost in the mail."

"We obviously can't be seen together. I'll go around the patio to the clubhouse."

As she turned to go I stopped her.

"When can I see you again?" I asked, trying not to sound needy.

She gave me a strange look. I couldn't tell if it was pity, or sorrow, or regret. Then she smiled, the slightest little enigmatic curl in the corner of her mouth. "I'm not sure you will," she replied. Then she disappeared into the night, heading toward the lights of the clubhouse.

Moments later, a shot rang out, someone screamed, and Don was dead.

The memory haunted me as I drove home. The timeline was right. I couldn't ignore that. She was at the right place at the right time. She *could* have done it, technically. But could she have, really? Was Kitty a killer? Could she be so cold as to make love to me moments before killing her husband? Was that why she'd taken me to the sand trap in the first place? I had caught her by surprise at the greenskeeper hut, I knew that. What was she doing outside the clubhouse? Just having a cigarette, or something else? Had I spoiled her plans and she had to improvise to get me out of the way?

My head was spinning with possibilities as I pulled into the driveway of the Pitch N' Putt. I didn't want to think that Kitty could do this . . . but, she had the opportunity to do it, between the time she left me in the sand trap and the time Don was shot.

Could it be? I didn't think she had a nervous bone in her beautiful body, but tonight she had been off, a little on edge. Why? What had she been so jumpy about? I honestly believed she couldn't have pulled the trigger. I wanted her to be the first suspect I ruled out, but I just couldn't do it.

Not yet.

# THURSDAY

## 3

The morning of the first day of the La Siesta Open, I woke up just before dawn, rolled off the pile of old rubber mats from the driving range that served as my bed, and landed with a thud on the cold linoleum floor. Almost instantly upon regaining consciousness, I was hit with a barrage of sharp stabbing pains shooting through my neck and back, my muscles screaming as they tried to untwist themselves from the knots that had formed overnight. Nothing unusual for me, just a typical morning for a man who plays golf seven days a week and sleeps in his car when he's too tired to make it to the next stop on the never-ending amateur tour.

I stood and stretched, untying a few of the knots and easing some of the pain. Then, clutching myself against the chill of the morning air, I shuffled across the office that served as my bedroom to make myself a cup of hot coffee. The room was bare of any decoration except for framed photos of my heroes, Ben Hogan and Thomas Magnum, hanging above the water cooler, which I'd converted into a tequila dispenser by replacing the bottle of water with an upturned bottle of Sauza. As a kid I had wanted to be one or the other: a great pro golfer, or Magnum P.I. Of course it hadn't worked out quite so perfectly, but they had inspired me to follow my two passions, professional golf and solving crimes, and for that I will be forever grateful.

After letting my chubby old Labrador retriever, Nicklaus, out for his morning constitutional and stretching some life back into my limbs, I went back inside and climbed through the hatch in the ceiling of my office and out onto the roof with my cup of coffee. I sat on my throne, an old folding metal beach chair, and watched as the sun rose and slowly turned the sky pink, revealing the town of La Siesta laid out below me to the west, stretching from the Pitch N' Putt by the highway all the way to the tip of La Siesta Point.

La Siesta California, a.k.a. The Big Snooze, is a sleepy little town, as its nickname implies. It's a quiet, relaxing, and peaceful island of wealth and privilege. Most of the time, anyway. A tiny, flawless jewel on the coast of Southern California, nestled just off the Pacific Coast Highway between San Diego and Los Angeles, a few miles south of Realito. La Siesta is most often described as "Beverly Hills by the Beach." The town is an oasis of lush, manicured lawns and large stately homes, an island of green separated from the dry, dusty, and brown rest of Southern California by the freeway, a demarcation point as clear as the Mason-Dixon line.

In Southern California, where the heat of the sun beats down like an oven, shade is the ultimate luxury, and you can tell how wealthy a town La Siesta is just by looking at all the trees. The enclaves and gated communities and little alcoves of La Siesta all sit in the cool dark protection of the shade trees that line the twisting suburban streets and provide much-needed privacy for the majestic houses sitting at the end of long winding driveways.

These days, La Siesta has become a tiny, exclusive enclave of the rich, the über rich, and the *Jesus-Christ-how-could-anyone-have-this-much-money* rich. A retirement community for people who retired at age forty, it's the perfect place to settle down after you've taken your company public and abandoned your first family for another, more attractive second family.

La Siesta has more income per capita than Dubai and more plastic surgery per household than Beverly Hills. Unfortunately, it also boasts a murder rate on par with Detroit or Chicago. Not that you'd ever know it from the news. Thanks to the media handlers and teams of lawyers and piles and piles of money, the crime rate in La Siesta didn't make it into the headlines much. But wherever you've got a high concentration of wealth, you're going to get a high concentration of people looking to get their hands on that wealth, even if they have to kill for it. As my dear old dad used to say, the brighter the sunshine, the darker the shadows.

The origin of the town was as unique and exotic as the people who now populated its glittering shores. Formerly an island, it was founded in the early twentieth century by a wealthy industrialist from back east who purchased the orange grove where the town now sits. A man of outsize vision and one not used to hearing the word no, Abe Shepherd decided he didn't like the way Mother Earth had separated this beautiful little island from the coast and took it upon himself to fill in the channel separating the island from the rest of California. This was during the era of the Panama Canal and other impressive earth works, and well, I guess a bridge just wouldn't do.

What remained was a breathtakingly beautiful promontory, a headland jutting far out in the ocean consisting of a tapestry of lush fields and rolling green hills bordered on three sides by the crashing waves of the wild Pacific. The town gets nicer and more expensive the closer to the ocean you get, with the nicest neighborhood of all being the former island itself, now known as Shepherd's Isle. At the heart of Shepherd's Isle is the La Siesta Country Club, and the nicest houses in the nicest neighborhood are all situated around the club itself.

La Siesta is a place so singular that even the weather here is different. In the middle of a heat wave that scorches the rest of California, La Siesta sits placidly out in the Pacific Ocean, caressed by a cool ocean breeze. The sign as you enter from the freeway says it all: LA SIESTA, CALIFORNIA - *A BEAUTIFUL PLACE TO LIVE.* That was true. But for some, it also became a beautiful place to die.

I had already been a cop for ten years with the NYPD when I moved here at age thirty-five, hoping to escape the harsh climate and the endless insanity of New York City, only to find that under the surface, this idyllic paradise was crawling with criminality. The difference here was the crimes committed by the residents of La Siesta tended to be white-collar financial crimes, and therefore go largely unpunished. That is, until someone's greed got the best of them and they did the unthinkable: kill for money.

Then it was my job to make sure they didn't go unpunished. Cooking the books is one thing, but killing your wife, your father, or business partner was not something I was willing to let slide, no matter how much money they tried to stuff into my pocket.

Not that I didn't need the money now. Getting let go from the force had deprived me of my steady income, leaving me to struggle to survive in this toniest of all towns. This was a place where people who rent instead of own their own home were referred to, without irony, as "the homeless."

From my vantage point on the roof of the Pitch N' Putt, I could just see the tip of La Siesta Point, atop which stood Don Osborne's house. La Siesta didn't have a lighthouse, but the Osborne home could easily fit the bill. Perched on the edge of a steep limestone cliff, it was a house built for a captain—not of the sea, in this case, but a captain of industry. A giant Cape Cod–style captain's house, the home was a rambling twenty-room mansion encircled by wide porches on all sides, its gray shingle exterior and whiter-than-white trim was traditional in every way except for its size, which was built on a scale more in line for a population of giants.

On the second story, there was a widow's walk off the master bedroom, a balcony built to stand and stare at the sea, waiting for answers. Kitty was that widow now, but the answers wouldn't come from the sea. I tried to imagine what Kitty was doing in that great big house, suddenly all by herself. I figured she was doing the same thing I was: trying to figure out who killed her husband.

As the president of the La Siesta Country Club and the town's most prominent citizen, Don Osborne had shined a light down on the rest of La Siesta. Now that light had been snuffed out.

I was enjoying the last of my coffee when my gaze drifted downward and I watched as my chances for a pleasant morning flew out the window. An El Camino with patches of primer on the hood and a Canadian flag sticker on its front bumper pulled into the parking lot of the Pitch N' Putt and skidded to a stop on the loose gravel, the sounds of "American Woman" by the Guess Who roaring from the car stereo.

*Shit*, I thought to myself, *I am not prepared to deal with Montreal mobsters today.*

I slid my folding chair back a few inches to conceal myself from view, and, crouching, watched as the Racquette brothers, Gordo and Barrie, emerged from the front cab, the fringe of their mullets rustling in the faint morning breeze. I had been hoping to delay this inevitable meeting until after the La Siesta Open, which would have given me at least the slightest chance of having the money I owed them, but unfortunately for me, it looked like they wanted their payment today.

I made this deduction based on the hockey stick in Barrie's hand. We have a lot to offer here at the Pitch N' Putt: batting cages, driving range, mini golf. But hockey isn't on the menu, so I figured whatever he planned on hitting with that stick, it wasn't a puck. I suppose I had this coming. Well, I suppose I don't *suppose* I had it coming, I did have it coming. In spades. It's what you get when you borrow money from the most crooked pair of Canadians our neighbor to the north has ever been kind enough to send our way. Descended from a long line of Montreal mafia, the Racquette brothers had to flee their native land after they illegally cornered the maple syrup market, not only defrauding the government of taxes and screwing the people of Canada in general, but also cheating their fellow partners in crime out of their fair share.

Now operating stateside in the sunny climate of La Siesta, they ran a very successful and legitimate construction company. It was so successful they didn't even have to dabble in the dark arts of loan sharking and smuggling anymore, but you can't ask a tiger to change its stripes, so they always kept a little side action going.

Today, I was that side action. I knew I never should have gotten into business with them in the first place, but after I was laid off from the force, I was in dire straits financially. I had no income and no credit, and I needed something to generate money while I played on the amateur circuit, and so I decided to buy the Pitch N' Putt. That's when I made my fateful error. I borrowed $80,000 from the Racquette brothers.

Now, here I was hiding on the roof while Barrie, an angry six-foot-six Canuck with bad breath and an insatiable hunger for violence, was beating on my door with a hockey stick.

Gordo leaned into the driver's side window and pounded on the horn.

"Ho there, Duffer!" he yelled. "Come on out and we'll have ourselves a little conversation, eh?!"

"Yeah, Duffer! Come on out, ya dipshit!" Barrie added, for clarity.

Trapped on the roof, I had to think quickly. One escape tactic I'd picked up along the way, more from criminals than from cops, was to use an opponent's weakness against them. I knew the Racquette brothers were hotheads, so I thought maybe if I could get them all riled up I could confuse them and slip away. In retrospect, what I came up with maybe wasn't the greatest plan, but shit, I was stuck on the roof and needed to do something.

I crept to the edge of the roof and yelled down.

*"Celine Dion sucks moose cocks!"*

When Gordo looked up and saw me on the roof I thought his head might explode.

*"You take that back you son of a bitch!"* he screamed. He ran to the office door, where Barrie had already begun beating in the glass front with his hockey stick, cursing and drooling with a thirst for revenge.

While they were occupied with my front door, I ran to the other side of the roof and jumped off the rear of the building, landing on the netting that surrounds the batting cages. I began crawling madly across the nets, heading for the back wall, but soon found the heavy netting much harder to navigate than I imagined.

*Shit.*

I was only halfway through my scramble across the netting, fumbling and stumbling, when the Racquette brothers emerged through the trapdoor in the roof, Gordo's head sticking up first, followed by Barrie. I scrambled as hard as I could and made it to the far side of the batting cage. I had just flipped myself over so that I was hanging from the underside when I looked down and saw the back door was wide open. I hung there by my fingers for a moment before reaching the depressing conclusion that I had nowhere to go, and my gambit had succeeded only in pissing the Racquettes off even further.

Barrie emerged from the back door of the office just as my fingers lost their remaining strength and I landed on the dirt floor of the batting cage with a thud. Before I could get up and make a run for it, Barrie was dragging me back toward the building as I struggled and kicked to break free. I was expecting him to drag me into the office so they could kick my ass in private, but to my dismay, Barrie stood me up at the back of the batting cage while Gordo bound my arms and legs with rope and tied me to the fence.

"Guys, guys, calm down! I was only joking! Celine is a gift. A beautiful songbird of the North. Please, whatever you're planning to do, it isn't necessary. Please, I'll get you your money!"

Begging for my life is not my best look, but I was desperate. I had a golf tournament to play, and I couldn't do it in a body cast. I was still struggling to wriggle free, bound to the fence like a condemned man in front of a firing squad, when I realized what they meant to do.

Gordo walked to the back of the cage and wheeled out the automatic pitching machine. He adjusted the canon-like barrel of the machine and aimed it at my head.

"Ho there, Barrie," he yelled over to his brother, "get me some quarters, eh?"

"Come on, guys, there's no need to do this, please, be reasonable," I pleaded, trying my best not to whimper.

"A reasonable man pays his debts, Duffer. If you were reasonable yourself you wouldn't be in this position," Gordo replied, keeping his composure.

"But I'm *going to pay you!*"

"Oh yeah, when?!" screamed Barrie. "We haven't seen one loony out of you, eh!"

Barrie had his face pressed up against mine. His hot breath, now directly under my nose, smelled like poutine and Molson Golden. I turned my head to avoid death by asphyxiation.

"Shouldn't you be fishing for quarters in the front seat of the El Camino?" I said, unable to contain the wiseass inside me. Barrie cocked his fist back and was a nanosecond from knocking my teeth out when Gordo called out.

"Never mind the quarters! I found the switch!"

Suddenly, a baseball shot out of the barrel of the machine.

*WHOOOOOOOOSH!*

A ninety-mile-an-hour fastball slammed into the fence half an inch from my head.

*CRASH!*

The impact from the ball on the fence behind my head sent shock waves through the entire cage. I swallowed hard and braced for what was coming next. At least the impact momentarily saved me from Barrie, who jumped out of the way.

"What the fuck, eh?!" cried Barrie, yelling at his brother. "Watch where you're aiming that thing!"

But Gordo was having fun now. With Barrie out of the way, he adjusted the machine and shot another ball at my head, this time just missing on the other side.

*WHOOOOOOOOOSH! CRASH!*

"Gordo! Please!" I begged, but he wasn't interested. He aimed the barrel at my torso and shot a third ball directly into my right shoulder. The pain from the impact exploded across my chest and down my arm, radiating outward like a shock wave. The air shot out of my lungs, and I would have doubled over if not for the ropes that held me up. By the time I caught my breath and my eyes uncrossed I could see them both at the pitching machine, big smiles on their faces.

"I'll get you your money," I spat. "I've got a plan!"

"Plan? What plan is this, now, eh?" Barrie giggled as he shot another baseball in my direction, this one mercifully bouncing off the fence. I could tell they were toying with me.

"The La Siesta Open," I blurted. "I'm going to win it."

They paused for a moment and looked at each other, then burst out laughing.

"*Golf?* That's your plan to pay us back?" Barrie scoffed, then aimed the barrel of the canon at my crotch.

"Wait! There's a half-million-dollar purse!"

But then Gordo stopped him.

"Say, isn't that the tournament at the La Siesta Country Club?" said Gordo, a sneer suddenly crossing his face at the mention of the place.

"Fuck that place, eh! Bunch a snobs is what they are," Barrie chimed in.

"Sure are. Wouldn't let me and Barrie join their fancy-pants establishment. Didn't think we were classy enough, I guess," moaned Gordo, clearly stung by the rejection.

"We're fuckin' classy as all fuck!" shouted Barrie. He grabbed hold of the pitching machine from his brother and shot another baseball in my direction, this one glancing off my left thigh before ricocheting into a pile of discarded baseball bats.

"Those stuck-up American so-and-sos don't know shit about us," cried Gordo.

"Well, they just don't know you like I do, Gordo," I stammered, as another baseball crashed into the cage behind me. "You and Barrie are fine and decent members of society. They don't know what they're missing."

"Fuckin'-a, right," said Barrie. "And that Don Osborne was a fuckin' asshole, eh?"

"Asshole!" said Gordo, sending a baseball at my head, which I barely ducked.

"That old pile of bones has stood in the way of every single real-estate deal we've ever tried to make in this posh piece-of-shit town."

"Every time!" yelled Gordo, punctuating his anger with another baseball shot at my head.

I dodged the ball as I tried to keep the conversation going. At least we weren't talking about the money I owed them anymore.

"You guys are in real estate? I didn't know that," I said, sounding about as casual as a man tied to a fence can manage.

"Hell yes, we're in real estate! We've been buying all sorts of classy shit. Car washes, strip joints, cannabis dispensaries, but thanks to that wrinkled old nut sack, we don't own jack shit in La Siesta."

"Wrinkled old nut sack," said Gordo, and then, surprisingly, he followed with, "I'm glad the old bastard's dead."

I straightened up.

"What did you say?" I asked, forgetting momentarily about the baseballs.

There was a moment of silence. Gordo and Barrie exchanged a look.

"I said I'm glad he's dead," said Gordo, a bit defensively.

"How did you know he was dead?"

"What?" said Barrie, suddenly seeming nervous.

"How did you know he was dead? The death hasn't even been reported in the news this morning."

"Come on, Duffer. This is a small town. Word travels fast."

"Not that fast. Where did you hear it?"

"Hey, who's asking the questions here?!" yelled Gordo. He shot another baseball into the cage behind me.

"We have our sources, Duffer," added Barrie. "You don't need to worry about us."

"I don't have to worry about the two guys who are shooting fastballs at my head?"

"Not if you pay us what you owe us."

"Well, if you want me to do that, you have to untie me and let me play in the La Siesta Open. It's the only way you'll get your money."

# 4

I pulled into the entrance of the La Siesta Country Club early, the morning dew still wet on the grass, and drove my Crown Vic slowly up the long, arcing driveway, taking in the beauty of the grounds. Lined with evenly spaced palms so tall you could barely see their tops, the drive led me past my first glimpse of the course itself off to my left, a luxurious blanket of green rolling toward the ocean on the horizon. On my right was a pond with a dancing fountain in its center. The jets of water formed elaborate geometric patterns on the surface, and the early morning sun created patches of rainbow in the fine mist surrounding it.

From the view at the bottom of the driveway, the clubhouse appeared fairly small and unassuming, but as you got closer you realized the long driveway played a trick on your eyes and the clubhouse was actually gigantic and assuming as hell.

The original clubhouse, a tiny little shack staffed by a lone groundskeeper who used a herd of sheep to tend the grass on the fairways, had been replaced with an enormous building the size of an ocean liner. Framed against the horizon in front of the end-less blue Pacific, it looked as if it could sail off at any moment, adding a new continent to the map in the process.

Built in the Spanish colonial style common in this part of the west, the club's main building was a traditional hacienda, but on an epic scale: a long low building painted a pale bone white, outlined with a deep red trim that gave shape to its ghostly form. It was a construction bold enough and grand enough, to stand up to the natural beauty of the plot of land upon which it was built. God may have given us the land, but Don Osborne gave us the La Siesta Country Club.

After Don had purchased the foundering club in the seventies, he brought in Paul Williams, a legendary Southern California architect, then in his seventies, to design a clubhouse on par with the great clubs like Augusta National, Shinnecock Hills in South-ampton, or the Lodge at Torrey Pines. The result was the kind of building regularly featured in architecture and design magazines, and held up as an example of what could be achieved when infi-nite resources met refined taste.

The clubhouse was shaped like a horseshoe, with the bottom of the "u" forming the wide facade at the top of the driveway, with a wing on either side extending out the rear toward the rest of the property. The simplicity of the club's grand facade was designed to accentuate the forms of the cars and people paraded in front of it. The main front doors were as tall as two men, guarded on either side by slim sculpted Italian Cypress trees in cube-shaped lattice planter boxes.

But a country club can't be great without a great golf course to match, so Don Osborne had spared no expense in hiring one of the greatest golf courses designers, not to mention perhaps the greatest professional golfer of all time, the "Golden Bear" himself, Jack Nicklaus, whose brand-new course at Muirfield Village in Ohio was being hailed as a masterpiece. Rumor had it Jack couldn't stand old Don Osborne and banned him from his office for being too demanding, but Don insisted on having not just a beautiful eighteen holes, but the most diabolically difficult eighteen holes he could come up with. Nicklaus didn't like it, but he did his job, crafting an old-fashioned links course that utilized the natural peaks and valleys of the rugged shoreline to challenge the golfers, while stopping just short of making it so difficult they'd want to leap into the ocean from the cliffs above.

Entering the grounds of the La Siesta Country Club felt like being transported to another universe. A universe of private jets, domestic help, and endless leisure time. A universe of beautiful people on permanent vacation. A universe of crisp white tablecloths, green fairways, and red Bloody Marys. A Shangri-la so exclusive that even movie stars and heads of state couldn't buy their way in, the membership strictly capped at 1,500 of La Siesta's best and brightest. Or maybe just its most ruthless.

On the left as you approach, still several hundred yards from the entrance, is a restored post-and-beam building that a century ago was a stable for horses and was now utilized as a garage for high-end automobiles, the hitching post replaced with a busy valet stand. A team of uniformed valets scurried around like worker ants, opening car doors and hauling heavy bags of clubs from the trunks of luxury vehicles that cost the price of a modest home in the Midwest.

Just then, a Rolls Royce rolled up the driveway in a color palate straight off a desert cart, its paint job a two-tone confection of latte-foam tan sitting on top of a rich chocolate-pudding brown. The Rolls Royce is a car built to seduce your eyes, the luscious lines of the handcrafted body rolling like the curves of a signature on the bottom of a big fat check.

Out stepped Kitty Osborne, her little black cocktail dress from the night before replaced with an equally little white tennis dress. Her tan athletic thighs and toned calves drew surreptitious glances from a few of the valets as she effortlessly glided toward the front door, her tennis racket slung over her shoulder and the tiny pom-poms on her ankle socks bouncing along with her perky black ponytail. She was the picture of innocence. And that's exactly what had me worried.

*What is she doing here?* I thought. *And why so early?*

•———————————•

When I arrived at the driving range, there was only one other person there: my caddie, far down at the end of the practice tees. He was sitting cross-legged on the ground in tie-dyed coveralls, meditating under a mulberry tree, his long shaggy gray hair matching the length of his wizard-like white beard. From where I stood, he was merely the hazy outline of a man, utterly still, a part of the landscape. As I drew closer, the man who came into focus looked like the very picture of inner peace, an ethereal aura of calm surrounding him. He was unlike any other man I'd ever met: an enigma, wrapped in a riddle, rolled in a big fat joint. I didn't even know his real name; I only knew him by his nickname, Grateful Ted.

Tall and rangy, he looked like one of those mystics who lived in the wilderness wearing a loincloth and searching for enlightenment. The reality of Grateful Ted's life wasn't far removed, I imagined, except that I had no idea where he lived, and he spent at least as much time searching for my ball in the weeds as he did searching for enlightenment. But the truth is I really knew very little about him, except that he was, hands down, the best caddie I'd ever had. More mystical than statistical, Grateful Ted had proved himself to be a guru of golf, a swami of the swing, a wizard with woods and irons.

I've known Grateful Ted since I picked him up for vagrancy my third day on the La Siesta Police Force. He wasn't really a vagrant, at least he wouldn't have been considered a vagrant quite so quickly in most other towns, but in La Siesta, he had been spotted wandering around Worthmore Avenue for *several hours*, and was therefore to be run out of town immediately. I didn't take kindly to the job, which I thought frankly ridiculous since he appeared to be just a stoned old hippie who wasn't harming anyone, but I accepted the assignment because, as I said, it was my third day on the job and I didn't feel the need to make waves just yet.

When I stopped him, he was ambling down Worthmore Avenue wearing the same pair of tie-dyed coveralls he wore today, and a large cone-shaped straw hat, like the kind you see rice farmers in Southeast Asia wearing to protect themselves from the glaring sun. I approached from behind, pulled up to the curb next to him, and got out slowly so as not to spook him.

"Morning, partner. Got some ID on you?" I inquired politely, and he seemed cooperative enough, stopping as if to chat with an old friend.

"No, sir. I don't believe in government documents," he replied, looking up at me with a quirky smile as if that was a perfectly reasonable answer.

"Sir, I'm afraid I'm going to have to ask you to come with me," I said, gently leading him by the elbow toward where my squad car sat idling at the curb. I was about to put him in the back of the cruiser and escort him out of town when I decided to give him one more chance.

"Okay, let's try this again," I said, stopping just short of putting him in the back seat. "What's your name?"

"They call me Grateful Ted," he said proudly.

"Why do they call you that?"

"I suppose it's because I have an encyclopedic knowledge of the Grateful Dead. I can recite from memory the set list from any concert the Grateful Dead ever played."

*Bullshit*, I thought. My older brother had been a Deadhead growing up, and I knew from him that the band played thousands of concerts over the years, and what made them special was that every concert had a different set list, different songs in a different order, every night. There was no way anyone could have all those set lists stored in their brain. It was impossible, but I had to see.

"Can you really do that?" I asked, looking at him with a slight tilt of my head that made my skepticism apparent.

"Name a date," he said, cool as you please.

"Just like that? Name a date?" I asked, amused by this curious old hippie standing in front of me, seemingly unfazed by the prospect of being placed in the back of a police cruiser.

"Name a date and I'll tell you what they played, in the order they played it."

"You're saying you can name all the songs, in order, of any date I pick?"

"Sure can. As long as there was a show that night. And there were a lot of shows, man. I'll bet you twenty bucks," he said, a glint in his eye.

"Bet me?!" I laughed. This guy really was crazy. "You do realize I'm a cop, right?"

"Come on, man, I know you're curious. I can see it in your eyes."

I couldn't believe the audacity of this guy, but I was beginning to like him. And he was right, I *was* curious.

"All right, you're on, but how will I know if you're right? I mean, you could be just bullshitting me."

"Pull out your smart phone and go to setlist.fm. They have them all listed right there. You can pick any show you want."

I pulled up the website, and sure enough, there it was, the set list for every show The Grateful Dead ever played. *All right, fine. Let's see*, I thought. I chose my deadhead older brother's birthday.

"Okay, here we go. How about, April 17th, 1971?"

Grateful Ted's eyes lit up.

"Oh, that was a good one!" He beamed, enthusiasm filling his voice. "A classic Pigpen show from Princeton, New Jersey."

"Pigpen?" I asked, confused. "Like in Peanuts?"

"No, not like Peanuts, man. Pigpen was *in the band*, he was a singer, a true blues man, some say he was the heart of the band in the early days. Sadly, he's no longer with us. But that show, that show will live forever."

Then, as easily as if he was reciting a poem he had learned by heart, he began listing the songs one after the other.

"They opened with what was then still a new tune, the soon-to-be classic, 'Truckin',' before launching into the old Tommy Johnson blues staple, 'Big Railroad Blues.'"

And from there he proceeded to list all nineteen songs, in perfect order, not missing a single one. I stared at the list on my phone in amazement as he barreled his way from the opening tune to the encore. For some reason, I found the experience of watching him recite the set list soothing, like a piece of performance art that freed my brain from focusing on the daily bullshit I was going through as a cop in a new town on a new beat. It was mesmerizing.

". . . ending the first set with a beautiful rendition of 'Sugar Magnolia.'"

I wasn't really tuning in to the names of the songs so much as just watching him go, his brain like a spinning top skittering across a flat surface. Part of me couldn't believe he was really doing it, and part of me found a certain kind of peace just listening to his voice.

"Set two started with another cover, the Young Rascals' 'Good Lovin','" he continued, his enthusiasm rising as the set list rushed out of him. It seemed almost as if he was there at the show, right then, in the audience living the concert as he told me about it.

". . . which really showed Pigpen in fine form and had a killer six-minute drum solo in the middle, before Bobby Weir took over vocal duties for 'Me and Bobby McGee,' a song made famous by Janis Joplin, who was rumored to be Pigpen's girlfriend at the time. . ."

It was unbelievable. He was like some sort of Deadhead Rain Man. He just kept rambling on, barely stopping for breath as the second set came to a climax.

". . . before ending with an *epic* twenty-minute 'Turn On Your Love Light' that featured one of the classic Pigpen raps of all time!" he finally concluded, breathless but exhilarated. It was as if just talking about the music had filled his fragile frame with life.

"Wow, that's incredible," I said. "You didn't miss a song. Were you there?"

The light in his eyes suddenly dimmed.

"No, unfortunately I wasn't around in 1971," he replied, his voice trailing off.

"Still, that's one hell of a parlor trick. You could win bar bets galore with that talent."

I handed over a crisp twenty-dollar bill, making sure nobody saw me handing money to a vagrant, which doubtless wouldn't look too good for a new cop. I was duly impressed, but he seemed to deflate after it was all over, losing some of his inner sparkle.

"Oh, it's nothing. It's really all I have . . ."

I felt bad for him now. I looked into his eyes the man I saw was more than just a filthy vagrant, and he certainly wasn't a dangerous man, but a sad old man with an emptiness in him. I opened the back door of my cruiser and gently placed my hand on his head, guiding him into the back seat.

Once I settled in behind the wheel and we were heading out of town I resumed our conversation. After witnessing his impressive talent, I wanted to know more about him.

"So what brings you to La Siesta?" I asked, his eyes meeting mine in the rear view mirror.

"I came to find the country club," he muttered, scratching at his unruly mop of matted gray hair.

"Oh, yeah?" I chuckled. "Thinking of joining?"

The thought of this crusty old hippie showing up at the gates of the La Siesta Country Club just about made my day, but he surprised me with what he said next.

"I'm a caddie."

"A caddie?" I asked, caught off guard. "Really? You know golf?"

"I've been a looper all my life," he said, as if resigned to a cruel fate.

I looked at him in the rearview mirror and somehow it actually made sense. The deep tan, the coveralls, the thousand-yard stare, the mystical air about him. I'd heard stories as a kid about otherworldly caddies, these quasi-magical creatures like Bagger Vance who show up at just the right time to guide a player to victory, like a golf guardian angel. I'd dismissed these at the time as complete hogwash, but that was before I'd played golf for thirty years, and the experience of playing, and losing, for that long, made me ready to believe anything. I thought, *If this guy is my golf guardian angel and I drop him off on the side of the highway, I'll kick myself for the rest of my life.*

So instead of running him out of town as ordered, I took him to the public course at the edge of town and got him a job as a caddie.

As it turned out, he was an ace. Maybe it was some perfect combination of magic mushroom trips and time spent baking in the sun, or possibly he'd just had one too many blows to the head, but Grateful Ted was an absolute genius when it came to reading a golf course. By some miracle of mental osmosis, the topography of the course burned itself into his brain. He could see the way the ball would break on any green without even checking the green book, as if he were wearing some sort of x-ray specs, and he could feel the yardage to the hole from any spot on any fairway just by using his thousand-yard stare. He factored in the weather conditions and their effect on the course as if the information lived in his bones, and he could hear exactly the way the wind was blowing without even tossing a blade of grass in the air. He soon became the most requested caddie at the course, and I heard players boast he could knock five shots off your score.

———————•———————

And now, Grateful Ted was going to be the key to my winning this tournament. Since the La Siesta Country Club was a private club, only members and their guests could play the course. Being a cop, a blue-collar civil servant in the city of La Siesta, I was not of the ilk that gets invited to such places, so I had never had the chance to actually play the course at La Siesta before playing the qualifier round this past Monday, a huge disadvantage. But with him by my side I'd managed to beat out an outstanding field of amateur golfers to qualify for the tournament.

Before having Grateful Ted as my caddie, I wouldn't have stood a chance against those guys, but he'd worked his magic, guiding me up and down the course like a Sherpa born and raised on Mount Everest, and here I was, playing in my first-ever PGA Tournament. I'd needed a miracle, and Grateful Ted had proved to be it. Now, I was hoping to harness that power to put me over the top and actually win the tournament itself. It would take four days of flawless golf, and I was putting all my faith in him.

Grateful Ted's eyes opened when he heard me approach, a smile parting the center of his long gray beard.

"You're walking softly today. That's good," he said quietly, as if trying not to disturb the still-sleeping country club. He stood up in one fluid movement, not using his hands for balance but unfolding upward like a ballerina rising from the stage in *Swan Lake*, suddenly standing six-foot-six and looming over the practice range like a benevolent redwood.

I put my clubs down and started to stretch when he stopped me.

"Not today," he said.

"But I need to warm up," I protested.

He put his hand on my chest, feeling my heartbeat.

"You're already warm," he said with a hint of concern in his voice. "Your spirit is restless. Something's bothering you."

*Shit. This guy really is good*, I thought. But I didn't have time to go into Don Osborne's murder, or my trouble with the Montreal mobsters, or my complicated relationship with Kitty, and I didn't really think Grateful Ted was the man to discuss it with. After all, none of this had anything to do with him, so I glossed over it.

"Let's just say I didn't get a very good sleep last night. A lot on my mind," I said and left it at that.

He nodded. "I understand," was all he said. From the look in his eyes, I knew it was true.

I selected my driver and bent to place my ball on the tee when he stopped me.

"No. No tee."

"No tee? What do you mean, no tee? You want me to hit it off the turf?"

"No."

He took the ball from my hand and without another word he sat down cross-legged once again. He held out his palm and closed his eyes, the ball resting in the center of his hand.

"Drive," he ordered.

"What? You want me to hit it out of your hand?!" I wasn't sure I understood what he was asking of me.

"Yes," he replied calmly, not opening his eyes.

"Are you insane, Ted? I'll break your hand. I need you for this tournament."

He sat impassively, his arm outstretched, holding the ball on the flat of his hand like the last crab puff on a plate of hors d'oeuvres.

"I trust you."

"That's nice to hear, but come on, bud, this is a bit too out there for me. I really don't want to hurt you."

"I trust you. In order to win, *you* must trust you," he said, looking at me once again. I thought about this for a second. I had no clue what it meant, but I decided to trust him, even if I didn't trust myself. I stepped into the box and squared myself off in front of my human tee. With nothing to lose but a caddie, I took my first swing of the day. I hit it clean, just barely grazing the palm of his hand, sending the ball arcing out over the range, straight and long, soaring over the two-hundred-fifty-yard marker before landing softly on the grass and bouncing along for another fifty yards or so.

I looked down at his outstretched hand, amazed.

Grateful Ted smiled.

"Trust yourself," he said.

5

Before my round got going and ate up the next four hours of lead time, I wanted to get started on the investigation into Don Osborne's murder, so after I finished up on the range, I headed over to the kitchen door. I couldn't go anywhere near the front door of the clubhouse without running into Chief Garrett, so I'd asked my old partner to meet me at the back door and give me an update on how the case was progressing within the La Siesta Police. He knew perfectly well it could get him in a shit-ton of trouble with Garrett if he saw us talking, but he also knew I had a better chance of catching the killer than anyone on the force, and the cop in him needed to catch that killer. He was just doing what any good cop would do, employing the best tool for the job, me.

As I approached the screen door he emerged with two paper cups of coffee and a couple of pastries.

"There's nothing but cops and caterers in there!" he said with a grin, the edges of his mouth glazed with sugar. Through the screen door I could see the kitchen was buzzing with activity, police everywhere drinking coffee and eating crullers.

"Sounds like a marriage made in heaven." I smiled, shaking his hand. "What's the latest?"

"The latest is that we've got exactly nothing. Zero point zero. Bubkes."

"Sounds like the La Siesta PD all right."

"We've got about as much chance of solving this murder as you have of winning this tournament." He laughed, slapping me on the shoulder.

"Thanks for the vote of confidence," I replied evenly, used to his ribbing.

He handed me one of the coffees and something that resembled a cruller, but fancier. I took a sip of the coffee and it was delicious. *Damn it.* Everything really is better on the PGA Tour.

"Who do *you* think did it?" I asked.

"Hard to say," he mumbled, chewing pensively on what I guessed was his third cruller. "Don Osborne wasn't exactly a popular guy, from what I understand, so I guess it could have been almost anyone," he managed to articulate through a mouth full of pastry.

"That's it? Almost anyone? Way to narrow it down for me."

I was disappointed but not surprised.

"Hey, that's about as far as I'm willing to go at the moment," he said with a shrug. "We're still interviewing people from last night."

"And what do these people tell you about old Don Osborne?" I asked.

"That he wasn't short of enemies."

"He was a powerful guy. Most powerful men have powerful enemies," I said.

"Holds true for Don. In spades. But it seems there was some grumbling among the members about the way Don ran the club."

"And how was that?"

"Like he owned the place."

"But he did own the place. Didn't he?" I asked.

"He did. The question I want answered is, who owns it now that he's dead?"

He thought about this for a moment, finishing his pastry. I had an idea about the answer, but I didn't want to say it out loud. Then he did it for me.

"You think it's the wife? Kitty?"

"It's a possibility," I said, then added a little too quickly, "I can look into that one."

"I bet you can." He smiled.

*Shit, maybe he knows about me and Kitty*, I thought. Then, maybe because he's a friend, he offered another possibility.

"There is a kid. Don has a daughter from a previous marriage. She might be in line to get it. But she doesn't live in La Siesta. I think they're estranged." He chuckled. "Estranged. Why is it that rich families become *estranged*? Regular families just fight and never speak again, but rich folks become *estranged*."

"It's different for people like Don," I said. "These people are so rich they even have their own words. Like *eccentric*. Normal people go crazy, but rich people become *eccentric*."

"Right." He laughed. "Normal people get in fights with their crazy relatives, but rich people become *estranged* from their *eccentric* extended families. Well, I guess we should find out just how *eccentric* Don's extended family was. See if anyone had their hand out."

"But a sniper job just seems so extreme for a family member or someone close to him," I said, the incongruity nagging at me. "Even if they hired someone to do the job for them, which I think is a distinct possibility."

"It does seem a bit cold."

"Cold. That's exactly it," I said, the word setting off an avalanche of thought. "The whole operation was precise. Almost clinical. Staking out the television tower. Timing the shot. Plotting the escape. It was a clean job, in and out, at a crowded country club. In order to pull that kind of thing off, it had to be carefully planned and executed to a tee."

"Executed to a tee?" He snorted. "Is that some sort of golf murder pun?"

"Sorry, no pun intended," I lied. I could hear myself starting to think out loud.

"Plus, whoever did this had to be able to get into and around the club with ease, which is a difficult thing to do at the La Siesta Country Club. But somebody who belonged here, who had an excuse to be on the grounds and not arouse suspicion would have a better chance of pulling it off."

"Unless they were good enough to go undetected," said Lopez. "Snuck onto the property through the golf course, maybe? That's a lot of empty land for one chubby guard on a golf cart to patrol. At night, with good camouflage, it wouldn't be impossible."

"Not impossible, but improbable. The golf course is bounded by the ocean for at least half of it, the parts that aren't guarded by the ocean are guarded by fences, walls, and guards. The only unblocked way onto the course is through the wildlife sanctuary at the bottom of the property, and that's some pretty thick marsh down there."

"What about a boat? They could've parked at the beach on that fancy hole," said Lopez, his eyes sparking at the thought. "What's it called? The one with all the little houses on the shoreline?"

"The thirteenth. The cabana beach hole. That's true, that's a possibility. But let's not overlook one important thing. Whoever pulled this off was disciplined, and a highly trained sniper."

"You thinking someone with military training?"

"Wasn't Don in the military?" I asked. I could remember seeing some military memorabilia in his study when I was in there with Kitty, but I didn't share that with Lopez.

"More than just *in* the military. It was the making of his fortune," said Lopez. He pulled out his notebook and started scanning his notes. "After his service was over, his association with the military continued, but this time he was a civilian contractor instead of a lowly serviceman. His business, Osborne Storage Solutions, owns half of the military surplus overflow storage facilities in the southwest. He made millions every year off his military connections."

"Surplus overflow? What is that?"

"That's what Osborne Storage Solutions does. They store stuff for the military."

"That's what they do?"

"Yeah, you didn't know that?"

"Why would I know that? I don't read the business page. I stick to the golf scores."

"Well, you're only playing in a tournament they sponsor," he said with a laugh, pointing at the banner hanging just behind me.

I looked around and realized he was right. Everywhere I looked there were banners and logos for OSS, Osborne Storage Solutions, the sponsor of the La Siesta Open. Everything at a PGA tournament is branded with a logo: the hats, shirts, the walls of every tent. I've even seen logos baked into the bread of sandwiches at the concession stand. I was going to have to start noticing details like that if I was going to solve this case.

"I'm sorry if I spent more time on my swing than researching the sponsor of the tournament. So enlighten me, would you?"

"It's all public record, but the short version is that Don made millions from the military for storing their surplus overflow, stuff they don't have room to store themselves. Then, Don took that money and made millions *more* investing in real estate, mostly in and around La Siesta. You add millions to millions eventually you get—"

"Billions."

"That is correct. Don Osborne was one rich-ass old dude, even by La Siesta standards."

"And all of that started by storing stuff? Just storing it?" I asked, marveling at the simplicity.

"It's a weird way to make money, I'll admit. But in the end, does it really matter how you make your money? As long as you make it, right?"

"Unless how you make your money plays a role in how you get murdered."

6

When I arrived, the locker room was silent and nearly empty, just a few scattered attendants getting ready for the day's special visitors, a hundred or so of the world's finest professional golfers. Like everything else at the La Siesta Country Club, the locker room was the nicest I'd ever seen. Most locker rooms are furnished with gray metal lockers, a rubbery floor that smells like foot spray, and towels so old and rough they rip your face to shreds. As I entered the La Siesta locker room, however, a subtle scent of lavender and hibiscus wafted gently under my nose. The carpet was a deep forest green, and by the door stood a tower of white terry-cloth towels so fluffy they appeared to be made from clouds. And everything, everywhere, was carved out of wood polished to a golden shine. It felt like the handcrafted hull of an enormous yacht, everything fitted with polished brass fixtures and gleaming under the soft yellow light from green shaded wall sconces.

The walls were lined with cherrywood wainscoting and hung

with old black-and-white photographs of the club back in the early days, when rich society swells from Los Angeles and San Diego used to venture to what was then the rural outpost of La Siesta for a few games of golf on the edge of the ocean. It was a novelty back then, a country escape with an old cowboy who rode around the property on horseback, corralling the herds of sheep they used to maintain the course.

Many of the pictures featured some of the celebrities who'd come to play eighteen holes. There was one of Charlie Chaplin balancing a club on his nose, and one of Bing Crosby in his signature sweater, a pipe dangling from his mouth as he stood over a putt on the eighteenth green. And it wasn't just show-business people in the pictures, but a few of the great old-time golfers in their prime: Bobby Jones, Sam Snead, and my personal hero, Ben Hogan. Hogan wasn't the most natural talent, but he believed that enough practice could turn anyone from a chump into a champion, and I had adopted that credo as my own.

I followed the lush, deep-green carpet along the aisles of lockers until I came to a locker with my name on it, written in elegant script on a little white card inserted into a brass nameplate. It looked positively regal and I stopped to admire it.

Francis Duffy McDermott. I had arrived. This was the equivalent of my name in lights. I sat on the bench that ran down the center of the aisle, took a deep breath, and luxuriated in my elegant surroundings. It was the first time I can remember feeling so cozy and comfortable in a locker room that I wanted to stay. Just hang out in here and feel rich for a while. But I had golf to play. The only way I was ever going to get to spend more time in rooms like that was to win the tournament and make it onto the PGA Tour. I had to focus.

I opened my locker to find it empty. This being the first day of the tournament, all it held was promise, but for me it symbolized something even greater. For the next four days, I was a member of this elite club, with a space of my own to call home. Since I had worn my own clothes and was already in my golf spikes, I had nothing to store in the locker, but I wanted to leave something to establish my presence on this hallowed ground, so I reached into my pocket and pulled out my ball marker, a quarter that my dad had given me as a kid. I'd been using it as a good luck charm for years, but I now realized, after twenty years of struggling to make the PGA Tour without success, perhaps it wasn't so lucky after all. It was time for a fresh start, time for a whole new me. So I took the quarter and placed it on the shelf in the empty locker. The old me could wait here while the new me went out and won this damn tournament.

I was feeling on top of the world as I sat down on the bench and took a moment to get my head together and prepare myself mentally for the day. When I looked up, I noticed the nameplate on a locker just a few doors down from mine.

Don Osborne.

All the other members had apparently had to clear out their lockers for the tournament, but being president of the club had its advantages, and Don's locker was allowed to stay as is. I recognized the lucky break for what it was, and quickly sidled over to Don's locker to take a look. I wanted to see what I could learn about Don Osborne, and something in his personal effects might hold a clue.

The first thing I noticed was that Don's locker was twice the size of all the others, a double-wide door that stood out as positively regal compared to the rest in the row, another perk of being club president, I supposed. All the other lockers were the size of a kitchen cupboard, but Don's was the size of a broom closet. It was big enough to store a body, it occurred to me, but I would be satisfied if all it contained were a few of Don's skeletons.

The locker was protected by a standard-issue Yale combination padlock, which I was surprised to find hanging open, the upper u-shaped shackle of the lock merely slipped through the metal hasp. I found this curious, but I assumed the La Siesta PD had already searched it, and, sloppy as usual, they had left it unlocked afterwards.

The wooden door swung open. Inside I found the usual items: a light rain jacket for the few times a year it rains in southern California, some shampoo and shaving stuff, including a bottle of cologne so noxious-smelling it seemed better suited to pouring on a handkerchief and knocking someone out than dabbing behind one's ears. The only thing that stood out was a bag of golf clubs. A country club as fancy as La Siesta was sure to be equipped with a bag room, an area dedicated solely to storing the clubs of each of its members, but Don Osborne kept his in his locker. Why?

As I was puzzling over this detail an attendant walked by.

"Excuse me," I said, stopping the young man, "doesn't this club have a bag room?"

"Yes, sir, it's right at the end of the hall, past the sauna."

"But Don Osborne didn't use it to store his clubs?"

A knowing smile crossed the kid's face.

"No, sir, nobody was allowed to touch Mr. Osborne's clubs but Mr. Osborne."

So that's why he kept his clubs in his locker, which also explains why it was twice the size of the others. At least I had one tiny part of the mystery solved. I figured since I had his attention, I ought to ask him another question.

"Did you have much contact with Mr. Osborne? What did you think of him?"

The kid thought for a moment, then looked around to see that the coast was clear. "Well, I guess now that he's dead I can finally say it out loud. Don Osborne was an asshole. Sir."

"Okay, then," I said. "Thanks."

*Boy, Don Osborne was really not a popular guy around here*, I thought to myself.

The kid walked away, and I turned back to the double-wide locker. On the inside door of the locker hung a framed photograph, creased in the middle and faded around the edges, showing five young men in Army Ranger uniforms. They were standing side by side in front of a Jeep with their helmets under their arms, smiling for the camera. Judging from the jungle in the background, I guessed it was probably taken during the Vietnam War. I scanned the men in the photo, and the unmistakable face of a young Don Osborne jumped out at me. He looked almost the same as he had the day he died, tall and reedy, with a long nose, bushy black eyebrows like two caterpillars, and a thick shock of black hair mussed from removing his helmet. The only difference between then and now was that his hair had gone white in the interim.

All the men in the photo were smiling, except for the one.

They looked happy, and it struck me as odd, cold even, that their youthful exuberance carried through in the face of so much death. But there they were, grinning for all the world, the *Osborne* stitched across Don's left breast pocket of his uniform confirming his identity for me. The others in the group were Dwyer, Graft, Schaefer, and Wilson.

I recognized the name Graft. I was friendly with a wealthy society doyenne named Elaine Bennington Graft, and her husband was a man named George Graft. It was a fair bet they were the same man. La Siesta is a small town, but the picture was faded and his face was hard to make out. The fifth man in the picture, standing slightly apart from the others, had his face obscured by a crease in the photograph, but the name stitched on the uniform, *Wilson*, was visible.

I couldn't be sure that any of these guys would have any relevant information. Hell, I couldn't even be sure any of them were still alive, but I made a note on my phone of their names. It wasn't much to go on, but it was a start.

When nothing else of interest caught my eye, I decided to search through the bag itself, a detail no doubt overlooked by the wizards at the La Siesta Police Department. I unzipped one of the pockets, and out fell a scorecard, dated yesterday, the day he died. Don's last round of golf. I looked at the scores and saw that Don didn't shoot too badly. Unfortunately, neither did the sniper that took him out later that evening.

Running my finger down the card I was surprised to see that it ended on the sixteenth hole. No score was recorded for seventeen and eighteen. That seemed strange. Did Don forget to record his score? Did he not finish his round? Why would someone play sixteen holes of golf and not finish? I looked at the tee time on the card, which read 9 a.m., so it didn't get dark on him, and yesterday was a beautiful day, so it wasn't weather that made him leave the course early. I made a note of the caddie's name listed on the bottom of the card and decided to head over to the caddie shack after my round to see if I could find the kid.

———————

At the sound of footsteps coming down the stairs toward the locker room I decided it would be in my best interest to head out to the tee as fast as possible. I made sure everything in the locker was back where I found it and shut the door, hastily putting the lock through the hasp and leaving it unlocked as it had been when I'd come across it. I was halfway out the door, but before I could make my escape, I heard a voice from behind that stopped me dead in my tracks.

"*Holy shit!* Is that Duffer McDingleberry?!"

There was only one person in the world who called me that name. The most obnoxious, arrogant, vile person on the planet. The bane of my existence since the age of twelve. The very person, in fact, who had coined the nickname "Duffer" that I'd carried around my neck like an albatross my entire life, a cruel epithet for a hack golfer that became a moniker I couldn't escape no matter how hard I tried. I've grown used to it, but it still stings a little every time I hear it.

The sound of his voice sent a chill down my spine. *Not now.* I thought. *Not today. Not him. Not . . .*

"Danny Master . . ." I said, cringing as I turned to greet him.

"THE ASS BLASTER!" he replied far too loudly, pointing his thumbs at his chest to indicate he was, indeed, referring to himself. "What's *up*, you douche nozzle?!" he bellowed, shooting me with a pair of finger guns.

Danny Master was the kind of guy who makes up his own nickname, and the fact that he's the kind of guy who would give himself a nickname like the "Ass Blaster" should tell you really all you need to know about him. In lieu of a handshake, he pulled me into a headlock and gave me a noogie, because, you know, that's how adults greet each other.

"Man, I haven't seen you since I was knuckle deep in your prom date," he said, laughing at his own joke. Danny had never been anywhere near my prom date. We hadn't even gone to the same high school, but for guys like Danny, conversation is just a constant stream of filthy sayings and crude jokes learned from a lifetime spent in locker rooms.

"What are you doing here, you toilet snorkeler? You come to watch me slay this field of weak-ass lady golfers?" he cried, his annoyingly handsome face now lighting up in a huge grin. The other golfers, who were now streaming in, turned and shot sour looks in our direction.

"I'm not here to watch, Danny. I'm here to play," I replied calmly. I was determined not to let anyone get under my skin, not today. It was too important.

"Bullshit, you turd burglar. You couldn't stay one stroke ahead of me in a circle jerk. What are you really doing here?" he said with a dismissive laugh.

"I'm really here to play, Danny."

He let out a laugh so loud I thought the ceiling might fall on our heads.

"And I'm really here to win."

This only made him laugh harder, doubling over now and holding his stomach for effect. Subtlety was never Danny's forte.

"I'm glad to see you find it so amusing," I said, waiting for the show to end.

He straightened up, putting a hand on my shoulder to balance himself.

"Oh shit, Duffer, you kill me," he said, wiping tears from his eyes. "Okay, great, I tell you what, I'll make you a bet . . . You beat me, and I will caddie for you at your next tournament. No matter what dump of an amateur course you're hacking around on."

"I'll take that bet," I said, genuinely eager to put this putz in his place. "And if I beat you, you caddie for me, and my next tournament won't be on a dump of a course, it'll be a certified PGA Tour stop, because if I win this tournament, I automatically qualify for a PGA Tour card."

"You're on!" he said, and we shook on it like men. Or like a man and a twelve-year-old boy trapped in the body of a man.

He walked off toward his locker holding his side from laughter.

Danny Master is a perfect example of what happens to someone when they win too much. When winning comes too easily, when you spend your whole life being told that you're the best at everything you do, and then you prove it by winning every tournament, well, after a while you start to believe you're invincible, and nobody felt as invincible as Danny Master.

The problem for me, and all the other golfers he came up

against, was that he really was that good. His swing was flawless, his putts were effortless, and his feel for the course was instinctive. I think deep down that's what I hated about him the most. It's what we all hated about him. And believe me when I say we all hated him. But he was just that good.

He was the most natural golfer I'd ever seen, born with a perfect swing somehow embedded in his DNA. He was also blessed with rich parents who paid for a parade of golf coaches and sent him around the country when he was a teenager to play the best courses and compete in tournaments against the elite golfers of his age group. Experience and training like that are hard to beat, but when you combine them with natural ability, well, you get Danny, a virtual golf machine.

My only hope against guys like Danny was practice. Practice, practice, and more practice. It may not sound like much, but believe it or not, sometimes it's enough. Practice is what brought Ben Hogan sixty-four championships and nine majors. Ben Hogan was so dedicated he was known to take a three-hour practice round just moments *after* completing a tournament. Sometimes even after *winning* a tournament. He just never stopped practicing. So I never did either.

From the age of twelve on, I dedicated myself to practicing as much as I could, wherever and whenever. I would putt into a water glass in my office, or practice chip shots out behind the police station. Any chance I got to improve my play, I took. If practice was good enough for Ben Hogan himself, then damn it if I wasn't going to practice my way into contention.

Now it was time to see if all my hard work would pay off.

7

When I stepped up to the first tee, I was so nervous my body felt like a tuning fork that had fallen down a flight of stairs. I was vibrating from the tips of my toes to the top of my head at a frequency only dogs could hear. My partner for the day, Lleyton Vanderfinch, was a recent college champion from Arizona State, hailed by the media as "the next step in the evolution of golf." That's quite a title to live up to, and I was hoping it would put a little extra pressure on him for this tournament, but one look at him told me that not only had the press not gone to his head, but they were right about him. He was young, cocky, and built like a superhero's stunt double.

There was a time, not long ago, when most professional golfers looked like average men. Talented athletes, to be sure, but not the perfectly sculpted uber-athletes in peak physical condition that you see today. Once upon a time it was okay to have a little beer gut like mine, but these days half the golfers on tour have a six-pack, and anything less than top physical condition and you're considered "out of shape," or as one fan on the internet called me, "a fat ass."

At twenty-two, Lleyton was already what I would never be: a phenom. This kid was a real talent, and nobody knew it better than he did. Well, maybe his wife, Rikki, a long and leggy Instagram model who hung on his every stroke. She'd caused quite a stir a few months back posing with his putter, and now there were as many photographers in the gallery taking pictures of her as there were snapping shots of him.

Seeing Lleyton's professional-looking setup—nice clothes, good sponsor, a giant Callaway logo splashed across a bag that he got for free—made me feel shabby. I looked down at my own attire and cringed at my wrinkled old pair of chinos and plain blue polo shirt. I looked like I was sponsored by Goodwill. My bag was a relic, a third generation hand-me-down from my father made of faux alligator skin, as was the fashion during the bygone era in which it was made. It was beat-up, but it had history, and I like to think a bit of character.

The sun was getting high in the sky, warming the morning, and I pulled a bottle of sunscreen out of my bag and gave my arms, face, and neck a good slathering with an industrial strength sunblock labeled SPF 1,000, "Irish-Grade Protection." Another hand-me-down from my father's side of the family was the ability to get a sunburn on even the cloudiest day. As my mother used to say, "You could catch a sunburn inside a bank vault." The last thing I needed was to play this tournament with severe sunburn, so I made sure to coat myself completely.

Grateful Ted was standing calmly by my bag, not saying a

word and looking out at the first hole with that thousand-yard stare of his. It was a look that made people slightly uneasy, but here, on the golf course, his thousand-yard stare was an asset, one I intended to put to good use. Hell, this hole wasn't even five-hundred yards long, which left him at least five-hundred yards of stare to spare.

"What are we looking at Ted?" I asked, pulling a glove onto my left hand and securing the Velcro clasp, just a bit too tightly at first. The nerves were getting to me. I had to focus.

"Four hundred twenty-five yards, par four, with a dogleg to the right. I walked the course this morning, and the conditions overall are pretty good. On this hole, the trees on the right are taller than they appear." He pointed to a stand of Scrubby Pine just beyond the gallery on the right. "So I'd play it safe and lay up, aim a little left."

"But if I go over the trees on the right, won't I be in better position?" I asked, eager to go for it. "I'd be a chip shot from the green."

"But if you hit into those trees you could be in trouble. Better to play it safe. It's only your first shot," he advised, sensing my eagerness to play the more aggressive line.

"But what about the rough on the left? It looks pretty long," I asked, concerned that if I missed the fairway long I might find my ball in a large clump of long beach grass on the opposite side. "If I hit it long, I could end up in that waist-high swamp."

"Then don't hit it long." He smiled.

"Thanks a lot," I said, not thrilled with our opening gambit.

Okay, I'll admit, there are times when I question my choice of caddie, but I had to trust him. A caddie can be a golfer's best friend and most useful tool. A caddie is there not just to help with club selections and reading greens, but to offer guidance, moral support, and strength. Golf is a famously solo endeavor, and nobody but you can hit the ball, but a good caddie is like having a teammate, a coach, and a friend all rolled into one. Since I'd started playing with Grateful Ted as my looper, I'd felt a calm come over me that I'd never found with a caddie before, and my game improved immeasurably because of it.

But you have to be careful. It can cut both ways. A caddie can have a negative effect on the outcome of the round too, particularly if he makes a mistake, which could cost a stroke, or worse, get you disqualified. The PGA doesn't mess around when it comes to the rules, and on top of that, this club in particular has very strict rules of conduct. Thanks to Don Osborne and his priggish nature, the La Siesta Country Club has a very strict "no foul language" rule, which carries over to the tournament itself. Any player caught uttering a four letter word was *automatically disqualified*. Out of the tournament. No exceptions. Done. *Sayonara*.

This was potentially trouble for me. I've been known to, on occasion, utter a vulgarity or twenty. But only when frustrated, angry, or otherwise peeved. Unfortunately, when you're playing a game as confounding as golf, it can be difficult to contain all the *fucks* from escaping your lips. I would have to watch myself every step of the way, because I knew the tournament officials would be on me like stink on . . . well, you know.

The announcer's voice came over the loudspeaker and introduced me.

"Now teeing off, from Long Island, New York, Francis Duffer McDermott!"

Son of a bitch. *Did he just announce me as Duffer?*

"It's *Duffy*! Francis *Duffy* McDermott," I said, peeved but doing my best to control it. I shook it off and concentrated on trying to contain my excitement as I walked onto the big stage for the first time. Standing in the tee box felt like being under a spotlight. All eyes were on me. It was an unsettling feeling. Playing in front of a crowd is part of playing professional golf. Unfortunately for me, playing in front of a crowd was the one part of professional golf with which I didn't have too much experience. Since I was an amateur, the crowds had always been relatively small. Sure, there was always a small cluster of folks following me around on the Korn Ferry Tour, but the PGA Tour was another level altogether.

Even on Thursday, even this early, the crowds were deep. The amateur tour was never like this. And it wasn't just hardcore golf fans either, the dimple-heads who come out early to every tournament. Here at La Siesta it was also full of celebrities, supermodels, and all sorts of corporate sponsors who could change my life with a single endorsement. I don't enjoy playing under any extra pressure. It's bad enough trying to sink a twenty-foot putt to win a tournament; I don't need John Stamos watching while I do it. Just thinking about who might be in the crowd made me so unsettled I resorted to my old nervous tic of chewing on a tee, not a great habit, but better than the cigarettes it replaced.

The crowd behind me was a sea of baseball hats buzzing with excitement as the intensity built up to a pressure that could only be released by hitting the first shot. This was it, the first shot of the tournament. After this there was no looking back. I had one chance to save myself. If I did well here and finished in the money, even just a top-ten finish, I could pay off the Racquette Brothers and keep them from breaking my legs, or worse. I could also save my business. But more important than all that, more important than my legs or my business or money, it was a chance to finally fulfill the dream I'd been chasing all my life. If I won, actually won the whole goddam tournament, I would earn my PGA Tour card.

I swallowed my fear.

I took my driver from Grateful Ted, who smiled beatifically, calm as the ocean on a windless day. I stepped into the box, took the tee from the corner of my mouth, bent over, and pierced the scarred turf at my feet. Setting my ball on top of the tee, my hands were visibly shaking. It reminded me of the way my father's hands used to shake when he needed a drink. All of the sudden I could see him sitting there, his nerves permanently rattled and his eyes bloodshot from too many grisly memories of too many grisly crime scenes, watching me on the Golf Channel.

I had to put all that out of my mind and drive this ball. For the next four hours my entire being had to be focused on this little dimpled sphere, and I couldn't look up until the job was done.

As I lined up my shot and took a few practice swings to loosen up, the gallery became quiet. For a moment, time seemed to slow down and my mind went completely blank as I settled over the ball. Somehow, through sheer muscle memory, I swung, and when the club head made contact with the ball, I was shocked back to reality by the satisfying *THWACK*. The ball shot off the tee like a bullet, a line drive straight and low down the fairway, zipping past the gallery lining the left side. Every head turned in unison to follow the drive. The ball zipped along for two hundred yards or so before finding the center of the fairway, taking a few short hops, and rolling for another seventy-five yards and disappearing into the long rough on the far side off the fairway.

"Aaaah, what the *FU*—!?" I barked, suddenly losing control.

There was an audible gasp from the gallery.

I had almost said it. I almost swore. I really had. But I didn't. I had stopped myself. *Jesus Mary and Joseph*, I thought, *I almost lost the tournament on the first stroke*. I looked over at the official at the edge of the tee box, who frowned and shook his head, but took no further action. I slunk back to my bag, lucky to have dodged a bullet. I would have to watch myself. Grateful Ted took my driver and tried to steady me.

"Easy, partner. It's only the first hole," he said in a soothing tone, patting me on the shoulder.

I was fuming, standing on the side of the tee box trying to regain my composure as I watched Lleyton Vanderfinch hit a high, loping drive that curved to the right staying above the small cluster of trees, cutting off the dogleg perfectly and landing safely on the fairway, spitting distance from the green. The small gallery let out a roar of approval, led by a whoop from Rikki. Lleyton picked up his tee with a confident smile and waved to the gallery.

I glared in Grateful Ted's general direction.

"Good thing I didn't hit it over the trees. I wouldn't want Lleyton's ball in my way."

Grateful Ted shrugged. "Just because you didn't do it right, doesn't mean it wasn't the right thing to do," he said, always ready with a bit of sage wisdom.

I was fuming, my temper already bubbling underneath, as I walked up the fairway to dig my ball out of the beach grass.

*Shit, I'm going to need to keep a lid on my temper this weekend,* I thought. Maybe I could get Grateful Ted to teach me a mantra or something, some hippie trick he learned in India or the parking lot of a Dead concert, to keep me calm. If I blow my big chance because I play crap golf, I can live with that, but if I let my temper blow it for me, I will never be able to forgive myself.

Anger management had been an issue in my game, and my life, for as long as I could remember. I wish I didn't have such a short fuse, I really do, but we're born with a certain set of attributes, and we have to learn to play the game with the clubs in our bag. The ability to control one's emotions is absolutely essential to the game of golf, whether it's anger, or nerves, or even, and sometimes this is the most dangerous of all, confidence. If you let any one of a million little things get in your head, you're doomed, and even the knowledge that you can't let anything get in your head can get in your head and drive you crazy. Sometimes it did this literally, as it did with my great-grandfather.

My mother always called it "the madness." To her, golf was a sickness that infected the family genes, passed down from one generation to the next on my father's side. She believed any natural inclination toward golf was a curse, not a blessing. My great-grandfather John J. McDermott Jr. was a professional golfer, and quite a good one. A champion, in fact. One of the first Americans to play the sport professionally, he was the first US-born winner of the US Open, in 1911 and 1912, and at age nineteen, is still the youngest to do so.

Grandpa Jack, as we called him, was a legendary figure in my family who loomed large over those who came after him, and in many ways set the template for all the McDermott men to come. The talent skipped a few of us along the way—half of my brothers couldn't hit the side of a barn with a driver—but my grandfather had the madness, and my father had the madness, and then, well, I got the madness in spades.

"It's a torment!" my mother would say. "Chasing a little ball around all day! And for what?"

I couldn't argue with her. It has been a torment. If it hadn't been for my dreams of playing golf professionally, I probably could've found a nice cushy job in the police department of a little town somewhere and coasted through life. In fact, that's what I thought I had done when I moved to La Siesta from New York. However, that was before I knew The Big Snooze was actually more trouble than a Second Avenue bar on St. Patrick's Day.

To a certain degree, the stories of my great-grandfather kept me going through a lot of the crappy tournaments and bad rounds I've had to endure over the years. The fact that I'm the great-grandson of a great golfer means I have golf in my blood. It's as much a part of who I am as my pasty white skin, my rugged good looks, my penchant for modesty, or my taste for cheap beer and expensive women.

Unfortunately, I also inherited his fiery temper, and my unfortunate habit of taking my frustrations out on poor unsuspecting golf clubs has cost me a fair amount in replacements over the years. I've broken them over my knee, thrown them at trees, and launched them into ponds. When the only other place to lay the blame for a crappy shot falls on yourself, it's handy to have a piece of faulty equipment to point to as the culprit, although truth be told, none of them were faulty until after I mangled them.

But it's true, golf is a torment. I've spent the last thirty years or so tormented by golf, giving it my every free moment, at the sacrifice of all else: family, work, a social life. I gave it all up to chase this little ball around, to chase this dream, and that was why I so desperately needed to play on the PGA Tour. I've already dedicated too much of my life to this to stop now. It's hard to explain to people who don't understand obsession.

My grandfather understood. He was obsessed. He burned out early and was essentially washed up by the age of twenty-three. He spent a good deal of the rest of his life in mental institutions and rest homes, suffering from what back then was referred to as "nerves." Some said that a shipwreck he survived in 1914 returning from the British Open had been the source of his troubles, and perhaps that was partly true, but my mother always assured me it was his obsession with golf, "the madness," that did him in.

Of course, I don't know for sure. I was a baby when he died. But at least he was a success. That was the difference between him and me. And perhaps that was the difference between obsessed and tormented. I'm obsessed, but I'm also tormented because I haven't found success. Yet. My great-grandfather retired with seven professional wins and two major championships, and he helped usher in a whole new era of golf in America. After John

McDermott came a host of American golf heroes and a surge in popularity that set the foundation for the PGA we have today. So even though it torments me, I guess in a way I feel like it's my birthright to play on the PGA Tour.

But now I had to swallow my past, step up and make my own history, carve my name in the family tree. This was the weight I carried on my back as I walked up the fairway and went to dig my ball out of the longest rough I'd seen in years.

# 8

After strolling up the fairway to the polite applause of the crowd, most of it for Lleyton I assumed, I found my ball buried deep in the rough. The grass was ankle high and thick as a shag carpet, my ball embedded so deeply it looked as if it had found a cozy bed and snuggled in to stay for good. I would be able to extricate myself, but it wouldn't be easy. I was still a good two hundred yards away, and I would have to swing hard to get it out of there.

"What do you think?" I asked Ted, although I wasn't sure I trusted him quite as much as I had a few minutes ago.

"Just don't miss it long," he said, helpfully.

"Isn't that what you said about that last shot?"

"Yep."

He had a point. To miss it long would mean landing behind the green in a sand trap the size of the beach at Normandy. I wanted to avoid the sand at all costs, which is probably why I hit my next shot directly into the sand trap.

"Ugh! What happened?" I sniped at Grateful Ted.

"You thought about it too much. You visualized the bad thing happening and you made it come true," he said, as if it were obvious.

"Well, why didn't you tell me not to do that?"

"I can't tell you what to do. Only *you* can tell you what to do."

He smiled serenely as he handed me my sand wedge. I let out a low grumble and trundled off to the trap.

"I'm gonna have to rent a camel to get across this thing," I moaned.

Meanwhile, Lleyton hit an easy nine iron onto the green, setting himself up for a birdie putt or, at worst, an easy par.

My ball was deep in the bunker, directly underneath the lip, which curled back toward me and provided ample defense for the virginal green laid out behind it. I positioned myself as best I could, careful not to disturb the sand around the ball and cause a violation. I gingerly placed my left foot uphill from the ball, set myself as square as I could, and took my swing. My heart skipped a beat as I saw the ball clear the lip and I rejoiced as I heard a cheer go up from the crowd.

Then, I listened as the cheer trailed off into a disappointed groan. By the time I climbed out of the trap I could see my ball rolling, and rolling, and rolling some more, all the way across the green and down toward the apron at the front, a good forty yards from the hole.

Shit. *Fast green*, I thought to myself.

There's nothing I hate more than a fast green. I have a natural tendency to putt the ball too hard, one of many natural deficiencies I've tried to overcome with practice, but it's still my Achilles' heel. If I putt too hard on a regular green I might have a chance, if I'm accurate, but when the green is dry and slippery and as fast as the felt on a pool table, I just can't seem to handle it. I fall apart. Of the myriad bugbears that can bedevil a man in this cruel sport, a fast green, above all, can be murder on my golf game.

Now on the far side of the green, I would need to sink a monster putt just to save par. Not exactly where I wanted to be at the beginning of the round. Lleyton meanwhile rolled his ball within an inch of the hole, then tapped in for an easy par, strutting off the green with the air of a man in control of his game. At this point I would consider myself lucky if I could control my bowels.

I stepped up to my ball, which lay just on the front fringe of the green, and gave it my best attempt at a "bump and run," trying not to hit it too hard, but hard enough to get it across forty yards of green to the flagstick. It wasn't a bad stroke, but once again I shot past the hole by a good five feet. Even on a putt from a mile away, I still manage to hit it past the cup. I let out a sigh of frustration, as my fear began to look like a reality. A course full of fast greens could be my ruination.

I somehow managed to get a handle on the speed to knock in the next putt, and I grumpily recorded my first bogey of the tournament. I wish I could say it was my last, but unfortunately it was the start of a trend, with four more bogeys, a double bogey, and a truly cringeworthy *four putt* on eight. I was driving all right, and my irons were solid, but I just couldn't handle the speed on these greens. My ball was slipping and sliding across the surface so fast it seemed to deny the existence of friction, like a billiard ball on a marble floor. I was falling apart, fast. I tried desperately to keep my shit together, but it was hopeless, and I headed into the ninth hole shuffling along with my head down, like a condemned man on the way to the electric chair.

I was currently ten strokes over par, *ten*, and trailing Lleyton by seven strokes. Of course, I wasn't playing against just Lleyton; there was a whole field of golfers to come in the next few hours and post their scores, but I had to use something as a measuring stick to see how I was doing, and at the moment I was not measuring up. I would have to do a lot better on the back nine if I had any hope of finishing the day in position to make the cut on Friday.

———•———

When we arrived at the ninth hole there was a backup, the group in front of us still waiting to tee off.

"What's the hold up?" I asked the tournament marshal.

"They found something in the cup," he replied.

"They what?" I asked, surprised at his answer.

He shrugged as he searched for the words.

"Something was blocking the hole. There was a . . . a foreign object, in the cup."

"What kind of foreign object?" I asked, curious. It seemed an odd reason for a delay.

"An egg," he said, trying to make the answer seem not bizarre. The look on his face, however, told me he was as baffled by the answer as I was.

"*An egg?*" I didn't think I'd heard him right.

"That's right, sir. An egg in the cup."

"What kind of egg? Were they holding an Easter-egg hunt for the kids or something?" I asked, sure he was putting me on.

"Nothing like that, sir. It's more like a quirk of nature, I guess you'd call it. The egg is from one of those birds that live in the nature preserve next door. *Pacific gnatcatchers*, I think they're called. They're endangered. And their nesting ground is right next door. And, well, for some reason they sometimes lay their eggs in the holes. It's happened before."

"Okay, well, I've laid an egg on several holes myself already today, so I guess I understand. But this is the strangest reason for a delay I've ever encountered."

"It'll just be a minute. They have to call in the people from the conservation group to come get it."

"Can't we just make an omelette out of it and get on with our lives?" I asked, impatient to get on with my round.

"It'll just be a few minutes, sir."

As he said this, a nerdy-looking guy clad in cargo shorts, Birkenstock sandals, and a t-shirt that read LA SIESTA WILDLIFE PRESERVATION SOCIETY ran by with a large pair of tongs and what looked like a bucket with a bird's nest stuffed in it. His ponytail and little round sunglasses made him look like John Lennon, if John Lennon had collected bird eggs with forceps for a living.

I tried to convince myself to use this time to get myself together, to relax and try to get back into the swing of things. I was sitting down on a bench to ride out the delay, when I noticed we were right next to the groundskeeper's shack. It looked like we had a few minutes to kill, so I decided to drop in on Mr. Lo and ask him a few quick questions.

When I arrived at the shack, Mr. Lo was sitting at his desk watching the tournament on a small black-and-white television.

"Morning, Mr. Lo. Who's in the lead?"

"Not you!" he said with a laugh, surprised to see me. "What are you doing here, Duffer? Shouldn't you be playing golf?" he asked, standing to greet me, then adding with a chuckle, "Or whatever it is you're doing out there."

I laughed it off. I liked Mr. Lo. He was a bit of a weird old bird but we got on well.

"What are you watching it on TV for?" I asked. "The real thing's right outside."

He waved his hand dismissively, sitting back down in his battered desk chair with a groan.

"Ah, I don't like crowds. What can I do for you, Duffer?" he asked, as impatient as I was to get back to the golf.

"I was hoping you could help me find a caddie. Who had Don Osborne's foursome yesterday?"

He reached over onto his desk and flipped through a stack of cards.

"That was a kid named Eddie Shamanus," he said, reading off the card.

"Do you have his address or anything?" I asked.

"Sure, it's all in his employee file." He got up to retrieve a file from an ancient filing cabinet. He riffled through the creaking drawer and pulled out a stack of papers bundled by a rubber band.

"Nice filing system. Don't you keep that stuff on computer?"

"Computers, I don't trust. Computers and left-handed golfers." He laughed.

"All left handers? That seems pretty prejudicial."

"A lefty has never won the US Open, so maybe God agrees with me." He shrugged, then took out a piece of paper from the file and copied down the address from the application.

"Say, Lo"—I smiled, watching him write—"isn't that your left hand you're using there?"

"What? I said I don't trust left-handed golfers and I don't. I should know better than anyone." He smiled and handed me the paper with Eddie's name and address on it. He lived in a run-down part of town on the edge of La Siesta—convenient since I also happened to live in the rundown part of town on the edge of La Siesta.

"Why do you want to talk to this kid?" he asked.

"I'm just curious why Don didn't finish his round. Do you know who else was in the foursome that day?"

He checked the card again. "Looks like it was a twosome."

"A twosome? I thought La Siesta was strict about four players at a time."

"Well, for Don there was always an exception."

"So he requested a special two-person tee time. With who?"

He checked the card. "Looks like Bill Dwyer."

I remembered the photo from Don's locker room. One of the guys in the photo was named Dwyer. Was it the same man? Was he living here in La Siesta?

"So only Bill Dwyer and Don played his last round?"

"Yep. Just Bill and Don."

"Where was the rest of the foursome?"

"Who knows? I don't question the club members about their

groups. I just give 'em their caddie assignments and otherwise my eyes are on the greens and fairways. I've got more important shit to do."

So Bill and Don played their last round together and didn't finish, I thought to myself. At least Don didn't. *Why?* My gut told me there was something to this, and I was eager to follow up with Eddie as soon as my round was over. But first, I had the back nine to play.

I thanked Mr. Lo for his help and hustled back out to try to improve my score and finish the day with a respectable showing. Just enough to keep me in the hunt would do for now. I would have to crawl back from a bad start, but I hadn't come here to give up after nine holes.

"Good luck out there," he called after me.

"Thanks," I said over my shoulder.

"You'll need it!"

I could hear him laughing as I walked out to play the back nine.

---

When I got back to the tee on the ninth hole, I finally saw Kitty in the gallery. I was able to pick her out of a crowd when I caught a glimpse of her sun hat, a gigantic straw construction that looked like something you'd see at the Kentucky Derby, or as shelter for a small animal. She turned her satellite dish of a hat in my direction when she saw me coming up the fairway, and something about her presence felt reassuring. Feeling her eyes on me felt good, and I suddenly started to play better. Grateful Ted and I seemed to find our groove, and with his knowledge of the course and calming influence, I was able to settle down and actually shave some strokes off my round. I recorded my first birdie on nine, and followed it with another on ten and a third on twelve. Just like that, I had erased three shots from my round.

The course at La Siesta is a classic links course, in the old Scottish tradition of short, difficult holes played on the rocky crags of an untamed shoreline, with nature providing much of the challenges faced by the players. A seaside stroll that meanders its way toward the ocean for the first nine holes and then, as the course winds around past the tenth tee, the fairways coexist with the coastline for the next three holes. It's a postcard view, a picturesque run of holes that are both beautiful and challenging, pocked with bunkers and riddled with boulders, and with the breeze off the ocean always a factor, not an easy run of holes either. The fairways of ten, eleven, and twelve are protected from the rocky cliff by just a small dune running along the outer edge, then the cart path leads through a small stand of Eucalyptus trees and the most glorious view of the entire property is revealed: the thirteenth hole, the world famous "Cabana Beach" hole.

I was starting to feel better about my game, but nothing will kill your confidence faster than getting your first look at the thirteenth hole at La Siesta. When we arrived at the edge of a cliff, all we could see from the tee box was miles and miles of churning Pacific Ocean the color of cold steel. You can't even see the flagstick on thirteen from the tee. In order to see the green itself, you have to be on the beach at the bottom of a two-hundred-foot cliff. The green is on an island in the middle of the ocean, about a hundred yards off the beach, surrounded on all sides by water. The only land between the shore and the green is a razor-thin bridge not much more than the width of a cart path, which, being paved, will simply bounce your ball directly into the water if you land on it.

The design is very simple, and very evil. It's all or nothing. You either land your ball on the green, or you land your ball in the ocean. You can't lay up anywhere, and if you miss, you shoot again. So many balls go in the water at the thirteenth hole that a small industry has sprung up of kids who dive for balls and sell them back to the club as range balls. Making it past the thirteenth hole was about faith, pure blind faith.

Neither Leyton Vanderfinch nor I looked over that cliff. We didn't need to. We knew what it looked like. We'd seen the pictures a thousand times and watched the La Siesta Open year after year as this hole broke the will of some of the world's best golfers. It was the world's most beautiful nightmare. It was rumored that Don Osborne had designed the hole himself, and that Jack Nicklaus had threatened to quit if he went through with it, but Don got his way. It helped explain why so many people seemed to dislike old Don. Only a sadist would design such a thing.

"This hole is a real beach," joked Grateful Ted, a smile curling across his face at the corny pun. It was one of those jokes that had been repeated so many times that it had long ago lost whatever humor it held, but was still repeated like a mantra by almost every player who stepped up to the tee at the thirteenth. It was just a dad joke, but like a lot of jokes, it was made to mask a deep fear of something that was dark and painful. This hole was difficult. I mean really, really, difficult. You'd better start with a smile on your face, because you're likely to be crying by the end.

The "Cabana Beach" hole was named after the little red-and-white-striped cabanas that lined the shore below the cliff. Nestled in a small cove hugging the coastline, the beach club was accessible only to the members of the La Siesta Country Club. In the center of the cove, there was a modest snack shack with a small patio and a bar with ten or so tables, fabled for its clam chowder and spicy Bloody Marys. It was tiny, with room for only about fifty people or so, which made it all the more exclusive and, therefore, all the more desirable. It was the best place to be if you wanted to watch poor unsuspecting golfers try their luck at what some say is the hardest hole in all of golf.

In front of the cabanas sat a few dozen rows of blue canvas beach chairs, neatly aligned along the shore. Having a chair on the beach at the La Siesta Open was like having seats on the fifty-yard line for the Super Bowl. From there, you could watch the balls come over the cliff, falling from the sky like shooting stars in the daylight. Normally, this tiny stretch of coastline is reserved for the senior-most members of the club, but during the La Siesta Open, it becomes home to some of the most coveted seats in all of golf. These were the VIP seats to end all VIP seats.

But the real prize, the ultimate in luxurious living, were the cabanas themselves, each one about the size of a small studio apartment, shaded by a billowing white awning that formed a makeshift porch on the sand. Staffed with waiters and beach attendants in shorts and crisp white polo shirts, the cabanas offered any delicacy you like at the snap of a finger. It was like having a luxury box seat at the beach. For practical purposes owing to the uniqueness of the hole's design, there were flat screens arranged around the common areas and in the cabanas so the lucky few with access to these prime seats could watch the putting action on television, filmed by drone. Otherwise, the best view of the action was looking down from the top, where the gallery was stretched out along the cliff, a thin rope between the onlookers and the abyss, as they craned their necks trying to get a peek.

———————————•————•———————————

I stepped up to the tee, cleared my head of all thought, and swung, sending my ball soaring out into the void. I watched it disappear over the ledge, and when a sudden roar from the crowd below rang out, I knew I had hit the green. Ahead of me on the lip of the cliff, Ted stood watching the ball land. He turned and gave me a thumbs up, smiling like a kid. I breathed a sigh of relief. I had avoided that particular disaster for today.

Unfortunately for him, I couldn't say the same for poor Lleyton. He over-hit his first drive by fifty yards, or maybe *leagues* I should say, and plunked it right into the ocean. He brushed himself off, stood in the tee box again and immediately hit another, which fell short of the green, overcompensating for his earlier effort, and sending a second ball to its watery grave. Much to the relief of the gallery and Rikki the Instagram model, he landed his third ball on the green. He let out a despondent sigh and we made our way to the wooden staircase that led us down to the beach.

As I descended the stairs, I looked out at La Siesta Cove, a normally empty and serene inlet that today was filled with boats of all description hosting parties to watch the tournament. Sailboats, speedboats, weekend fishing cruisers and luxury yachts were anchored for the afternoon, their decks lined with bikini-clad beauties and party-hardy billionaires, all watching the action. Only one vessel in the cove wasn't hosting a party, a weather-beaten old sailboat, which sat listing lifelessly on the edge of the cove, seemingly abandoned, with the name *Bill's Baby* printed on its stern. It looked out of place, and I wondered briefly why it hadn't been hauled out to sea and sunk.

When Lleyton and I arrived on the beach, we were greeted with a round of applause from the crowd. It felt like putting on a soft warm sweater on a cold night, a nice fuzzy feeling, like being surrounded by static electricity. At a moment like this, play-ing in a PGA Tournament on one of the most beautiful holes in the world, winning seemed a faraway concern. Playing was the only thought in my head. I let the applause wash over me like the ocean at my feet. It was golf nirvana.

Lleyton leaned over and flashed me a wry grin.

"I think it's safe to assume the applause is for you, partner," he said magnanimously. It struck me then that this kid was more than a phenom, but a class act.

Even though Lleyton had sunk his first two drives into the ocean before finally reaching the green in three, his ball was still farther away, so I needed to mark my ball to allow Lleyton to make his putt unobstructed. However, when I reached into my pocket I realized I had nothing to use as a marker.

"Ted, would you mind marking my ball for me?" I asked, which immediately triggered a reaction from Lleyton.

"Wait a minute, wait a minute. A caddie can't mark a player's ball. That's against the rules!" he cried, quickly reverting to the hypercompetitive young man I'd met on the first tee.

"Oh, I didn't realize you were such a stickler for the finer points of the game," I said, pretending to be impressed with his erudition.

"This game's all about the finer points," he replied, a smug little grin on his face.

"Well, then you should know they changed that rule, amendment to rule fourteen, subsection one-B. As of 2019, a caddie is allowed to mark and lift the player's ball anytime the player is allowed to do so."

He looked over at the rules official, who simply nodded to indicate that I was, in fact, correct.

"Well, look who's the stickler for the finer points now," he said, grudgingly impressed.

"Golf is all about the finer points," I replied, enjoying having put him in his place perhaps just a little too much.

That settled, Ted bent down to replace my ball on the green. He reached into his pocket and pulled out what appeared to be a small flat coin.

"What's that marker, Ted?" I asked, wanting to make sure it was regulation.

"It's my dong," he replied.

"Your *what*?" I gasped, almost choking on my water bottle.

"It's called a dong," he repeated. He held it up so I could see it: a gold coin about the size of a quarter, but with a wavy edge, giving it an almost flowerlike shape. "It's a coin. I carry it for good luck. Makes a great ball marker."

I shook my head. Grateful Ted was full of surprises.

"You want to rub it for good luck?" he asked.

"No, that's fine. I don't want to rub your dong for good luck."

I wasn't much for good-luck charms, talismans, or other mystic mumbo jumbo. I believe in practice, not luck. But that was the thing about Grateful Ted. Somehow, his mystical mumbo jumbo seemed to work. So I figured what the hell. Let him use his dong to mark the ball.

"Okay, well, as long as it's regulation, I guess it's okay."

"Oh it is," he assured me. "Any small flat object is usable as long as it doesn't obstruct the other player's ball on its way to the cup," he said, reciting the rules he knew by heart. "We could use almost anything as a marker as long as it's reasonable." He smiled, then stuck his hand in his pocket and pulled out an array of small flat objects. "I've got a guitar pick, a penny—"

"No, no, that's fine," I finally said, growing exasperated. "I can't believe I'm saying this, but, go ahead and use your dong."

He picked up my ball and marked the spot where it had once sat, allowing Lleyton the opportunity to step up and sink a solid twenty-foot putt from the outer edge of the island green, miraculously escaping with just a bogey. I followed his lead and sank my shorter putt, to my great surprise and relief recording my fourth birdie in a row on the hardest hole on the course. It boosted my confidence, and the next couple of holes I actually managed to play some decent golf, recording par on fourteen and fifteen. Who knows, maybe Grateful Ted's dong was a lucky charm after all? But then on my walk to the sixteenth tee I passed the leaderboard, and all the wind went out of my sails.

Looking at the scores posted already, I saw even Lleyton was in danger of not making the cut. The guys at the top of the leaderboard were racking up the birdies, and the number to beat was looking a lot further away than it had when it was just me and Lleyton. To make things worse, Kitty disappeared from the gallery on the sixteenth tee. I saw her hat disappearing over the ridge, headed back to the clubhouse. I tried to hide my disappointment; I couldn't let anyone connect me to Kitty. Not while I had golf to play, and, well, hopefully not ever.

I limped across the finish line with a bogey and a par, leaving me hopelessly behind the pack at the end of the first day's play, circling the drain at twelve strokes back. *Twelve strokes!* Dear sweet Jesus. I was going to need a miracle on Friday if I was to have any chance of making the cut and playing for the money over the weekend. I slunk back to the clubhouse with my tail between my legs and decided it was time I turned my attention to the other pressing matter weighing on my mind, finding out who killed Don Osborne. Perhaps if I could solve that particular problem, my chances on the course tomorrow might just improve.

# 9

When I arrived at the caddie Eddie Shamanus's house he was out front working on his car, a beat-up old Dodge Duster. A blast of steam from an overheated radiator blew him out from behind the hood and he noticed me.

"Help you?" he asked, a touch of suspicion in his voice. He couldn't have been more than sixteen, a long skinny kid of about six feet who looked like he might have another six to go.

"You Eddie?" I asked, trying not to sound too much like a cop.

"Yeah," he replied, a look on his face like he was in trouble for something. "What's this about?"

"Mr. Lo tells me you were Don Osborne's last caddie," I said.

"Yeah, so?"

"I mean his last one ever. He's dead."

The kid seemed genuinely shocked.

"Whaaaaat?" He exhaled, sitting down on the front bumper of the Dodge. "He didn't seem that old. What happened? Did he have a heart attack or something?"

"He was shot by a sniper last night."

Eddie looked as if he'd been shot himself when he heard the news.

"Shot by a sniper? Whoa, that is seriously fucked up. Who would do that?"

"That's exactly what I'm trying to find out."

"You a cop?"

"I was. Now I'm a golfer."

He made no attempt to hide his laugh.

"Yeah right, and I'm an auto mechanic."

A blast of steam from the radiator punctuated his sarcasm.

"Look, I didn't come to talk about my golf game. I came to talk about Don's."

"Mr. Osborne was pretty good. Usually shot in the low eighties."

"What about his last round yesterday? Anything unusual about it?"

His eyes darted away as I asked him. A sure sign something less than truthful was coming.

"Not that I can think of . . ." he said, doing a poor job of acting.

"According to his scorecard, he didn't finish the last two holes."

The kid looked up at me like he'd just been caught with his hand in the till.

"Oh, that," he said. His eyes suddenly found the tops of his shoes very interesting.

"Yeah, that. Why didn't they finish the last two holes?"

I could see him struggling with how to answer the question so I pressed harder.

"Did something happen on the sixteenth hole?"

He sighed, giving in, and spilled what he knew.

"I'm not supposed to say anything about it."

"Not supposed to say anything about what?"

"The fight."

"What fight?"

"The fight between Mr. Osborne and Mr. Dwyer."

Now we were getting somewhere.

"Don and Bill had a fight? About what?"

"I don't know. I couldn't tell. They were trying to keep their voices down so nobody could hear. They kept walking off toward the woods, but it was pretty clear they were going at it good. Mr. Osborne's face got all red, and I thought for a second he was going to burst a blood vessel, he looked so mad. He had a vein throbbing on the side of his head the size of a garden hose. That's why I asked about the heart attack. I thought maybe the stress of the argument killed him."

"Do you know what they were arguing about?"

"I couldn't really tell. They were too far away most of the time."

I took in this new information. Bill and Don had a fight the day he died. A fight bad enough that they didn't finish their round of golf. What did it mean? Was it connected to Don's murder?

"Who told you not to talk about the fight?"

"Mr. Dwyer. He wasn't messing around either. He said if I told anyone about the fight it would mean my ass. He'd get me fired, he said. And I need that job. I need to buy new parts for this old junker."

"Bill told you not to tell anyone?"

"In no uncertain terms."

I thanked him for his time and let him get back to work under the hood, and as I headed back to my car, I decided it was time to call my old friend Elaine Bennington Graft, the one person who knew everyone and everything that went on in La Siesta.

I knew she could fill me in on all the juicy details from the society swells at the country club and I was hoping she could illuminate me on the life, and possibly the death, of Don Osborne.

•————————————•

Traffic moved with ease as I cruised down Worthmore Avenue in search of a spot to park my old Crown Vic, which stood out like a pimple on a supermodel's ass on this street full of Bentleys and Ferraris. Not a lot of people would consider the Crown Victoria a muscle car, but I loved it, and wouldn't trade it in for a fancy pants sports car if you paid me the price difference. It was fast, roomy, and built like a tank. Driving it reminded me of being a cop, its big block engine rumbling under the hood and its wide body commanding the lanes of the freeway unlike any car made today. I backed it into a spot at the end of the boulevard and headed out in search of libation and useful information.

The main drag of La Siesta, Worthmore Avenue, is world-famous as a paragon of luxury, a parade route of the rich and famous, five fabulous blocks of high-end shopping, dining, and dodging paparazzi. The entire street is a shimmering beacon of consumerism, a wide four-lane boulevard lined with perfectly placed palm trees reaching into the sky and a center divider filled with more flowers than a mafia funeral. To be seen shopping on Worthmore Avenue was to let the world know you've arrived.

On any given day, the spotless sidewalks are populated with affluent influencers, richer-than-you'll-ever-be assholes, and the pampered crème d'elite, frittering away their time and money in boutiques from exclusive brands like Louis Vuitton, Hermes, and Balenciaga. The window displays alone offered a glimpse into a world most people could only follow on Instagram. The restaurants almost all boast a Michelin star or two, and in most, a reservation could take months, even years to acquire, assuming one had the star power and social heft to get one in the first place.

Nobody ever seemed to be in a hurry in La Siesta. In other centers of wealth, New York, Tokyo, or even Beverly Hills, you can feel the energy of people in a hurry, of people wheeling and dealing and buying and selling and running themselves ragged, all in a desperate bid to make money, money, and more money. In La Siesta, everyone has already made their money, so what's the hurry? Of course there's always more money to be made, but once you reach Worthmore Avenue, your money is making more money all by itself.

This is where the ladies who lunch come to have lunch, and this evening I had come to have a drink with one of them, the queen of them all, to see what she knew about Don Osborne. Elaine Bennington Graft is the wife of George Graft, the man I was fairly certain was in the photograph with Don on the inside of Don's locker. If it was him, they were obviously old friends, going all the way back to the war, and I wanted to learn more about their relationship. I also wanted to see what Elaine had to say about Don's death. If there was scuttlebutt about Don around town, Elaine would know every salacious detail.

I had first met Elaine at a fundraiser when she served as a chairwoman to the Policeman's Auxiliary Fund, and I was forced to sit through an agonizing dinner of rubber chicken and fumbling speeches. We bonded over the open bar, and she quickly became a useful source of information about the who's who of La Siesta. We got along, I think, because she was too smart for this town and easily bored, so any connection to the cops, to danger, to dirt, attracted her. During my years on the force she gifted me with what she knew and I returned the favor with lurid tales of the criminal class.

We met for drinks once every few months back then, at Vernetti's, a venerable old standby on Worthmore Avenue. Housed in an old brick building from the 1920s located right in the center of the golden five-block stretch, its ivy-covered facade is famous the world over as a symbol of decadence. Out back its luxurious patio is full of private alcoves and lush greenery, perfect for being discreet, or at least trying to look like you're being discreet, which made it a favorite among the many visiting celebrities who love to be seen "trying not to be seen."

I was waiting for her at our favorite table, ogling the sizzling steaks that whizzed by on waiters' trays, when I looked up to see Elaine standing next to the table. She was a small woman in her early seventies with a perfect poof of white hair and a diamond ring the size of a doorknob weighing down her left hand. If you looked closely, you could see that her left bicep was just slightly more toned than the right, a result of hauling that ridiculous diamond everywhere.

"Aren't you the lucky one," she said by way of hello, a big smile on her perfectly pulled back face.

"How do you mean?" I stood up to greet her with a peck on the cheek, pulling out her chair for her.

"Well, for starters you're alive. That puts you one up on old Don Osborne," she said. "Plus, now you can keep fucking his wife without having to worry about him finding out!" she added in a loud voice before letting out a sharp cackle of a laugh.

I almost dropped my beer.

"What do you mean?" I feigned, trying to laugh it off. I looked around to see if anyone had heard her, but thankfully everyone seemed too wrapped up in themselves to notice.

"Oh, don't dick around with me, Duffer," she said, sitting down. "Everybody knows you've been sleeping with Kitty Osborne for months."

I swallowed hard. This was not the information I had come here hoping to get. It was good to know, important, but unexpected, and I dare say unwelcome. I really didn't need my affair with Kitty coming to light in the middle of this investigation.

"Everybody?" I asked, hesitantly.

"Well, not everybody knows," she said with a conspiratorial smile. "But among those who know, we all know."

She caught the eye of a passing waiter, who nodded his head and then snapped his finger at the bartender who, upon looking up and seeing Elaine, immediately began making her a martini.

"Does Chief Garrett know?" I asked, anxiously.

"Chief Garrett doesn't know which shoe goes on which foot."

We shared a laugh, mine tinged with a dose of relief.

"How did you know?" I asked, curious what had given us away.

"Well, for starters it was obvious a woman like that wouldn't be satisfied with just old Don Osborne. We knew there had to be somebody. It was just a matter of whom."

"And what led you to me?"

"She did, of course."

"How did she do that?"

"Well, not too many ladies in La Siesta ride an Italian motorcycle around town, so she's not hard to spot. And that sure is a fancy bike to see parked outside a dump like the Pitch N' Putt on Highway Five."

Damn it. The Ducati. I should have known that bike was too conspicuous. I should have told her to take an Uber.

"I feel like such a heel." I hung my head. "I should never have gotten involved with another man's wife," I said, genuinely contrite, although I'm not sure if it was only because I'd gotten caught.

"Oh, relax. Nobody cares that much. Besides, you know as well as I that Don was a first-rate asshole. The world is better off."

Just then a waiter gingerly set down a large shimmering martini in front of Elaine. She looked down into her reflection and smiled, then reached into her purse, took her cell phone out of her bag, and placed it on the table, checking the time.

"Are we on the clock?" I asked.

"I'm supposed to take my pills at six o'clock."

She reached into her purse and extracted a small jeweled pillbox. She shook out a small pink pill and swallowed, washing it down with a large gulp from her martini.

"Doctor says I have to take them with gin," she said with a wink.

"Does your husband feel that way? That Don was an asshole?"

I asked, trying to steer the conversation in a direction that better served my needs. "I was under the impression they were old friends," I said, leading into the reason I was there, and away from my affair with Kitty.

"Ugh. George's never been able to shake him," she said, placing the drink gently back on the table so as not to spill, "but that doesn't mean he liked him."

"So George and Don didn't get along?"

"Oh, George just tolerated him because they're old army buddies. They were in the war together, and then of course George went to work for OSS as his operations manager."

"Wait, you're telling me George worked for Don?" I asked, surprised at the news.

"He did, that is before getting the ax just last week," she said, her tone turning sour.

"George was fired last week?"

She nodded.

"Rather unceremoniously I might add. You'd think after all that time, after what they went through together in the war and everything, that Don would give him the benefit of the doubt. But, hothead that Don is, he just flew off the handle and fired him."

"What prompted this?"

"Don claims George had something to do with some missing inventory, but as God as my witness, George Graft never stole a thing in his life."

She could tell from my expression I found this all very interesting.

"Unless you count my heart," she added with a playful wink,

an attempt to deflect the possibly damning information she'd just given me, I suspected.

"And you say this happened just last week?" My mind was already running down the road, and she could tell I was hot on an idea, so she tried her best to walk it back a bit.

"Yes. It was just last Friday. But you couldn't possibly think George would have anything to do with Don's murder. I mean, the man's not capable, I promise you."

I sat back in my chair, taking a pull on my beer and letting the bubbles go to work on this new information.

"Look, I can promise you George had nothing to do with this," she said, seeming anxious to clean up her mess. "If you'd like to speak with George about all this, I'm sure I can arrange that. He's privy to more detail than I."

"That would be a great help. Thanks," I said.

I nursed my beer. I was starting to put some pieces together. All three of these guys were in the war together, Bill, George, and Don, and then all of them settled in La Siesta. A sniper is certainly an unusual way to kill a person, but not necessarily for a group of Army Rangers. But if Don was their cash cow, why would they kill him? And certainly none of these guys had a ponytail. They were as straightlaced as ex-military come. They could certainly have hired someone to do it, and it sounded like they had the money to do it, but again, why? As I had hoped would be the case when I'd set up this meeting, I now had a few avenues to follow for clues, but I was still as far away from solving this case as I was from making the cut tomorrow.

# 10

had just gotten back from having a drink with Elaine, which never seems to stop at just one, when trouble showed up on my doorstep. I was flopped in the desk chair of my office in the Pitch N' Putt, exhausted, and had just finished sweeping up the mess of broken glass from my shattered front door, when Kitty appeared in my doorway. She was wearing a too-short tennis skirt that showed off her perfectly tan thighs, with pleats that made it look like a curtain that could open at any moment. I let out a defeated sigh. I knew I was in for trouble, but I also knew I needed to see what was behind that curtain.

"Kitty, don't tell me you've come to play putt-putt," I groaned, not sure I was ready for what was coming.

She smiled coyly and flashed her green eyes in my direction.

"I need help with my swing," she purred, swaying her hips ever so gently.

She stepped inside, the light from the flickering ceiling fan casting her in alternating stripes of light and dark. Her black hair was pulled back, a visor just covering the top half of her down-turned face like a veil. When she looked up at me and turned the full power of her smile in my direction, I had to use my hand to steady myself against the desk, despite the fact that I was already sitting down.

I knew I was making a mistake, but I was unable to resist her. I'd sworn to myself that I would break it off months ago. Having an affair with a married woman was always trouble; I had done it enough times to know better. But having an affair with the wife of the most powerful man in town was downright suicidal.

And now the situation was potentially even worse. Now that Don was dead and the La Siesta PD was searching everywhere for his murderer, any association between Kitty and I could spell a hell of a lot of trouble for me. If it came down to it, she was my alibi, but I was hoping it never came to that. So what was I thinking even letting her into my office?

But I wasn't thinking. That was just it. Kitty possessed the kind of beauty that switched a man's brain right off. I was a zombie by the time she was halfway across the room, and when she came around and perched on my desk, sliding one leg over the corner and the other planted firmly on the ground, I was helpless. I had to fall on my knees and take a peek under the curtain.

Forgive me Lord, for I am weak.

When the building finally stopped shaking, we lay sprawled on my bed of mats, gleaming with sweat and panting like a couple of huskies after finishing the Iditarod. I got up, crossed the room to the water cooler, and poured myself a paper cup of tequila. Kitty lay staring at the ceiling, seemingly far off in thought. I decided asking her a few questions while she was vulnerable and unguarded might be fruitful, but I tiptoed into the water carefully. I didn't know what I was going to find lurking under the surface.

"I don't get you, Kitty. You're a thrill seeker in every aspect of your life, but you were married to a man as old as Methuselah. Where's the danger in that?" I teased her.

"If you don't think having sex with a man's who's had two heart attacks is dangerous, I've got news for you."

"Hell, I'm lucky to survive you at my age," I replied.

She slapped me playfully as she got up and tiptoed naked to the bathroom. I always loved the way she tiptoed to the bathroom when she's nude, almost prancing across the floor. She'd never walk that way fully clothed, with a little skip in her step, but something about the lack of clothes made her feel light and dainty. Or maybe she was just cold.

"But what was it, really?" I said through the crack in the door. "Was Don Osborne really enough for you?"

There was a pause, then the door opened a crack and she stood there in the doorframe, her naked silhouette backlit by the bathroom light.

"Clearly not or I wouldn't have been with you," she said, wearing only a sultry smile, her green eyes shining.

"Point taken. But the word around town is that Don was, how shall I put this, an asshole. So what drew you to him?"

"Oh, he was. I can't deny that. But never to me. He was very sweet to me. I saw a side of Don that he showed to very few other people. I don't know why, really. I guess something about me just brought out the kitten in him."

She opened the bathroom door and let the light from inside illuminate her naked body, showing me exactly what turned the tiger into a kitten.

"So why did you marry him? Was it the money?"

"That's what everybody thinks. Of course most of the gossips around this town who think that married for money themselves. But no, it wasn't that."

"Then what?"

"I was in a very vulnerable place when I met Don, and he turned out to be just what I needed to get through it. My first husband had just died and I was a mess," she said, padding back to the makeshift bed, tossing out the death of her first husband like it was nothing unusual, a trifle. I took in this new information calmly, without reacting.

"What happened to your first husband? If you don't mind my asking."

"He was killed."

The information hit me like a punch in the face, but I didn't flinch. Things were getting complicated fast.

"Okay. You care to tell me how he was killed? There must be some story there."

"What does it matter?!" she snapped, her voice rising in annoyance.

"So you *do* mind if I ask. My mistake. I didn't mean anything by it. It's just a question."

"Yeah, well I've had plenty of questions over the years, believe me. And you'll forgive me if I don't need a fresh round from you."

I downed my shot of Sauza and poured one for her, returning to the bed.

She sat on the edge of the bed and turned to me, taking the shot and downing it, then crumpling the paper cup and tossing it into the wastebasket by the side of the desk.

"I'm sorry, Duffer. I don't mean to snap. It's been a rough couple of days, and when the subject of Billy came up, it was just too much."

"Billy was your first husband."

She nodded, her face down, not wanting to look at me as the tears welled up behind her eyes. From anger to tears just like that. What was with this woman?

"You okay?" I asked, gently whispering in her ear, but she just stared off into space, facing the wall, a slow trickle of tears falling down her cheek. After a moment she turned back to me.

"I can't believe this is happening again," she moaned, her head in her hands, the frustration obvious in her voice.

"Okay, why don't you tell me what happened with your first husband? It might do you some good to talk about it."

She looked down at the floor, avoiding my eyes.

"He was shot."

"He was *shot*?!" I was unable to hide my surprise.

She nodded, still not looking me in the eye.

"Who shot him?"

She looked up at me, stung.

"It wasn't me, if that's what you're asking."

"Hey, forgive me, but twenty years as a cop has taught me

to start with the simplest question and move on from there. So forgive me if I repeat myself here, but who shot Billy?"

"They never found out. It was a drive-by shooting."

I stood up and crossed the room for another drink, unconsciously putting some distance between us. Suddenly, she seemed dangerous. I slugged back another shot of Sauza and steadied myself before continuing.

"A drive-by? What the hell? Was he in a street gang or something?"

"Of course not! He was a doctor at Mercy Hospital in Dana Point."

"Okay, fine. But what kind of doctor gets killed in a drive-by shooting?"

"A doctor with a drug problem," she said, finally looking up at me. "He was in debt up to his eyeballs to some very bad people."

"Which very bad people?"

"He wouldn't tell me. All he said was that he owed some guys from up north a lot of money, and that he was afraid for his life."

"Up north? Like Los Angeles? San Francisco?"

"He didn't say!" she cried, "I've already been through this with the police years ago. Please, can we just drop this?"

"I'm sorry, but it seems relevant in light of what just happened to your second husband."

"I know it looks bad. I do. But I swear on my life I had nothing to do with any of it."

"So where were you when your first husband was killed?"

"I was at home."

"Alone?"

"I was with my brother. He was helping me pack my things. I was leaving him."

"So your husband was killed the night you were leaving him. I have to say, that's pretty convenient."

"It's a coincidence. That's all."

"Hell of a coincidence, two husbands dead of gunshots," I said, more of a statement that an accusation. She was sobbing now.

"Oh, Christ, how the hell did I get myself into this mess?"

"Hey, no fair, that's my line."

# FRIDAY

# 11

When I woke up on Friday morning and heard the steady patter of rain beating on my office window, it was music to my ears. I sat up and looked out to see fat gray thunderheads hanging low over the coastline, soaking the normally sun-scorched Southern California ground. Rain was a good omen for me. I love to play in the rain. When most golfers see the clouds rolling in, they pack up their clubs and head to the clubhouse for a hot beverage and a lot of speculative conversation about how well they were shooting "until the damn rain came and blew my big round."

I'm different. When I see the clouds rolling in, I know I'm about to knock a few strokes off my game. I suppose it comes from growing up in the northeast, where, unlike sunny Southern California, the weather was bound to be mostly crappy three out of four seasons of the year. Under the circumstances, if you wanted to play golf in the northeast in November, I mean really wanted to play, *needed* to play even, then you had better learn to play in all kinds of conditions.

So that's what I did. I played in howling gales, dodging hail bigger than my golf ball, and even right on through the nor'easters that rode the spine of Long Island out to sea every year. No matter the weather, I was out there hacking away with my clubs, my feet spread wide to steady myself against the wind, and squinting to keep the rain from running into my eyes. I would play until I was soaked through, the only one on the course, a lone little boy fighting against the forces of nature to play the game he loved. The only thing that would stop me was lightning, and even that didn't really stop me until my mother came out onto the course wrapped in a raincoat to physically take the club away from me.

"You're holding a lightning rod, you dummy! You want to *fry yourself* like Ben Franklin?!" she'd yell.

My mother, for some reason, always maintained that Benjamin Franklin had electrocuted himself and died when he famously flew a key into the clouds and harnessed electricity, and throughout my childhood she used him as an example of the dangers of electricity.

"Don't stick your finger in that socket, you'll *fry yourself* like Ben Franklin!"

This, despite the fact that every history book in America could confirm that Benjamin Franklin had survived his encounter with lightning. How else could he have reported his findings had he not? But the facts were not to be foisted upon my mother, and she saw my fanatical desire to play the game of golf even under the worst weather conditions as more evidence of "the madness."

So I played in the rain, and the wind, and even played in the snow with bright-orange balls so they could be found among the blanket of white. Then a strange thing happened. I found out I played well in the rain. Better, in fact, than I did when conditions were fair. Like a racehorse who loves to run in the slop, I discovered that I was a foul-weather wunderkind, happiest in the mud and muck. Somehow, when the added factor of the weather pushed the unpredictability of the game to such an absurd level, with swirling gusts of wind and waterlogged fairways, with puddles the size of ponds and visibility down to zero, I found a certain freedom. Having no idea how the ball was going to react when you launched it into the air, whether it was going to sail toward the green or blow back in your face, allowed me to stop worrying and just swing.

But the biggest effect the rain had upon my game was in my putting. Nothing slows down a fast green like rain. When the greens are so full of water that it feels like putting through wet cement, it worked to my benefit. I usually putt the ball too hard and overshoot the hole, so a dry, fast green is a nightmare, but with the rain-soaked green offering resistance, I could finally find the perfect tempo.

So I was ecstatic when I woke up to find that on the second day of the La Siesta Open, the most important day of my golf life so far, a day I needed as badly as the bone-dry ground needed this rain, the heavens opened up and gave me a chance. Every drop that hit the window was another drop of hope. I had to make the cut today. If I didn't make up at least twelve strokes on the field today, I would wind up below the cut line and out of the tournament, out of the money, and out of chances.

I rolled off my bed of mats, cursed whatever god made my

spine so fragile, and shuffled over to the coffee machine, ignoring the symphony of pops and cracks coming from my joints. As the coffee brewed, I pulled out my phone and decided to do a little research on Don Osborne. I needed to know more about him, other than the fact that I had been sleeping with his wife. There had to be something in his history that would point me to his killer. Lucky for me, a successful businessman and socialite like Don Osborne left behind a long digital trail of newspaper articles, magazine profiles, and society column mentions, so a simple Google search yielded dozens of hits and a string of articles.

Going all the way back to the mid '70s, when he came back from the war and took the town by storm, Don Osborne had always loomed large in La Siesta. One of the earliest articles I could find was a piece in the Orange County Register about his purchase of the La Siesta Country Club. Located at the very tip of La Siesta Point, the country club sat on five hundred acres of pristine Southern California coastline, with dramatic cliffs falling into the sea and rolling green hills of the type that make real-estate developers have to change their pants. The club had been scheduled for demolition and the course itself was a wreck, a rough patchwork of bald greens and dried out fairways, but Don had seen the potential for revival and bought it. This hadn't sat well with those who were eagerly awaiting the opportunity to take back that land and develop it, and there seemed to be a long list of people shut out of a lot of potential profit when Don shut the door and elected instead to keep La Siesta a private country club, a place where he and his wealthy friends could cloister themselves from the riffraff and have the ocean all to themselves.

The list of the aggrieved parties seemed to get longer with every click, as articles about Don zipped by my eyeballs as fast as my coffee was going down my throat. The Racquette brothers, my dear old friends, had been publicly feuding with Don over real-estate deals, construction projects, and just about anything else they had their hands into ever since they'd emigrated from the great white north. Gordo was widely quoted as saying Don Osborne was going to ruin La Siesta by standing in the way of development, that he was "wasting all that beautiful land on a stupid game for rich people, eh?"

The local chapter of the Wildlife Preservation Society wasn't too happy about Don's purchase either. The land the country club sat on was a nesting ground for a species of endangered birds, California gnatcatchers, *Polioptila californica* to be specific, who made their nests in the low coastal sage brush along this particular stretch of coast. This must have been one of those birds that laid the egg in the ninth hole yesterday. Sure enough, one of the next articles I clicked had a picture of the hippie with the tongs from yesterday. The caption identified him as Shiloh Greene, head of the Wildlife Preservation Society.

I replayed the scene from the previous day in my head. It had been such a peculiar sight on a golf course, a long-haired hippie with Birkenstocks and a pair of elongated forceps. The Wildlife Preservation Society had planned to expand the existing sanctuary at the edge of town to include the land the country club now sat on. But then Don stepped in, and, well, I was about to play eighteen holes on that land, so I didn't have to read the whole article to see how it turned out.

Don had secured the land, fought off the competition, and signed the deal thanks in large part to his ace lawyer, Bill Dwyer. Bill had helped fend off challenges from the Racquettes, the Wildlife Preservation Society, and even the town of La Siesta itself to make the deal possible. Dwyer was a "crack legal mind," Don was quoted as saying, and he wouldn't be where he was today without him. I scrolled through a half dozen more links on my phone and decided it might be a good idea to pay old Bill Dwyer a visit. After all, he was last person to play a round with dear old Don

I Googled the number of his office and called to see if I might somehow get an appointment, and the line was answered by a chirpy young receptionist who informed me that Mr. Dwyer was out of the office on a call with a client at the moment.

"But I thought Mr. Dwyer only had one client? Don Osborne, who just so happens to be dead right now."

"That's correct sir, but now Mr. Dwyer's sole client is the wife of the deceased, Mrs. Osborne."

"Kitty Osborne hired Bill Dwyer? Why would she do that?" I asked, surprised that Kitty had not only hired a lawyer so soon after Don's murder, but Don's own lawyer at that.

"Mr. Dwyer wondered the same thing. That's why he went to see her at the Osborne estate."

"Do a lot of lawyers make house calls?"

"Not in my experience, sir. But Mr. Dwyer and Mr. Osborne had a very unique relationship."

"And now that relationship continues with his widow," I said, ruminating on the possible implications.

"I suppose so," she replied.

She had been friendly and helpful, and I wasn't sure I wouldn't need her assistance down the line, so I made sure to be solicitous as I signed off.

"Well, thanks for your help. You've been very kind. With your boss out of the office and his only client dead, you must be bored sitting around that office today."

"Not for long," she piped up enthusiastically. "Mr. Dwyer gave me the rest of the day off, and two passes to go see the La Siesta Open! I'm leaving right after this phone call.".

"That was awfully nice of him," I said, trying to match her enthusiasm.

"Oh, Bill's the best," she gushed. "I mean, Mr. Dwyer," she followed, dampening her tone to hide her enthusiasm, which I found more than a little telling. It's possible there was something more going on between Bill Dwyer and his secretary, but frankly, I was more interested in what was going on between Bill and Kitty.

"I only wish it wasn't raining."

"Oh, I wouldn't worry about that," I assured her. "Some golfers play better in the rain."

I hung up the phone and decided immediately that I needed to get into Bill Dwyer's office and get a look at his files, and one look out the window at the storm outside confirmed I would have some time before the tournament could begin. Lightning crackled across the sky, and despite the fact that ol' Ben Franklin had survived his encounter, the PGA wouldn't expose players to that risk, so they'd be forced to delay the tee-off until the sky was a little less dangerous.

I drained my coffee and decided to head over to Bill Dwyer's office. I had learned a lot about Don Osborne in a short time from Google—that was the beauty of the world wide web. But Google only tells you the things people want you to know. The information I was after was sure to be more closely guarded.

## 12

The storm was showing no signs of letting up, the dark gray sky blooming periodically with bright flashes of lightning, as I pulled into the parking lot behind Bill Dwyer's law office. I would have to make this fast if I was going to get back before my tee time. The rain wouldn't hold out forever. There were only a few cars in the lot, and I was hoping his office would be empty. I didn't know what I was looking for exactly, but I knew Bill had closer ties to Don than anyone else, so I decided to have a look around. If he was a person with dirty little secrets—and I suspected Don was—the only person he would trust would be the only person sworn to secrecy, his lawyer.

I parked my car at the far end of the lot and popped my trunk. I rooted around among my clubs and all the other crap until I found what I was looking for: an old jumpsuit, the kind worn by caddies. I slipped it on over my regular clothes and grabbed a box of cleaning supplies I kept in the trunk. It wasn't the most elaborate disguise, but I made a passing resemblance to a janitor.

Otherwise I had no real cover story, no reason for being there, so I had to make it in and out clean.

The manifest in the lobby listed Dwyer & Associates on the second floor. I took the stairwell in the hopes of passing as few people as possible and made my way down the hallway, a baseball cap pulled low over my eyes to avoid any unnecessary eye contact. I had my hand on the knob to the office and was about to pick the lock when a voice from behind stopped me cold.

"Hey! Janitor!" someone yelled down the hall.

*Shit. You've got to be kidding me,* I thought. I turned my head as little as possible, not wanting to show my face to whoever this was.

"Hey you! I'm talking to you," he called after me, his voice raising in volume. "Someone puked all over the men's room."

"Okay. I'll get to it right after I clean this office!" I called back to him, hoping that would be the end of it.

Nope.

"You'll get to it when I say you'll get to it, *pal.*"

*Shit.* That *pal* sounded aggressive, I thought to myself.

He was coming toward me now, a towering hulk with a neck as thick as a tree trunk bulging out of his blue blazer and a head shaved bald. He looked like a steroidal wrestler on his way to the high school prom. I desperately wanted to tell this guy to piss off, but I was in no position to make a scene. I tried to play nice.

"No problem, sir. I'll get it all cleaned up for you right away. I just have to take care of something urgent in here."

He was closer now, and I could see from the flare in his nostrils he didn't like what he was hearing. He was bearing down on me like a charging bull and I turned to face him, my hands in the air.

"Don't make me drag you down there myself." His face was flush with the rush of confrontation, and the veins were beginning to bulge across his temples, making him look like an angry hard-on. He was practically on top of me, close enough for me to smell the creatine powder and raw eggs he'd had for breakfast on his breath.

"No problem. You got it. Anything you say, sir," I said, doing my best to appear submissive, to bow and scrape to this ape in the hopes of somehow avoiding further confrontation.

I bent down to get my box of cleaning supplies, but, to his great surprise, when I stood back up I was holding only an aerosol can. A look of confusion registered in his eyes for a brief second before I jammed my forefinger down on the nozzle and blasted him with a face full of furniture polish. He shrieked and pawed at his eyes, burning from the toxic cloud of lemon-fresh scent. Eyes red, nose running, and coughing like a man drowning on dry land, he was helpless at my feet in a matter of seconds.

*What the fuck was that all about anyway?* I thought. *Who is this steroid jockey?* Then I looked down at the writhing mass and saw a taser in a holster on his belt.

*A taser?*

Then I noticed the name tag on his suit, SEASIDE SECURITY.

*Damn it.* He was the security guard. The exact last person I wanted to encounter. Now I'd maced him into a slobbering mess. He was still in agony, in the fetal position, which gave me a second to think. I grabbed the taser out of its holster, arming myself against any retaliation this monster was planning, and considered my options. I had to get into that office and find out what I could about Bill Dwyer and Don Osborne's business together, but

I couldn't just assault a security guard, then go through with the crime and hope not to get caught. I had to think of something.

And that's when I saw the thong. A little pink lacy whale tail sticking out of the back of the big oaf's suit pants. As he rolled around on the ground his shirt had come completely untucked, and with his shirt tail hanging out I could see the panties. I realized, *this guy is wearing women's underwear.* Perfect. I love a little blackmail. It can be an incredibly useful tool.

I zapped him with a quick jolt from the taser, sending him into a fit of convulsions before conking out on the floor. When I was sure he was out cold I used his keys to open the office door, then dragged him inside and shut the door.

By the time the oaf came to, I had him tied to a chair in the waiting room with his pants around his ankles. He was clad only in a pair of pink Victoria's Secret panties, with his uniform jacket still on to clearly display his name tag. I snapped a picture, and when he heard the familiar clicking sound he opened his eyes to see me standing in front of him focusing an iPhone on him.

"Smile for the camera!" I said as he came back to consciousness. *Click. Click. Click.* "Pink really isn't your color, by the way." *Click. Click.*

"Shit," was all the lummox could muster.

"I didn't even know Victoria's Secret made panties that big." I chuckled.

*Click. Click.*

"You know this is nothing to be ashamed of. This kind of thing is perfectly healthy," he spat, defiant. "So I'm kinky. *So what?* You can't shame me."

"I completely agree," I said. And I do completely agree. I personally have no problem with whatever anyone wants to do, or wear, or whatever. But I took one look at his tough-guy persona, the muscles growing out of his muscles and the neck tattoo, and I called his bluff.

"So who should I send these to?" I asked. "Your whole contact list?"

His eyes went wide.

"This is your phone, by the way. My pictures are already living happily in the cloud." I reached into my back pocket and pulled out my own iPhone and waved it at him.

"Your thumbprint was easy to get when you passed out in your pink panties. I'd say as a security guard, that's going to look bad on your performance review."

He said nothing, but I could see the fight go out of his eyes.

"That's what I thought. Now I'm going to have a look around and then I'm gone. I'm not going to steal anything. And I'm not going to send those pictures to anyone, if you just be cool. All right?"

He breathed a sigh that I took as a yes.

"Cool. Now just sit tight," I said with a smirk. I headed toward the inner office—and hopefully some of Bill Dwyer's secrets.

———————•———————

They say a messy desk is a sign of intelligence. If that's true, Bill Dwyer must be some sort of genius. The carpet of papers spread across the large antique mahogany desk was thicker than the carpet on the floor, several inches of legal briefs, books, and manila folders spilling their contents.

*Shit.* I was prepared for some digging, but didn't this guy have a laptop? I was in possession of a handy little tool, a program that could be easily uploaded to any computer with a thumb drive, that would allow you to bypass the security password on the home screen. It wasn't really all that groundbreaking a hacking tool, fairly routine in the intelligence and law enforcement communities. It couldn't decode encrypted messages or anything that was really well-protected, but I find that most of the people I've used it on, particularly older people like Bill Dwyer, didn't have much more than the basic gatekeeping setup. I took it off a hacker we busted while I was on the force, and I guess it must have ended up in my box of personal effects when I got let go. Funny how that happens.

A lot of good it did me staring at a stack of dead trees. I rooted through his desk drawers and found the usual stuff, a lot of dried-up pens, a two-year-old copy of *Golf Digest* with a dog-eared article, "How to Improve Your Swing in Six Easy Steps," and a fully loaded nine-millimeter handgun. You might think finding the gun was an a-ha moment for me, but the truth is that in modern America, a gun is as common an item to find in an office as a water cooler. They're everywhere. There were times as a cop when I became more suspicious when I *didn't* find a gun, because that meant someone had most likely removed the gun. But Bill's was right here in his desk drawer, right where it ought to be, so that didn't raise any red flags for me.

Stacked next to the desk were even more papers, these in

bound bricks the size of cinder blocks, enough to make an igloo for a small family of Inuit, and against the far wall, boxes of legal documents stacked in towers. They were marked in black magic marker on the side: *The Wildlife Preservation Society vs. Don Osborne, The Wildlife Preservation Society vs. La Siesta Country Club, The Wildlife Preservation Society vs. Osborne Security Systems.* Box after box of lawsuits, all of them waged against one man, Don Osborne. I thought it was ironic that an environmental group could generate so much paperwork. There must be a forest's worth of paper in these boxes.

I could hear the security guard outside the office door struggling to get free, so I figured I'd better hurry up before he tried something heroic. I didn't have time to look through the boxes, so I glanced around the office, searching for anything else that might hold a clue.

There was a bag of golf clubs in the corner, a wet bar in another, and over by the window, what looked like a small display case: a wooden table about the size of a scrabble board with a clear glass box sitting on top, a protective shell encasing a miniature display inside. Like every other surface in the office, this had stacks of papers piled on top, but when I slid them to the side and peered down into the display I saw an architectural model. It looked like a perfect little town for a model train set, complete with fake little trees and green felt lawns. Except I've never seen a model train set with enormous mansions overlooking the ocean.

I cleared off the paperwork and got a better look at what appeared to be a luxury planned community. Surrounded by a low wall around the perimeter, the model showed a group of houses, gigantic ones from the scale of it, built around the outside of a wide circular drive. In the center of the houses was a large lagoon, and it was bordered the rear side by a cliff that dropped off steeply into the ocean. All of this was rendered in loving miniature detail, down to the little sign on the front gate that read LA SIESTA DUNES.

I thought for a second. *La Siesta Dunes?* No such place exists. I was sure of it. The entire town of La Siesta itself was no bigger than a bump on the Pacific coastline. Not only was there no La Siesta Dunes, but there was no place to build one even if you wanted to. Every inch of this town was already taken, and the only land that hadn't been bought up and built on was the wildlife preserve, but that was protected from being developed by environmental laws.

So where was La Siesta Dunes supposed to go?

As I stared into the glass box, it occurred to me there was only one place left in La Siesta it could go. The wildlife sanctuary.

# 13

The sky was still spitting rain when I arrived at the country club, the driveway a river of umbrellas as the more dedicated dimple-heads slogged their way through the inclement weather on their way to watch the day's action. A true golf fan is an all-weather fan, so I wasn't surprised to see a line of golf faithful snaking down the driveway as I drove the Crown Vic at a crawl toward the players' parking area, moving slower than a golf cart to make sure I didn't run anyone over. The difference between a group of golf fans standing together in the rain compared to a regular group of people is that golf fans all bring along their extra-large golf umbrellas. The amount of coverage was so complete, it formed a virtual roof, like one long tent of stripes and sponsorship logos. I could have walked all the way to the club-house without getting wet.

For a game that was born on the rocky and rainy country-side of Scotland, golf has since become a much gentler pastime, one associated with warm climates and sunny skies. Places like

California and Florida and Arizona have softened the game to make it more accessible to the average weekend player. After all, a hobbyist with his one day off all week doesn't want to hack his way around a course in the middle of a squall. But a true dimple-head loves it. Anyone afflicted with "the madness" could feel the connection between the game and nature that was truly awakened when the weather showed up and came into play as a factor.

I parked my car and headed toward the clubhouse, but instead of entering directly through the back door to the locker room, I took a detour and went around the side toward the back patio. I wanted to take a quick look at that TV tower the sniper had used as a roost. I rounded the corner and there it stood, not much more than metal scaffolding holding up three stories of platform. The entire structure was wrapped in a tight plastic skin in the Golf Channel colors and hung with various sponsorship banners and corporate logos. The top level had a large television camera, which at the moment was unmanned. The story below was obscured by the signage from sponsors, but I could tell from where I was standing that the second level was the height the sniper needed to get a clean shot at Don in the ballroom.

I wanted to get into that second story and look around, but the place was buzzing with activity. Crew members of all sorts from the Golf Channel and the PGA were running around in a state of semi-panic trying to get ready for the day's broadcast. I took a chance that they would be so focused on doing their jobs that they wouldn't notice me, but I had to make it look good. Along the low patio wall, next to some large equipment boxes, I noticed a pile of cables wrapped in bundles. I picked up one of the bundles and walked casually toward the TV tower. As I reached the ladder, I looked around at a sea of distracted faces, then swung the bundle over my shoulder and climbed up the ladder to the second level, pulling myself through the small entry flap between promotional banners.

I crouched down and peered around at the small, cramped space, filled with boxes and more piles of cables. *Christ, how many miles of cable are these people gonna lay?* I thought, before adding my bundle to a pile in the corner. Surrounded on all sides by banners and advertising, it was impossible for anyone to see in, but peeking out from the cracks between the banners from the inside was no problem. From where I stood, I had a clear sightline not only to the ballroom where Don was shot, but a complete three-hundred-sixty-degree view of the entire area. The sniper could have seen anyone coming from almost any direction just by peeking through the banners.

I looked around at the boxes of equipment and coils of cables for some kind of clue, a dropped cigarette butt or candy wrapper, but there was nothing. It occurred to me that none of the stuff that was now in this space was there when the sniper was. That was Wednesday, before the tournament started, and it had been empty. After that, the crime scene had almost immediately been taken over by the television crews, and of course Chief Garrett and the La Siesta Police had taken no measures to seal it off from contamination.

I was creeping around, trying to be quiet and not knock into anything, when my foot brushed up against something on the floor. I looked down and saw a little brass disk, about the size of a quarter, with a serrated edge that made it look like the blade from a miniature buzz saw. My first thought was that it was a gear from the inside of a watch, but when I bent down to pick it up I realized it was a gear from the top of a sprinkler head.

Golf courses have literally thousands of sprinkler heads, so it shouldn't have been too surprising to find one on the property. But up here? The scaffold had only been here for a few days. It's possible that some member of the grounds crew had been up here and dropped the sprinkler wheel out of their pocket, but what reason would they have had to climb up onto a scaffold? There was no other sprinkler equipment up here, no pipes or sprinkler heads—just TV stuff from what I could see. It could belong to the killer. But a sprinkler head? What could it mean?

As I was puzzling over the meaning of the gear, I suddenly felt a presence on the tower. I could feel the pull, like a small tug on the screwed together structure, of someone climbing up the ladder. I froze in place, bracing for a confrontation and preparing to do some serious bullshitting, but the man on the ladder climbed right past the second level and continued to the third story. I figured he must be the cameraman, and I realized that meant the broadcast was about to start. I was about to make a hasty exit when I heard three familiar voices coming toward me, the television announcers for the Golf Channel: Joe Roebuck, Jill Smelt, and Wee Jackie Argyle.

*Shit.* Now was not the time to make my casual escape with a bundle of cables. They would recognize me. I would have to wait it out. I could hear their voices coming closer, and it sounded as if Joe Roebuck was not having a good morning.

"Jesus Christ, Jackie, could you lay off it until at least lunch? I can smell the Scotch on you from here," he said, his deep baritone immediately familiar to anyone who watched golf on television.

"Oh *fer fucksakes*, lad!" said Wee Jackie, having none of it. "It's cold as a dead dog's knob out here. There should be whiskey in the water fountains on a day like today."

"Really, Joe," said Jill, coming to Jackie's defense, "if we have to put up with watching you scratch your nuts all day, I think we're all entitled to a little nip." She laughed.

"Aye! Now that's a lass," cheered Jackie, taking a nip from his flask.

I could hear them settling into the booth below me. I peeked through the crack between the banners on the front side and could see the main camera being wheeled into place in front of them. It looked like I would be stuck up there for a moment. I couldn't help but listen in.

"Jesus, between the two of you and the rain, it'll be a miracle if we don't float away today," grumbled Joe Roebuck, settling into his chair. Then, like flipping a switch, there was a complete change in his tone.

"Okay, game faces everyone, I'll open her up and then throw it to Jill. Jackie, you stand by for when we need the ramblings of an old drunk."

A crew member stepped up to the side of the camera and began to count down.

*Five, four, three, two . . .*

"Screw you, ya wee cu—"

*One.*

"GOOD MORNING, GOLF FANS! And welcome to day two of the Golf Channel's coverage of the La Siesta Open coming to you live from the Big Snooze, beautiful La Siesta California. I'm Joe Roebuck, and with me today is the two-time LPGA Tour champ and now my talented colleague, Jill Smelt."

"Morning, Joe! It's so good to see you!" gushed Jill, her chipper on-camera persona slipping on as easily as an old pair of shoes.

"And to my left, if you can see him behind his coffee cup, *he-he*—"

"I'm right here, boy-o!" piped up Wee Jackie, cheerful as a cartoon character.

"Oh, there he is! It's none other than Wee Jackie Argyle, with us as always for a little color commentary."

"Cheers, Joe. A've not seen a gray day I couldn't paint a little brighter with me humble words."

"Well, we're gonna need you today, Jackie. It's so rainy, it looks like your homeland out there," said Joe.

"Aye, she does remind me of bonnie ol' Scotland. No doubt the weather will play a major role in today's outcome."

I couldn't believe the sincerity coming out of these three people who'd just been sniping and clawing at each other moments ago. I have to say, I was impressed. They were professionals.

"No doubt about it, Jackie," continued Joe. "Now, Jill, let's take a look at this field of golfers. Some really strong players at the top of the leaderboard going into today."

"That's right, Joe. At the top of the leaderboard, we have the usual cast of characters such as Danny Master, Buong Ho Park, and Lleyton Vanderfinch. Master set the pace on day one with a blistering six under par through the front nine, and just kept burning up the greens all the way through eighteen holes and really showing how to play this beautiful, if unpredictable course, finishing with an impressive round of sixty-seven."

"It really was something to watch," said Joe. "Now, Jill, you mention the usual cast of characters, Park, Master, Vanderfinch and the like . . . but what about the *unusual* characters out there? I'm speaking of course about Lleyton Vanderfinch's partner for the day, the retired police officer Duffer McDermott."

*Son of a bitch.* I fumed. *Did Joe Roebuck just call me Duffer on national TV?!* The bastard would pay.

"Ha ha, yes," chuckled Jill. "Mr. McDermott is an unusual presence on the course. Kind of a throwback, you might say."

"Aye," chimed in Jackie, "a throwback to a time before personal trainers."

Their laughter ran through me like a jolt of electricity. Joe especially seemed to be loving it, really letting loose with an over-the-top phony laugh.

"I guess it's true what they say about cops and doughnuts." Joe chuckled.

*Did he just call me fat?* I couldn't believe my ears. I was being slagged off by the goddamn Golf Channel. Even *Wee Jackie Fucking Argyle* was taking shots at me.

"It was not a great day for our crime-fighting friend," said Jill, "who found more trouble on the greens than he ever found in the mean streets of La Siesta. He shot a cringe-inducing *four putt* on eight that seemed to last forever."

"A've seen fewer shots in a game of pool," added Jackie.

"Oh, that was truly ugly, Jill." Joe sighed. "I had to watch a replay of Danny Master's beautiful eagle on eleven just to wipe the memory out of my head. And what about that awful approach on fourteen? If he spent any more time whacking weeds in the rough, I thought the grounds crew was going to make him an honorary member!"

Everyone shared another hearty laugh at my expense.

*Screw you, Joe Fucking Roebuck, you chisel-chinned asshat*, I thought to myself.

I was fuming. How dare he mock me on national television?! What a prick. I realized I'd had enough. I couldn't sit up here and listen to this shit any longer. It was going to get in my head. I had golf to play. They were about to see what a true throwback looks like. Not a pampered poodle with a personal trainer, but a blood-and-guts golfer who could not only master this course, these players, and this weather, but a golfer who can master himself, under all conditions. Today was going to be different. I was in my element. This was the kind of day that separates the sunny-day dreamers from the all-weather true believers. So fuck Joe Roebuck and his crew of merry Muppets. They'd just have to wait and see.

I was climbing down the ladder at the back of the scaffolding when my eyes became level with a small mark embossed onto the metal poles that made up the frame: PROPERTY OF RACQUETTE BROTHERS CONSTRUCTION.

*I'll be damned.* I thought. *The Racquette Brothers put up this scaffolding?* They had said they weren't allowed anywhere near the club, but it turns out they provided the infrastructure for the tournament. That means they would have had full access to the grounds and they would have known exactly where the television tower would sit. And they sure had an ax to grind with Don. With him dead, they could expand their business and who knows, maybe make enough money to join the fancy-pants golf club. Sure they said they hated the place, but that's only because they weren't allowed in. The Racquette brothers wanted to be rich and fancy like everyone else.

# 14

I was chewing on a golf tee, deep in thought, when my partner for the day came up behind me and slapped me on the back, almost causing me to inhale the small piece of sharp pointed wood in my mouth.

"What flavor tee you chewing these days?" he asked, having a good chuckle as I coughed and sputtered.

"Piña colada. I have them specially made," I replied, spitting the tee into my hand.

"Well, shit, partner, if you got the hook-up on some tasty tees, get me some would you?" He laughed, sticking out his gloved right hand for a friendly but firm handshake.

Today I was paired with Byung-ho Park, an old friend from the Web Dot Com Tour. He and I had bonded over many consolation beers after losing rounds out on the road, and I was happy for him when he had finally gotten his tour card last year. Born in South Korea to conservative, golf-obsessed parents, Byung-ho had arrived at the University of Florida ten years ago on a golf scholarship and very quickly adapted to life in America. By the end of his freshman year, he was not only number one on the golf team but also the "keg stand" champion of his fraternity. Gone was the shy, polite young man from Korea, replaced with a beer drinking, tobacco chewing, good ol' boy from the swamps of Florida that his friends nicknamed "Bung Hole."

"It's good to see you Byung-ho. How's the tour treating you?" I asked, with genuine affection.

"Shit, hoss, up until now I couldn't win a beauty contest on a hog farm. But I feel like my luck is about to turn around," he replied with a wide smile.

"What makes you think that?" I asked.

"Because they paired me up with you!" He let out a loud hearty Southern laugh and slapped me on the back once again. "You're like a lightning rod for bad luck, so I figure the safest place to stand in a shit storm is right next to you."

"Thanks for the vote of confidence," I replied, shaking it off as good-natured ribbing. Giving each other shit was a player's time-honored duty on tour, and I wasn't one to gripe about a shot to my ego.

Grateful Ted was standing serenely at the edge of the box, his eyes open but his thoughts clearly miles away as I approached to discuss our game plan.

"So, Ted, rainy day today, good for my putting game. What's our strategy?" I asked, hoping for some pearls of wisdom.

He contemplated this for a second, or at least I hoped that's what he was contemplating. You never really could tell, before he said, with certainty.

"Long and low."

"Long and low?"

"Your drives. I want you to keep them low. The wind is coming in off the ocean and it's going to play havoc with the ball. So keep it long and low and slice through it like a laser beam. Wind can't affect a beam of light."

"Wind can't affect a beam of light?" I wasn't quite sure if I knew what he meant by that or not, but like all things with Grateful Ted, there was a lot more going on than just what was on the surface. At least, I hoped so.

I took my driver from the bag and prepared to take a few practice swings.

"No, Duffer. No practice."

"What? No practice? Why? I thought practice makes perfect," I protested.

"It does, but you already practiced. You're perfect. Just hit the ball."

I'd given up trying to decipher the words that came out of Ted's mouth a long time ago and had found that the best way to take his advice was literally. The pronouncements often sounded complex, but they were hidden behind simple instructions, so I learned to just follow the instructions.

"Just remember. Long and low."

I stepped into the box, set my ball on the tee, and, without a warm-up stroke, crushed a laser beam down the middle of the fairway, long and low. Despite the stiff headwind coming in off the sea, my ball sliced throughout the air with ease. Unlike the day before, I had avoided the long grass, hitting a slight fade to the right and landing in the dead center of the fairway, a safe but solid shot to start the day.

I turned to Grateful Ted, pleased.

"Wind can't affect a beam of light," I said with a smile.

He smiled back. We were in the groove already. A good feeling. Even Byung-ho was impressed with the drive.

"Yee-haw!" he whooped "You slapped the snot outta that sumbitch!"

As clear a sign as the starter pistol of a race, that first drive signaled the beginning of a great opening nine holes for me. I was three strokes under par by the turn, and I was beating the pants off Byung-ho so badly he started to lose his Southern accent. The rain continued steadily for most of the morning, with the wind coming off the ocean in bursts and thunder crashing overhead like sonic booms. Players were struggling from the beginning, and the pace of play was a slow grind, as player after player splashed his way from puddle to puddle. The wind swirled in unpredictable eddies and blew the rain sideways, dampening spirits and beating down some of the best golfers in the field. Even Danny Master was having a bad day, slogging his way to a four over par for the front nine. The greens were soaked, club grips were slick, and the wet weather showed no signs of abating. It was a "duck's day out," as my father would have said, and I was loving every minute of it.

I was soaked through to the skin and shivering by the end of the tenth hole, but I'd never been happier. I was playing out-of-my-mind golf. On the dreaded eighth hole that I'd had a meltdown on the day before, I sunk a twenty-foot putt for par, stroking the ball as hard as I could and watching with glee as the ball pushed its way through the waterlogged green like a groundhog through fresh dirt, slowly but firmly plowing toward the cup and in.

PLUNK.

I was ecstatic. On that same hole, Byung-ho got stuck in a swamp and wasted three strokes trying to get his ball out from under two inches of water, a disaster by any standards, but cruel fun to watch as he slammed and slashed his nine iron at the submerged ball. As we rounded fifteen I caught a glimpse of the leaderboard, and to my delight and amazement my name was on it. Right below the cut line, there it was: F.D. MCDERMOTT. Starting the day a dozen strokes back, I was amazed to have made up so much ground, but the storm had added so many strokes to the other players' scores that I had closed the gap considerably.

I was close. I could taste it. I needed to make up just two strokes on the last three holes to make the cut and continue to play for the money on the weekend. I hadn't seen Kitty in the stands all day, but with the weather as nasty as it was, I didn't think too much of it. Probably that was for the best. I didn't need to think about Kitty right now. I needed to think about golf. But the thing about Kitty was once she got under your skin, she was always there. I couldn't shake her, not even in the one place I go to completely forget everything else, the golf course.

"You all right there, boss?" asked Grateful Ted, breaking my momentary reverie.

"Yeah, yeah," I assured him. "Let's make some weekend plans."

I shook off the minor Kitty-induced coma on sixteen and knocked in a birdie, aided once again by a green as slow and soggy as a manatee fart. I was feeling good heading into seventeen, need-ing only one more birdie in the next two holes to make the cut, when something odd happened, which was, unfortunately, typical for me. As soon as things are going well for me on the course, it seems something always pops up to try and throw me off.

We arrived on the seventeenth tee and the strangest thing set my mind off on a tangent. Ironically, on the rainiest day in La Siesta Open history, the sprinkler system inexplicably switched on, suddenly spraying great jets of water onto the already water-logged fairways. It lasted only a few moments before Mr. Lo arrived and managed to shut it off, but seeing him reminded me of the night we met, a couple of years prior, when I was still on the force. I had been called out to a domestic disturbance, and I was preparing myself for another entitled La Siesta jerk slapping his wife around, but what I found instead was a very drunk Mr. Lo stumbling around his backyard ranting and raving about the Vietnam War.

When I arrived at his modest ranch house out back of the club he was waving a pistol above his head yelling, "Come and get it, G.I. Joe!" and it took some delicate negotiations to get him to put the gun down and head back inside. What I saw when he opened the back door was a little unnerving, a veritable arsenal of weaponry strewn about the living room, ranging from decorative samurai swords hanging on the wall, to boxes of ammunition and several handguns lying on a table. A pile of rifles lay dumped in a corner. It seemed a dangerous situation, given his state of ine-briation and anger level, so I had a couple officers come out and confiscate the lot for safekeeping until he sobered up, but he had come to the station the next day with permits for everything, so we gave everything back to him with a warning to keep his cool, or we might have to make the arrangement more permanent.

I hadn't thought about that night for years. Mr. Lo and I had since become friendly and I never saw him that way again, so I'd long since written it off as an aberration, but seeing him on the course just then sent my mind going and I started making connections in my head. I suddenly knew where I'd seen a wheel like the gear I found in the TV tower. The idea struck me, and suddenly I wasn't concentrating on golf anymore, but thinking about Don Osborne's murder. I needed to focus: only two more holes to go, and I needed a birdie on at least one of them. I had to reach within myself and find the discipline to concentrate on golf and nothing else. Just two more holes.

Unfortunately, when I stepped up to the tee on seventeen, I tightened up. Suddenly, my arms felt an inch shorter. I sent my drive high into the air, where a sudden gust of wind knocked it back at me as if in contempt, prompting a disappointed groan from the small crowd that had started to follow me as news of my steady ascent had circulated among the dimple-head faithful. My ball sat maybe one hundred fifty yards in front of the tee, splashed down in a puddle so deep I'd need Moses to come and part the damn thing.

I managed to dig myself out of the water and advance the ball another hundred yards or so, but even with a nice recovery on my third shot to land on the green within shouting distance of the hole, I would be lucky to make par on this hole.

I was not lucky. I two-putted for a bogey and suddenly I found myself in the same position the other golfers had been in all day, going backwards. Now I was two strokes away from the cut line with only one hole to go. How the hell was I supposed to do that? The chances of me getting an eagle two on the par-four eighteenth hole were next to zero. Just like that, I was screwed. My only hope was that the other players behind me continue to do so poorly that the cut line moved. I just had to be in the top seventy golfers to qualify, so if someone screwed up, I could still make it in.

It was a long shot, but I still had to try. I had to play the eighteenth as well as I could and hope for the best. Now was not the time to pull a stunt and try to go for an eagle. It was too difficult, too aggressive a line. But something deep within me wanted to go for it. *To hell with long and low*, I thought. I wanted to swing full out and go for a monster drive, do anything and everything I could to get myself that eagle and secure my place in the tournament for the weekend.

Grateful Ted could sense what I was thinking and tried to talk me off the ledge.

"Easy there, partner. There's no sense in letting that last hole rattle you. It was bound to happen. One more hole. Let's not do anything crazy," he cautioned. "You can still make the cut if they move the line, on a day like today, that's a pretty good bet," he said, a steady and rational argument.

This is why I had hired Grateful Ted. To be the yin to my yang. To be sensible, if a bit mystical. I have him around to talk me out of doing stupid things.

"I want to go for it," I said, a slightly insane sparkle in my eye.

"Come on, buddy. You saw what the wind just did to you.

You don't want any part of that. Long and low like we talked about, remember?"

"Fuck long and low, Ted! I want to hit the shit out the ball."

At the sound of the word "fuck" leaving my lips, Grateful Ted's eyes almost popped out of his head. He instantly shushed me and I realized what I'd done. I'd said a curse word! Two in fact! I could get kicked out of the tournament right here! Luckily, when I looked over at the referee, Charlie Winer, he was huddled under the hood of his raincoat so deeply he hadn't heard me.

We both breathed a sigh of relief, but the moment made me stop and come to my senses a bit. I couldn't lose it here. I had to keep it together. I had to do the smart thing. I decided I'd better listen to Grateful Ted.

I exhaled deeply, letting go of the bad luck of the last hole, and stepped up to the tee.

"Remember, long and low," repeated Grateful Ted, a deadly serious look in his eyes. "Trust me, Duffer."

I nodded my head. I understood. Then, despite all reasoning, and completely ignoring what was good for me, I swung full out, crushing a high, arcing, rainbow of a shot. At the moment my ball reached its apex, the wind suddenly caught hold of it, carrying it aloft like a feather and propelling it forward. The ball soared over the gallery, landing three hundred yards away and smack dab in the center of the fairway, just a few dozen yards from the green. I don't really know how it happened, I had decided to play it safe, but somewhere along the way my body must have overridden my mind and just gone for it.

The crowd loved it.

I turned to Grateful Ted as they applauded.

"What happened to long and low?"

"Ted, I trust you, but sometimes a man has to make his own decisions," I said, slapping him on the back as we set off down the fairway. I was a chip shot from the green, and I could feel the pull of the hole begging for my ball. I knew I had to go full out. To play it safe and wait for the other golfers to fall behind just wasn't my style. I wanted to make the cut by playing great golf, not by hoping others play bad golf.

After watching Byung-ho splash his way down the fairway, out of one puddle only to land in another, I approached my ball and said a silent prayer. I held the grip of my nine iron softly, like I was holding an egg, took a deep breath and swung. The ball popped off the club head and launched into the air, much higher and much further than I had intended.

My heart sank as I saw the trajectory of the ball taking it far beyond the green, but then mother nature suddenly came to my aid once again, and a gust of wind knocked it down, seeming to freeze the ball in its tracks and drop it like a rock onto the green. I couldn't believe my luck, and was already salivating over my coming birdie putt when a miracle happened. The force of the ball's backspin began dragging it toward to hole and, to the utter astonishment of everyone assembled, it plunged into the cup for an eagle.

*A fucking eagle!* I screamed inside my brain. I threw my arms up in triumph, tossing my pitching wedge high into the air.

The crowd went bonkers. Umbrellas flew into the air and strangers hugged each other, jumping up and down with glee. The roar was deafening, louder even than the thunder that had rolled across the sky all morning.

I stood on the fairway stunned. I couldn't believe what I'd witnessed. A goddamn miracle. I had done it. An eagle two on the par four eighteen had put me right at the cut line. I was in. I had made the cut. I was going to play on the weekend, for the money, and, maybe, just maybe, for a chance to win the tournament.

Grateful Ted was speechless. He turned to me with an enigmatic smile and just shrugged. "Well," he finally said with a chuckle, "I guess you can't always trust me."

# 15

After my round I wanted to follow up on my momentary revelation on seventeen, so I decided to go see Mr. Lo. The groundskeeper shack was empty when I arrived, and I used the opportunity to take a quick look around the chaotic room, a cross between an indoor office and outdoor garden shed, with walls on three sides and open to the golf cart parking lot on the fourth. In one corner was a desk piled with employee time cards, seed catalogues and other bric-a-brac. Stacked on the cement floor were boxes of lawn mower parts and broken leaf blowers, while rakes and Weedwackers leaned against the wall. Then, on the workbench below the pegboard, I spotted a box of sprinkler gears. It was torn open, its contents spilled out, and little piles of gears, just like the one I found in the TV tower, sat on the bench in stacks like poker chips.

I turned the corner and found Mr. Lo just outside the shack, bending over a lawn mower. He must have heard me coming, and he stood up and turned around.

"Duffer. What's up, man?" he greeted me with a smile.

"Oh, just thought I'd drop in and say hello," I said, trying and failing to sound nonchalant.

"Okay . . . Well, hello . . ." He stared at me for a moment, seemingly trying to size up my real motive. "Was there something else you wanted?"

"Well, it's nothing, really," I said, soft-pedaling my segue. "It's just that, I stopped by the other night to see you and you weren't here."

"The other night?"

"Yeah. Wednesday night. The night Don Osborne was murdered. I came to say hi and you weren't here."

"So?" he said, a bemused smirk crossing his face. "I don't live here twenty four hours a day, Duffer. I'm not Bill Murray in *Caddyshack*."

"So where were you?"

"I was at home!" he said with a chuckle. "Come on, Duffer, what is this?" he asked, more pointedly.

"This is nothing. Just wondering where you were and if you saw anything that night." I lightened my tone, not wanting to scare him off.

"Well, I was home, and I saw nothing." He sounded as if the conversation was finished, at least as far as he was concerned. "Congratulations on making the cut."

He stood his ground and looked me square in the eye. It seemed as if he wanted to send me a message. Never in my life has "congratulations" sounded so much like "fuck you."

I turned to leave. As I was heading out the door, I turned and asked one more question.

"You didn't like Don Osborne much, did you?"

"Don Osborne was an asshole," he shot back, a sudden anger rising in his voice.

"That's what everyone says, and I'm starting to believe it. But, there was nothing more to it than that?"

"Like what?"

"Well, like, for starters, the fact that the good ol' USA waged a long and painful war in your country. And Don Osborne played a big part in that."

He looked down. "The war was a long time ago. I was just a kid."

"Still, it can't have felt good to have to work for a man that did that to your people. And then to take shit from that man every day . . ."

When he looked up, I saw a flash of anger in his eyes.

"It did *not* feel good. But I *never* took his shit. He threw it at me, you bet, but I never took his shit. I let it pass right through me." He took a deep breath as if letting his anger flow out with his exhalation, then looked me square in the eye.

"Duffer. As my friend, I swear to you. I hated that man. But I didn't kill him."

I looked into his eyes and wanted to believe him, but the sprinkler head, and the prior incident at his home kept me skeptical.

———

The sun was coming out from behind the clouds and warming the late afternoon, the rays of light glinting off La Siesta bay transforming it into a glittering, twinkling field, as if the stars had come out in the daytime. I was heading to the Osborne estate to see if I could have a conversation with Kitty. I wasn't sure if she wanted to see me, but I wanted to ask her a few things about husband number one. I had a feeling it might give me a better idea of what had happened to husband number two.

I decided it was best to bypass security at the Osborne estate. Ever since Don's murder, there'd been a detail of the La Siesta Police Department stationed across from the estate, with more scattered about the Shepherd's Isle neighborhood. I parked my car at the edge of the neighborhood and waited for my ride to show.

Moments later, an oversized pickup with LA SIESTA LANDSCAP-ING pulled up, and I jumped into the back, piling in with four landscapers, a load of sod, and some bags of wood chips bound for the Osborne estate. I had known Phil, the owner of the company, since I'd helped him recover his stolen gardening equipment a few years back. We found it easily, when the meth fiend who'd stolen it couldn't resist firing up a leaf blower at five in the morning, and everyone within a mile radius called the police to report a noise complaint. I knew Phil worked the Osborne estate and asked him to get me past the gate, and he readily obliged.

I pulled a large sun hat over my face as we were waved through the security gate and made our way up the serpentine driveway toward the house. I parted ways with the landscaping crew at the garage and made my way around the back of the house.

I had gone to the Osborne estate looking for Kitty, but she was nowhere to be found. On my way out, I was surprised to run into a different Mrs. Osborne entirely: Don's first wife, Cheryl. She immediately looked familiar, and I realized I recognized her from an old family portrait on the mantle in the house. She was crossing the back lawn, heading toward the guest bungalow at the back of the property with a bottle of Scotch under one arm and a baguette under the other.

I caught up with her just as she reached the threshold of the small cottage, a cute little gray-shingled hut festooned with rose bushes and engulfed by lattice and climbing vines.

"Excuse me, ma'am. Are you Cheryl Osborne?" I called out as she reached the threshold.

She stopped and turned to me, a look of annoyance on her face. I thought she was going to give me hell for that "ma'am." A lot of women hate being called that, but I can't help it if I still talk like a cop: polite, if a bit old-fashioned. Instead she let out a weary sigh and corrected me.

"It's Schaefer, now. Cheryl Schaefer." She took a hungry bite from the end of the baguette.

"My name's McDermott. I was hoping I could talk to you for a moment about your ex-husband, Don." I flashed what I thought of as my disarming smile, hoping she'd be swayed by charm. She didn't seem to go for it.

"Don't you cops ever give it a rest? I just spent half the afternoon being grilled by that blob of a police chief and . . ."

"Garrett was here?" I interrupted.

She nodded. "That explains why you won't find any food left in the kitchen." She gestured with the baguette. "This was all I could wrestle out of his paws before he finally left."

"It also explains the bottle of Scotch."

She looked down at the bottle, slightly embarrassed.

"Anyone would need a drink after talking to Chief Garrett. He's like a garbage disposal with a badge."

I thought she wouldn't break her patrician resolve, but then she smiled, and I knew I'd broken the seal.

"What did you two talk about?" I followed up, trying to dive in while I had an opening.

"Next to nothing, really. That man's a moron. Truly. All he wanted to know is if I stood to gain from the reading of the will. He was insistent. I told him Don and I were *divorced*, why would he leave me anything? But he wouldn't listen. He seems convinced this whole thing is about money."

"And you don't think so?"

"I don't know what the hell this is about, but I don't really feel like talking to another cop for an hour," she said, turning to go.

"I'm not a cop. I'm a private investigator," I said, trying to stop her. "And I couldn't agree more that the chief is an idiot. That's why I'm trying to solve this case myself."

"Well, as long as somebody's *actually trying*, I guess that's okay with me," she said, softening. "Don wasn't the greatest guy in the world, maybe, but he didn't deserve to die. Not like that." She looked at me with a rueful smile. "Are you a drinker?" she asked, holding up the bottle of scotch, a twelve-year-old Balvenie.

"I can be persuaded."

She pushed open the door and beckoned me in. "Join me for a belt."

I followed her into the little storybook cottage, which was

decorated like something out of a little girl's fantasy, a place where Alice in Wonderland might have had a spot of tea. Frilly white lace curtains hung in the window, and the walls were painted the palest of powder blue. In front of the fireplace sat a comfortable-looking overstuffed couch and there was a colorful bouquet of flowers arranged neatly in the center of a small table by the window. She set the bottle on the coffee table, retrieved a pair of crystal cocktail glasses from the sideboard, and poured two stiff shots, neat. She handed me one and then held hers aloft in a toast.

"To Don," she said, a small hitch in her voice.

I clinked my glass to hers.

"To Don. And to finding his murderer," I added.

We both drank deeply. Then she refilled her glass and settled back into the couch. I took the chair across from her, hopeful she'd have something useful to tell me.

"So what do you want to know about Don and me?"

"Well, I guess let's start at the end," I said. "Was it an ugly divorce?"

"Ugly?" She looked at me like I was an idiot. "No, it was a laugh riot. It was the world's friendliest divorce." She laughed sarcastically and took a long pull on her drink. "Of course it was ugly, dipshit, it was a divorce."

I let her slight rebuke brush right past me. I liked this woman. She didn't dick around.

"And yet here you are, sitting in his guesthouse. I presume you came out for the funeral on Monday?"

"Oh, well, Don and I had our differences, sure, but we worked most of them out over the years. It's amazing what three thousand miles of distance can do for a relationship."

"So you moved away from La Siesta after the divorce?"

"And never looked back," she said with apparent relief.

"Where did you go?"

"New York City. I married again pretty quickly, so Katherine and I decamped for Park Avenue with my second husband."

"Katherine is your daughter?"

"That's right."

"She get on well with her father?"

"Of course, she did. Why wouldn't she?"

"Just a question. Sometimes families don't get along. I've seen it plenty."

"Well, despite whatever gossip you might have heard, that's not the situation here. Katherine loved her father. That's why she went to work for him."

"She worked for him?"

"Indeed. She's a senior VP at OSS." She stopped herself. "Well, I guess now she'll be taking over the company. Now that Don's dead."

I took a drink, trying to take all this in. "She's next in line to take over Osborne Storage Solutions?"

"Of course. She practically runs the place already anyway."

"And where is she now?"

"At work, as usual. She's a workaholic just like Don," she said with a touch of distaste, sipping her scotch.

I sipped my own and thought for a second. I wanted to talk to Katherine Osborne, but first I'd see what else this scotch could help me extract from Cheryl.

"So you were saying that you remarried quickly after your divorce from Don?" I asked.

She nodded, taking a cigarette from her purse and lighting the tip with a thin gold lighter.

"Very soon afterwards, yes."

"Why so quickly after an ugly divorce?"

I handed her a heavy crystal ashtray from the side table. She took a long drag on her cigarette, a thin tendril of smoke hanging in the air above her like a question mark.

"The man I married after Don was my childhood sweetheart. He was the man I should have married in the first place."

"This is Mr. Schaefer?" I thought back to the picture in Don's locker. I was certain that one of the other Army Rangers in the picture was named Schaefer.

"Would this be the same Schaefer that was in the war with Don?" I asked.

"Yes. That's how we all met. Ethan was my childhood sweet-heart, and he was stationed with Don in Vietnam. Ethan and I were a couple at the time."

"So how did you end up marrying Don Osborne instead of Ethan Schaefer?"

"Ethan was captured during the war and ended up in a POW camp. Of course, we didn't know he was in a POW camp at the time. We didn't know what had happened. For years he was MIA and presumed dead, and during that time, Don and I grew very close. While we were waiting for news of Ethan, we fell in love. Eventually, when Ethan didn't come back after a few years, we gave up hope. Then we got married and had Katherine."

"And then Ethan came back?"

"Yes. He was freed in late 1975, but by then it was too late, we were married with a kid."

"How did he take it?"

"As well as could be expected I guess. I mean, it must have been weird, his girl and his best buddy. But given the circumstances, he understood. He had been presumed dead. Life goes on."

"Until it doesn't." I reached for the bottle and helped myself to another snort. "Did your husband come out for the funeral as well?"

Her shoulders drooped. She bowed her head and reached for her drink.

"My husband's dead," she said, flatly.

"I'm sorry. How did it happen, if you don't mind my asking?"

"He was murdered," she replied, almost in a whisper. As she took another drink I noticed her hand trembling a bit.

The news stopped me in my tracks. I'd barely had time to digest the fact that her second husband was the other man in the photo with Don, when she dropped this on me.

"Murdered?" I couldn't hide the surprise in my voice.

"That's right," she said, her eyes suddenly focused somewhere far off in the distance. "Strange, don't you think? Both husbands murdered. What are the odds?" Her eyes teared up ever so slightly and she shook her head at the absurdity of the universe.

The odds of having two husbands murdered were low, I thought, that was for sure. However, the odds of the two murders being connected were much higher.

"Strange is one word for it. It's certainly a hell of an odd coincidence," I agreed. "How was he killed?"

"He was shot. In our apartment."

"Did they catch who did it?"

"They didn't have the first clue. We lived in a doorman building on Park Avenue with tight security. There were cameras every ten feet, and they never showed anyone entering or leaving the building that night."

"Was your husband suicidal or depressed? Years in a POW Camp can weigh heavily on a man."

"That was not Ethan. Not to say that it didn't weigh heavily on him—it did, but because of his experience, he was happy every day of his life since he'd been freed. After going through hell, every day was like heaven."

"So you two were happily married?"

She looked stricken at the insinuation. "Blissfully," she spat, finishing her drink. "If you're thinking I had anything to do with his death, you can shelve that thought."

"I'm not thinking anything, just trying to understand. Was anything taken? Could it have been a robbery?"

"They searched and all my jewels and the silver were there. The only thing that seemed to be missing was Ethan's Medal of Honor."

"His Medal of Honor?"

"Yes, it always sat on his desk. And the night he died, it disappeared."

I took a sip and let all this sink in.

"Where did they find the body?" I finally asked.

"In the garden," she replied, refilling her glass. This was clearly not her favorite topic.

"The garden? But I thought you said he was killed in your apartment in New York City."

"We lived in the penthouse. There's a garden on the roof. He was killed next to his prized rosebush."

How bizarre. Another murder, another buddy from the war, a missing Medal of Honor?

"When did this happen?" I asked, my mind beginning to race. "Was this recent?"

"No, this was a long time ago. 1987. We had ten good years together, then he was gone. Again."

1987 was a hell of a long time ago, I thought. Thirty plus years is a long time between murders, but I still couldn't help think that somehow they may be connected.

What's more, if the person who murdered Ethan Schaefer was the same person who murdered Don, then Kitty couldn't have had anything to do with the murder. She was only seven years old when it happened. If I could connect the two, I could clear Kitty, and if I could clear Kitty, then maybe I could clear myself.

I finished my drink and got out of there, leaving Cheryl in a puddle of tears and twelve-year-old scotch. I was hoping I could catch Katherine Osborne before she left the office for the day. On the way to the car, I called my old buddy Milt Jackson of the NYPD to see what he knew about this thirty-year-old murder.

# 16

I arrived at the Osborne Storage Solutions headquarters just as the sun was slipping below the horizon, the exterior of the tall glass building a perfect mirror image of the ocean and sky stretched in front of it. I took a moment to watch the sunset lighting up the sky in a garish display of spectacular colors: pinks and yellows and oranges fighting it out to see who would sink into the ocean last. The storm had finally moved out to sea, the last of the clouds disappearing over the horizon on their way to Hawaii, and the air felt crisp and clean.

I had to get my head around everything I'd learned in the last twenty-four hours or so. I desperately wanted to solve the case and get back to what was really important, golf. Hell, I wasn't even a cop anymore, I shouldn't have been mixed up in all of this. But that was the problem. I *was* mixed up in it. And as long as it looked like Kitty had something to do with it, then it looked like I had something to do with it.

To that end I wanted to speak with Katherine Osborne. I wanted to talk to her about OSS and the work they did for the military. A sniper is too rare a killer outside the military to not want to look inside the military industrial complex for answers. Maybe Don had stumbled into something he shouldn't have? I was also anxious to see what she knew about her stepfather Ethan Schaefer's murder.

Peering up at the building in the darkening sky, I noticed a solitary light on one of the upper floors. A few late-working employees were just leaving as I slipped into the lobby, once again wearing the coveralls from my trunk and carrying cleaning supplies, which had worked well enough to get me in and out of Bill Dwyer's office. I was afraid I may have gone to the well one too many times with this flimsy disguise, but it was all I had at the moment so it would have to do. When I'd lost my badge, I'd also lost the ability to walk into any building I choose, no questions asked, and now that I had to sneak around and talk my way into places, I was realizing I wasn't exactly a master of disguise.

The lobby was a spacious glass-enclosed atrium with polished black marble floors and a long red carpet leading directly to the security desk about fifty feet from the front door. One thing I love about these long walks to the security station is that they give you a few extra moments to get your story straight, or in my case, come up with a story, but as luck would have it, the security station was unoccupied, just an empty chair in front of a bank of monitors. I looked around briefly, glancing at the monitors just long enough to spot my own image standing in the lobby checking out the security setup. I didn't like the way that would look to anyone reviewing the footage, so I tried to act casual, like I was just looking for the guard, then slowly made my way to the elevators, cool as could be.

When the elevator doors opened on the top floor, I was surprised to find a man in coveralls almost exactly like mine staring at me like he'd been waiting for me.

"Where the hell have you been?" he asked, clearly peeved. "I called down twenty minutes ago about the bathroom!"

*The bathroom? What the hell is he talking about?* I thought. Then it hit me. *Shit, it's happening again. The same fucking thing as last time! He thinks I'm the janitor.*

"Sorry, sir. I uh, got held up . . ." I stammered. I had no choice but to roll with it. I guess that's what I get for dressing up like a janitor. *Damn this stupid disguise!* I cursed myself as I followed him down the hallway.

He was leading me down the hall in a hurry as if a bomb was about to go off, pushing a large cart full of cleaning supplies including an industrial-sized mop. He looked down at my little box of Windex and Lysol bottles.

"What do you think you're going to do with that?" he asked, incredulous.

"Um, clean the bathroom?" I guessed, which seemed to amuse him for some reason.

"Good luck." He chuckled, shaking his head. "Boy, you really are new around here."

"I'm just trying to be prepared, boss," I said, playing my part as best I could.

"The men's room is completely flooded. Some joker crammed rolls of toilet paper down the john. But don't worry. I've got everything you need right here."

*Great. Now I have to clean a bathroom for real.* I cursed my luck.

This was not what I needed right now, but I really didn't want to have to assault another person after the incident at Bill Dwyer's office, so I put my head down and followed. *Screw it*, I thought, I've cleaned the bathroom at the Pitch N' Putt a thousand times. How bad could it be?

"Okay, sir. I can handle it. I've seen a flooded bathroom before," I said obligingly, hiding underneath my baseball cap as best I could. We arrived at the men's room door, and I could see the water streaming out into the hall from under the door.

"Not like this." He opened the door onto the most utterly and completely destroyed bathroom I'd ever seen, and I was in a fraternity in college. It was a more horrible sight than any crime scene I'd encountered in all my years on the force, and smelled much worse.

*Shit.*

Whoever had trashed this place really went all the way, flooding the floor, overturning the trash and smearing the walls with, well, let's just leave it at smearing the walls. It took all my intestinal fortitude not to vomit right then and there. Another thing I'd have to clean up.

"Good luck," said my new boss with a chuckle. "I'll be right out here in the hall waiting for you when you're done."

"Wait, you're not going to help me?"

"Son, it's your first day and my last, so, no, I'm not. Consider it your initiation into your new job. But don't worry. I'll be here to supervise if you need me."

He turned and walked out, leaving me knee deep in bathroom soup. I cursed my luck and grabbed a mop. *Damn these coveralls.* This would teach me to play dress up. I should've just talked my way in. instead I got a little too cute and wound up knee deep in shit, literally. I rolled up my sleeves and got to work.

———————•———————

When I was finally done mopping up the mess, I exited the bathroom to find the hallway empty, the cleaning cart standing abandoned. I peeled off my coveralls and stuffed them into one of several overflowing trash bags. That would be the last time I tried that trick. The hallway was quiet, and I was relieved to find myself on a nearly deserted floor. As I turned down the hallway, I thought I saw the shadow of a person entering the stairwell at the end of the hall, most likely my "boss" on his way to tell the rest of the cleaning crew a funny story about the new guy, but otherwise, the only sign of life was the distant clicking sound of someone typing.

I followed the sound down the hallway until I found Katherine Osborne in a conference room. I knew it was her immediately since she was, unfortunately for her, the spitting image of her father, with small black eyes, a long aquiline nose and a thin, pinched face. Her hair was pulled back so tightly I was afraid the hairband holding was going to snap and fly into my eye. She was sitting at the far end of a long table working on her laptop. I knocked lightly on the door and she looked up as I entered.

"Can I help you?" she asked curtly.

"Katherine Osborne?" I asked.

"Who's asking?" she snapped, seemingly fed up already with my very presence on Earth.

"My name's McDermott. I'd like to ask you a few questions if you don't mind," I said, hoping she might soften.

She didn't.

"Are you another cop?" she sneered.

"Not exactly," I replied, purposefully vague. Then, "*Another cop?*"

"Yes, the chief of police was just here," she said, as if I should already know that.

*Damn it.* Once again it looked like Chief Garrett beat me to a witness. For once the slob seemed to be one step ahead of me. He was questioning all my leads; however, was he asking the right questions?

"I thought it smelled like French fries in here," I said, which actually made her crack a smile.

"So what then? What are you doing here?" she asked, already turning back to her work.

"Trying to solve your father's murder."

"Isn't that the job of the police?"

"It is, but you've met the man in charge. Did he strike you as La Siesta's finest?"

I could tell from the look on her face that she saw my point.

"I wouldn't hire that man to find a missing dog in a kennel." She sighed. "All he wanted to know was how much I stood to inherit. As if I would kill my father for an inheritance that was already coming to me. Besides, I loved my father. Sure, he had some sharp edges, but he was still my father."

"So you won't mind if I ask you a few questions? See if I can't narrow the suspect list down to, say, some actual likely suspects."

She acquiesced, putting her glasses down on the table and gesturing for me to have a seat.

"You live in New York City, is that correct?" I asked, pulling out a high-end Aeron desk chair and parking my weary haunches in its soft contours. Between a full round of golf and cleaning that swamp of a bathroom, I was bushed.

"Yes, ever since Mother and I moved in with Ethan," she replied, closing her laptop and giving me her full attention.

"And you came out for your father's funeral on Monday?"

"Actually, I was already in La Siesta on business."

"What business is that?"

"I was looking into an . . . irregularity," she said, trailing off.

"What kind of irregularity?"

"There was some missing inventory, in one of our warehouses."

"Missing inventory?"

"Guns, to be specific."

"Guns? That unusual?"

"Very unusual. Of course, what kind of operation do you think we're running? We didn't earn the trust of the US Military by letting weapons disappear."

"Okay, so why don't you tell me what happened?"

"Five hundred rifles that were stored in our nearby warehouse went missing. Not that it's any of your business."

"What kind of rifles?"

"AR-15 sniper rifles."

"They just went missing?"

"They had been stored there for years. Then a routine inspection by the army revealed that one of the storage sheds had been burglarized. All the crates were still there, but they were empty."

"Did your father know about this?"

"He was the one who called me about it. He suspected it was someone within the company."

"Any idea who?"

She shook her head. "We never got a chance to discuss it before he was . . ."

"Shot by an AR-15 rifle," I finished for her.

The reminder of her father's grisly end clearly shook her. I didn't want to push her too hard under the circumstances, but I had to pursue all the avenues I could.

"Is there anything else?" she asked, clearly growing weary of the whole sordid situation.

"Just one more thing, I wanted to ask about your stepfather, Ethan Schaefer's, murder," I said, watching to gauge her reaction.

"What about it?" she asked, perking up a bit at this new thread.

"It strikes me as one hell of a coincidence, both your father and stepfather being murdered," I said.

"You can say that again. It confirms my suspicions."

"What suspicions?"

"That my stepfather knew his killer," she said with conviction.

"What makes you think that?"

"His Medal of Honor went missing after he was killed."

"Yes, I understand the police believed it may have been taken during a robbery."

"But that couldn't be. It didn't go missing until after the wake.

So that means the person who stole it was someone he knew," she said, her eyes filling with excitement. This was obviously a subject she was passionate about.

"And you think the missing medal had something to do with the killing?" I asked, beginning to put the pieces together.

She nodded emphatically. "I'm sure those two things were connected; I just can't figure out how."

"You said it went missing after the wake?"

"Yes. We had a wake for Ethan after the funeral. About a hundred or so people came up to the apartment. There were so many people there it was hard to tell who everyone was exactly, but the guests were all people he and my mother knew, people from his business, old friends, even some of his old Vietnam buddies. After the wake, I noticed his medal was missing."

"Are you sure it was there after the murder?"

"I'm sure of it. I had been in his office the morning of the funeral and it was there. I know it was there."

"Your mother seems to think it was stolen the night of the murder."

"I know my mother swears it went missing the night of the killing, and the cops too, but I know that's not true. I think she just got mixed up. The whole thing was such a shock and all."

"Why would someone come to a wake to steal a medal from the deceased?"

"That's what I've been trying to find out for thirty years."

"Do you think the murderer would be bold enough to attend the funeral of a man they'd killed?" I wondered aloud, a question more for the universe than Katherine herself perhaps.

She appeared shaken at the memory, fear creeping into her eyes as she thought back on the horror of it all.

"If they did, they'd surely have to be a sociopath. Who else could do such a thing?"

"Did you go over this with the police?" I asked, not wanting to lose her to her memories.

"I did, but they didn't want to hear about it after a while. They thought I was mistaken about the timing of the medal being stolen. But I'm sure I'm not. They were convinced that someone had gotten into the apartment somehow and not been seen, but I didn't believe it. Security in the building was airtight. There had to be an explanation. After a few months went by with no leads, they dropped it altogether. After that, I was on my own."

"You mean you continued your investigation?"

"I never gave it up. I wanted to find who killed my stepfather," she said resolutely, the determination in her voice rising, "and now I want to find who killed my father."

"So what did you do?"

"I traced the only clue I had. I've been tracking the Medal of Honor."

"How do you track down a stolen Medal of Honor?"

"Buying or selling a Medal of Honor is illegal, and there's a nonprofit veterans organization that monitors any that show up in pawn shops, jewelry stores, places like that. And just last week, I got a hit."

"The Medal of Honor showed up?"

"Someone hocked it at a pawn shop, right here in La Siesta."

# 17

After leaving OSS headquarters, I went to meet Lopez at Mulligan's, a tacky little golf-themed bar out by the freeway that catered more to the tourists that flocked to see the wealthy residents of La Siesta than to the actual citizens themselves. The scene made it less likely anyone would recognize either of us. It reminded me of a bar on Hollywood Boulevard, full of tourists from the Midwest who come to see famous movie stars and then find themselves looking at nothing but other tourists from the Midwest.

He was already at the bar when I arrived, drinking a glass of bourbon so big there was no need for him to tell me how his day was. He was holding the glass to his forehead, letting the condensation from the ice lower his core temperature, when he looked up and saw me.

"Going that well?" I inquired with a smirk, before flagging the bartender down for a beer. "Need a refill?"

"This *is* a refill." He removed the glass from his worried brow

and applied it directly to his lips for a long swallow of liquid vacation. The relief registered almost immediately as the muscles of
his face relaxed and his shoulders lost their tension, but as soon as
I paid for my beer and turned back around, he was back to looking
miserable. It reminded me of how I looked after a day of work on
the force. Say what you will about my golf career, but a bad day
on the golf course is still better than a good day as a cop.

"So what's the latest?" I asked.

"They're focusing on Kitty," he said, point-blank.

I took a deep breath, absorbing the information. "Okay, well,
what do they know that I don't?" I replied, readying myself for
his answer, but instead he turned to face me and asked a question
of his own.

"How much do you know about Kitty? I mean really know,
about her past?" he asked, looking deadly serious.

"I know she couldn't have done this," I said, only half believ-
ing it.

"Are you sure?" he asked, his skepticism apparent on his face.
"Did you know she was a former Olympic athlete?"

"Well, I knew she was *athletic*," I said, coyly.

"I bet you did," he replied, a slight grin on his face, which
quickly disappeared. "So you didn't know that she was a biathlete?"

"Listen, whatever she did with her fellow athletes in the privacy of her bedroom is between her and my fantasies."

"No, dummy." He sighed. "Not a bisexual athlete—a *biathlete*—as in the *biathlon.*"

"What's the biathlon?" I asked, the word only vaguely ringing
a bell.

"It's an Olympic winter sport, fairly obscure but fun to watch. It's a combination of cross-country skiing and marksmanship."

"Marksmanship?" I asked. A cringe slowly crept up my back. I knew what marksmanship was, of course, but I didn't like where this was going and I wanted to delay the impact of the information.

"They ski through the woods and shoot at targets with rifles. That's the whole sport. They're basically snipers on skis," he said, the look on his face letting me know he was beginning to suspect Kitty as well.

*The biathlon.* I remembered seeing that weird sport on television as a kid, people in skintight suits skiing through the woods and shooting at targets with sniper rifles. I couldn't believe it. I took a sip of my beer and let the bubbles go to work on this new information.

*Kitty was a trained sniper.*

"Okay, well, I guess that doesn't look so good," I finally said.

"You're right about that, and you know what else doesn't look so good?"

"What's that?"

"Your relationship with her."

"Who knows about that?" I asked, unhappy to hear that particular cat was out of the bag.

"Apparently, everyone. When Chief Garrett found out, I swear he practically jumped for joy. He's convinced you had something to do with this, and he's champing at the bit to nail you."

"Me?! Why would I have something to do with this?" I protested.

"Look at the facts, Duffer. You were in love with another man's wife. Now he's dead and she's about to be rich. It looks like you get the girl and the cash."

"But I didn't get anything! I'm just trying to win a goddamn golf tournament. I don't care about Don Osborne's money, or Kitty's past, or any of that bullshit. I just want to play golf."

"Oh, yeah, shit, I almost forgot. How's the tournament going?"

Suddenly, my whole mood shifted. With everything I'd learned since the morning, I'd almost forgotten that this should have been one of the best days of my life. I sat up straight and proudly delivered the news.

"I'll have you know I made the cut today."

His pained expression lifted for a moment, and I could see he was genuinely happy for me.

"You did? You actually made the cut? Duffer, that's fucking awesome, man! Congratulations."

He stood and gave me a hug. A true friend understands what's important.

"Man, we didn't think you were *ever* going to make a fucking cut. I just lost twenty bucks on you," he said with a chuckle, sitting back on his barstool.

Okay, *true friend* might be a bit strong.

"Thanks, pal," I said, half-heartedly.

"Oh, come on, man, you know I'm just giving you shit. Really. That's cool," he said, knocking me on the shoulder.

"Thanks. Now all I have to do is play perfect golf for the next two days and beat out some of the best golfers the world has ever known," I said with a rueful smile.

"And solve a murder," he added, helpfully,

"So it's officially up to me, is it?" I shot back, a little incredulous.

"Duffer, you know as well as I that Chief Garrett couldn't

catch a glimpse of his ass in a mirror factory. How the hell is he going to catch a killer?"

I drained the end of my beer, and we both sat there in silence for a second. When I looked up, I noticed the television above the bar was tuned to the Golf Channel with the sound off. They were recapping the day's play from the La Siesta Open, and I looked up just in time to see an image of myself flash by on the screen. I grabbed the bartender by the shirtwaist.

"Hey, turn it up, will ya? They're talking about me," I excitedly informed him.

He grabbed the remote and raised the volume just in time to hear Joe Roebuck.

"And in our surprise performance of the day at La Siesta, a forty-year-old former local cop played a hell of a round and made his first PGA cut today."

The smile on my face as I watched myself walk up the fairway on national television would have put the Cheshire cat himself to shame. The bartender turned around matching my grin.

"Hey, that's you!" he exclaimed.

Lopez was standing next to me and he nudged me with his elbow. "That's cool, bro!" Suddenly the whole bar was watching the television intently as Joe Roebuck continued.

"Duffer McDermott, a former police officer who's been hacking away on the amateur circuit for decades, has finally made it into his first PGA Tournament, and I gotta say, as much as I love this story, I don't think this is going to have a happy ending."

The smile fell off my face.

"Oh, he doesn't stand a butterman's chance in a toast factory," chimed in Wee Jackie with a gleeful little cackle of a laugh. "But it'll be fun to see the tubby old boy give it a try."

The two of them shared a hearty back slap at my expense. I stared at the television, stung.

"Did Wee fucking Jackie just call me a *tubby old boy*?" I yelped, stung by the insult.

Lopez put a conciliatory hand on my shoulder. Everyone in the bar, who just moments ago had been excited to be in the presence of a real pro, turned back to their drinks and conversation as the bartender once again lowered the sound.

"Fuck that four-foot munchkin," said Lopez. "Now you've got motivation to prove him wrong."

He tapped my beer bottle with his glass in a cheers, and I knew he was right. Lopez was always there to offer another perspective. Turn it around and see the positive. I relaxed back onto my barstool.

"You're right. I've got my motivation for tomorrow. But what was the motivation to kill Don Osborne?"

———•———

I was just getting back to the Pitch N' Putt when my cell phone rang, the number showing 212 for New York City. I quickly opened the door to the office and let Nicklaus out to do his business before I picked up.

"What are you still doing up? Isn't it past your bedtime there?" I said by way of greeting.

"I'm still up because some asshole needed information on a

decades-old murder, and I was too stupid to say no!" Milt Jackson replied, with only the slightest hint of amusement in his voice.

"Listen, old man. I appreciate you putting in the time, I really do," I replied sincerely. Milt was an old friend and a good cop, the kind of guy you could count on to dig up dirt without kicking up too much dust, thorough but discreet. I was hoping for information about Ethan Schaefer's murder, but not expecting much given the amount of time that had elapsed.

"So, what have you got?"

"What I've got is a lot of people asking questions about why I'm asking questions about this murder. It seems like everyone around back then remembers this, but nobody wants to talk about it," he said, the frustration evident in his voice.

"Why not?"

"I suspect it's because it stumped them. They came up completely dry on a motive, a suspect, anything. He lived in a doorman building with security cameras all over the place and they showed nobody coming in or out. But get this. They think it was a sniper."

"Did you say a *fucking sniper*?!" I gasped, disbelief choking my voice to a squeak.

Suddenly, Nicklaus wasn't the only one taking a dump. I nearly shit myself.

"I did indeed. The building next door was under construction at the time, and from the upper floors it would have been possible to fire down into the roof garden."

"Holy shit! Why didn't anything come of this?"

"They couldn't prove anything, and the idea seemed fairly ridiculous, so, they dropped it."

"What's so ridiculous about it?"

"The thing is, like I said, the building across the street was unfinished. It was nothing but a steel frame at the time. For anyone to make that shot, they would have had to place themselves way out on a suspended steel girder. It would have been next to impossible for anyone to pull off that shot."

"Next to impossible. But not impossible. Why did I never hear about this? Something like this would've surely been all over the news."

"Nobody heard about it. They kept it quiet at the time because they didn't want to start a panic. Can you imagine what that would do to Manhattan if people thought there was a wild sniper sitting on a rooftop just waiting to pick people off?"

"I see your point."

"So when no other shootings took place, they basically dropped it."

"They just dropped it?"

"No other crimes matched the MO. No other sniper shootings took place."

"Until Wednesday night," I said.

I let Nicklaus back inside and settled into my comfy desk chair as I let my brain have a go at this new information. A sniper murder thirty years ago and then another one Wednesday night. It couldn't be a coincidence. And the fact that the first victim was Don's one-time best buddy, and married to his first wife? The connection was too strong to ignore.

"This is a lot to take in, Jackson."

"You think there's a connection between this and your murder?" he asked.

"I can't see how there *isn't* a connection."

"But thirty years is a long time."

"Not for someone holding a grudge."

# SATURDAY

# 18

The morning of day three of the La Siesta Open, I stood out on the driving range at the Pitch N' Putt, driving tennis balls off the tee for Nicklaus to retrieve. It's a little game we like to play, and he's a fairly decent retriever as long as he doesn't get distracted by a dropped hotdog bun or stray potato chip. I wanted a nice easy warm-up, and this worked for both my body and my mind. I couldn't stop thinking about Don Osborne's murder, but I knew I had to find a way to focus on golf if I was going to have any chance of finishing at the top of the leaderboard.

I had written the names of my leads in the Don Osborne murder on the back of a discarded mini-golf scorecard. Whoever had used this particular card had gotten a seven on the windmill hole, and that's where I felt like I was right now with this case, on a windmill going around and around. The list of possible suspects, in my mind at least, was longer than I'd like it to be.

To begin with, there was Mr. Lo, the head greenskeeper. He checked a few of the boxes in my head. The sprinkler head I'd found in the television tower seemed to tie him to the crime scene, not to mention he also had a grudge against Don Osborne that went far deeper than just Don being a boorish asshole, a bitterness that went all the way back to the childhood trauma of war. I wasn't sure if he was capable of such a thing, but then I didn't really know him all that well. He seemed friendly, but so did Ted Bundy—before they found a sorority full of corpses. He certainly knew about the television tower and had access to the country club, which was a key factor common to all those on my suspect list. The La Siesta Country Club's security wasn't exactly airtight, but they were used to keeping out the riffraff, so whoever killed Don was likely to be someone who had access to the club, at least temporarily.

Right below Mr. Lo were the Racquette Brothers. La Siesta's most colorful Canadian crooks had a longstanding feud with Don over real estate and construction in La Siesta that seemed to have left a bitter taste in their mouths. They stood to gain a lot from Don being out of the way, and they had a long criminal history, so I had little doubt they were capable of pulling the trigger. Plus, they'd put up the scaffolding the sniper used as a roost, which gave them access, and then they had lied about it. Of course, if the Racquette brothers went to prison for Don's murder, that would be the ideal situation for me, since I wouldn't have to pay them back, and they wouldn't be able to break my kneecaps with a hockey stick. Unfortunately, in my experience, the ideal outcome is very rarely the outcome that arrives, so I felt that theory might be a little too perfect.

Then there was Bill Dwyer, Don's old army buddy and lawyer.

He's a member of the club and has military training. Don and Bill Dwyer had an argument the last day Don was alive, but I wasn't sure about what. Kitty had hired Bill immediately following Don's death, which seemed a bit odd, and I wondered if there were more to their relationship than I had previously been privy to.

On top of that, Bill Dwyer was also an old army buddy of Ethan Schaefer. Could he have killed both of them? It seems likely that he would have been at the wake in New York City, and he lived here in La Siesta, so he could have been the one who'd stolen the Medal of Honor and hocked it. But why hock it? Bill seemed to have plenty of money. And why now? The more I thought about it, the more I realized it was time to talk to Bill Dwyer himself. He and Don were up to something concerning the wildlife preserve, the possible future real-estate development known as La Siesta Dunes, but I wasn't sure what. Could Don's murder have something to do with the wildlife preserve?

Thinking about the preserve led me to thinking about Shiloh Greene, the ponytailed egg wrangler who'd swooped in to save the gnatcatcher's offspring yesterday. He had spent the better part of twenty years fighting Don in court over the last remaining piece of pristine land in all of La Siesta. Things couldn't have worked out better for Shiloh and the gnatcatchers when Don turned up dead. The security guard at the country club had mentioned he saw someone with a ponytail running off into the night after Don was murdered, but a hairstyle wasn't much to go on.

Then, there was whoever killed Ethan Schaefer, assuming it wasn't Bill Dwyer. Katherine Osborne had plans to go to the pawn shop to track down whoever pawned the Medal of Honor, and I was planning to meet her later after my round to find out what she had discovered.

*Who could it be?*

I couldn't help but think back to the photograph in Don's locker of the army buddies. Who was the unidentified man in the photo? The man whose face was partially hidden by the crease. Was he even alive? And if so, did he live in La Siesta? All the other men in the photo had settled in La Siesta, so it was a reasonable possibility. Of all the known suspects, this person would have known both Ethan Schaefer and Don Osborne from the war. If he was still alive, it's possible he either had something to do with this or could at least have valuable information. I decided to see if I could get another look at that photo in Don's locker if I could get the chance.

Then, of course, there was Kitty. I didn't want it to be true, but I couldn't help seeing that it was starting to line up that way. She had one hell of a motive, more money than she could ever spend in a lifetime. She had access to the television tower. In fact, she had been just a few yards away right before it happened. What's more, I now knew that she had the skillset to pull it off; she was a trained sniper. Add to that the possibility that she may have killed her first husband, and suddenly my choice in lovers looked like a worse decision than my choice in careers.

The worst part of it all was that it put me right in the middle of it. Right where Chief Garrett wanted me to be. The list of suspects in my pocket didn't seem to matter as much as the fact that my name was at the top of Chief Garret's own list. That man had wanted to get his revenge on me for years, and now he had me almost dead to rights for a murder I didn't commit. To him my motivation was obvious, with Don dead I got the woman I love and all her husband's money.

My main problem, as far as I could figure, was that my alibi was crap. I was a few yards away from the scene of the crime with the man's wife, with whom I was known to be having an affair. My alibi was her alibi. If she was a suspect, I was a suspect. We were together right before the shot was fired. Just a few yards away. I had to admit it didn't look good. I had to find the killer to clear my name, and that meant that I had to seriously consider that Kitty could have done it.

But could she be that cold, that callous, to make love to me one minute and then run off and kill her husband with a bullet to the heart the next? She'd have to have ice water in her veins. She'd have to be, well, she'd have to be some sort of sociopath, someone either able to suppress her emotions to such a degree that she could compartmentalize, focus on the task at hand without raising her heartbeat or taking an extra breath. Of course that's exactly what they train you for in the biathlon. If it was true, as an athlete I almost admired the self-control. If I could master myself like that as a golfer I could be unstoppable. Emotionless. A robot.

What had I been thinking getting mixed up with a woman like that? I cursed myself, but I still wasn't willing to admit to myself that she could have done it. Not yet. I guess I just wanted to keep hope alive. I needed that today. I had to play the best golf of my life if I stood a chance to win this tournament. The list of names in my pocket would have to wait until I finished my round.

⎯⎯⎯⎯⎯⎯⎯⎯

I was almost finished working my way through the bucket of tennis balls when the unmistakable sound of Rush blasting from the speakers of an El Camino rattled the windows of the Pitch N Putt, the tale of "today's Tom Sawyer" pumping the blood of the Racquette Brothers full of testosterone and Canadian pride.

Another day, another visit from my favorite pair of lunatic loan sharks. I knew it was no use running. They'd always find me, if not at the Pitch N' Putt, then on the golf course, and I'd much prefer to take a beating in private than in front of a crowd.

"Ho there, Duffer," Barrie cried. "Saw ya swinging the sticks on the old TV last night. Pretty fair play, but you're no Moe Norman, eh?"

"Too true, Barrie, he's no Moe Norman," agreed Gordo as they approached.

"Who the hell is Moe Norman?" I inquired, a question I didn't anticipate being as offensive as it seemed to be to them.

"*Who's Moe Norman?!* He's only the most famous golfer to come out of Kitchener," Barrie said.

"I'll have to take your word for that."

"You don't remember Pipeline Moe? What are ya, soft in the head?" asked Gordo looking at me like I'd insulted all of Canada.

"Story goes he had to drop out of the Masters because he practiced too much," said Barrie. "Hit eight hundred drives and mangled his thumb before he ever teed off in the tournament."

"Impossible. There's no such thing as too much practice," I countered, now the offended party.

"Well, maybe not, but there's a lot of ways a golfer could end up with a mangled thumb."

"Too right, Gordo, too right."

They moved toward me, an air of menace coming over them as they approached.

"Now listen, fellas. What good would it do to mangle my thumb, when playing golf's the only way I'm going to be able to get your money?"

"I see your point there, Duffer, I do," said Barrie. "But the problem here is that you make the assumption that we'd enjoy the money more than we'd enjoy taking our payday out of your ass."

"Now, listen, you leave my thumb and my ass out of this."

"We've got plenty of money, there, Duffer," Barrie continued. "You Yanks around here are practically pissing pennies."

"And I haven't kicked the crap out of anyone in ages!" cried Gordo, finishing his brother's thought. "Frankly, my knuckles are getting itchy," he said, working his left fist into the palm of his right hand like a first baseman loosening up his glove.

"Then why don't you take it out on some other poor sap," I spat, defiant. "I've got two rounds left and then you'll have your money. Until then, leave me alone."

"The thing is, Duffer, we know you're up to more than just golfing. You like to ask a lot of questions," barked Barrie, the statement coming out like an accusation.

"A *lot* of questions," said Gordo, cracking his itchy knuckles.

"And we don't much take to people poking around in our business."

"I'd be happy to poke around in your personal life if it makes things easier," I quipped, unable to stifle my inner wiseass, as usual.

"Don't get smart, Duffer. It's a dumb thing to do."

"Yeah, don't get smart, dumbass."

"Now listen to me, Duffer, with both ears, eh? We've got a lot of business deals going on here in La Siesta, and we don't need some golfing gumshoe sniffing around and messing things up for us."

"Like the deal to handle the infrastructure of the tournament? Your name's all over the grandstand, the vendor village, even the scaffolding outside the clubhouse bears your imprint. Pretty sweet gig."

I watched to see if there was any reaction when I mentioned the scaffold, but their faces belied nothing, only the usual barely contained rage.

"It *is* a sweet gig. One we'd like to keep for years to come, if you follow me."

"What's interesting to me is that you told me you weren't allowed anywhere near the country club. You said that Don Osborne hated you."

"Don Osborne was an asshole!" blurted Gordo.

"Too true, Gordo, too true. And yes, old Don had no love for us, but we have our ways of getting around that."

"And what else do you have brewing that you'd like to keep going? Perhaps the building of a place called La Siesta Dunes?"

"See, there ya go with the questions again!" Gordo was really champing at the bit now.

"There's no such place as La Siesta Dunes, Duffer," said Barrie, ever the pacemaker of the two.

"Not yet. But if it does get built, there'd be a hell of a lot of construction work to come your way. Only, with Don Osborne in charge, you wouldn't stand a chance of landing the contract, would you?"

"Well, that's not a problem anymore now, is it?" Barrie smiled.

"That's exactly my point. With Don out of the way, you'd stand to make a pretty penny."

"You should worry more about your putts than your points, golfer boy."

"What are you going to do, Barrie? Kill me? I'm on national television nightly as long as this tournament is being played. You don't think anyone would notice if I suddenly disappeared?"

"He's got a point, Barrie."

"Shut up, Gordo!"

I had them where I wanted them, confused and turning on each other. It was the only way I knew to escape from sharks.

"Listen to me, Duffer. I'm only going to say this once. Stay out of our business."

"Or what, exactly?"

"Or Gordo's going to make sure you lose a lot more than a golf tournament."

"It'd be a shame if they found one of your balls in a sand trap," said Gordo.

"Too right, Gordo, too right. And Lord only knows where they might find the other one."

———————•———————

I scratched Nicklaus on the head for good luck and was heading out to play what would hopefully be the round of a lifetime, when I turned around to find Lopez standing in my doorway. The look on his face told me immediately that something had gone cockeyed.

"Katherine Osborne is missing," he blurted, seemingly relieved to get the information off his chest.

"What? Since when?" I asked, shocked, putting my clubs down.

"She didn't show up for the reading of the will this morning. They checked with the hotel where she was staying, and she never returned from work last night. Her room was untouched."

"But that doesn't make sense. I just spoke with her yesterday evening."

"I know," he said, with the same cockeyed look he'd arrived with.

"You know?" I asked, my stomach moving slowly toward my Adam's apple. "How do you know that?" I was having a hard time wrapping my head around what I was hearing. I didn't know what it meant yet, but I had a feeling it wouldn't be good for me.

"I saw the security video from the OSS building. There you were, clear as day, walking past the security station in your coveralls. Nice disguise, by the way," he said with a slight chuckle.

"But, she was there when I left!" I protested. "She was fine. Working away on her computer. We had plans to meet later after my round and after she followed up on a lead at the pawn shop."

"Well, she hasn't been seen since you paid your little visit, and now the chief is salivating to arrest your ass."

"Arrest me?! He can't do that! I have golf to play!"

Lopez gave me a look like I'd grown an alien head. He shook his head in disbelief.

"That's all you're worried about?" he asked. "Golf? The chief of police has you in his sights for two murders . . ."

"*Two* murders?!"

"Yes, Don Osborne *and* now you're tied to the disappearance of Katherine Osborne."

"A disappearance is different than a murder, Lopez. We don't know she's dead. We don't know anything," I protested pointlessly, stalling for time as my thoughts raced.

"Okay, okay, fine. You're being tied to a murder investigation and a *missing person* investigation, and all you're worried about is golf?! Your mom was right. It really is a madness with you."

"Hey, come on. Let's not bring golf into this. Golf did nothing wrong here," I said, appealing to reason. "And, look it's not that I'm, you know, *not worried* about possibly being implicated in a murder and a disappearance. Sure, I get it. This is serious. But come on, I have my priorities. *I'm in the goddamn La Siesta Open!* I could win this fucking thing, Lopez. Do you realize what that means?!"

He looked at me like a frustrated parent. "It means you get your tour card," he said in a bored monotone, as if he'd said it a million times before.

"*It means I get my goddamn PGA Tour card!*" I exclaimed. I could see him starting to come around, a small smile creeping into the corner of his face, but he was doing his best to hide it.

"And besides, let's be honest here," I continued, reeling him in, "I didn't do it. I had nothing to do with Don's murder, or Katherine Osborne's disappearance. I know I didn't do it, and you know I didn't do it, and *I know you know* I didn't do it."

He nodded, seemingly on my team, for now at least.

"*Right?*" I continued. "So the chief can go fuck himself. I had nothing to do with any of this, and I'll be happy to prove it to him, *after* I finish the tournament." I brushed past him and headed for the car.

"How are you going to do that?" he said, following me. "How are you going to prove it?"

"I don't know, but I'll figure it out. Besides, why would I have anything to do with Katherine's disappearance?"

"To help Kitty," he said, looking in my eyes to gauge my reaction.

I gave him nothing but a blank stare. "How does that help Kitty?" I asked, genuinely curious.

"Well, that's the other thing," he said with a sigh, a sure sign that another shoe was about to drop. I slammed the trunk.

*Oh God*, I thought. *I don't like the sound of that.*

"What other thing?" I asked reluctantly.

"It seems there was an anomaly at the reading of the will," he said, enjoying his ten-cent word.

"An anomaly? What does that mean?"

"It means something strange, out of place . . ."

"Thanks professor, I know what anomaly means. What kind of anomaly are we talking about here?"

"It turns out there's more than one Katherine Osborne."

"What? You just told me we don't even know where the first Katherine Osborne is, now you're telling me there are two Katherine Osbornes?"

"Kitty is also named Katherine Osborne."

"Wait, what?" I asked, genuinely confused.

"Kitty's real name, it turns out, is Katherine, thereby making her Katherine Osborne, the same as his daughter, Katherine Osborne."

"That's, um, unusual."

"It certainly complicates things. I'll tell you that."

"And Don's will?" I asked, the implications of the anomaly slowly becoming clear to me.

He nodded. "Don Osborne's will left everything to Katherine Osborne, but it didn't specify which one. Now, with his daughter, Katherine Osborne, missing, the only one around to collect is . . ."

"Kitty." I sighed, finishing his thought for him.

He nodded. And there it was. The other shoe had dropped, with a sole full of golf spikes right onto my head.

"It looks bad, Duffer," said Lopez with obvious concern. "Kitty's involved in this in some way, and you're involved with her, and now this Katherine Osborne thing . . ."

"I told you! I had nothing to do with Katherine Osborne disappearing! And I sure as hell didn't have anything to do with Don Osborne's murder," I insisted, trying not to sound desperate.

"I know that, Duffer. I really do. But you have to see how bad this looks.

"Listen, this isn't about his wife or his money! I just want to win this fucking golf tournament! I want to hit a little white ball into a little round hole and go home with a goddamn trophy. What's so crazy about that?"

"What's crazy is that you're in a world of shit and you're still worried about this golf tournament, which, let's be honest, you haven't the slightest chance of winning!"

"That's where you're wrong! I have *exactly* the slightest chance of winning, which is a better set of odds that I've ever faced in my life. Don't you see, Lopez? This is as close as I've ever come to realizing my dream, and I'm not going to let anything stop me—not you, not the chief, not even if I have to climb over a pile of dead bodies to get to the eighteenth hole on Sunday."

He was silent for a moment. He knew I was serious. He knew there was nothing he could do to stop me. I opened the driver's side door of my Crown Vic and got in.

"Just give me thirty-six holes, Lopez," I said, putting the key in the ignition and pumping the gas, the engine roaring to life. "Please. Put off the chief, occupy him somehow, stage a robbery at McDonald's and have him search the French fries, anything, but I have to finish this golf tournament."

He nodded, and I was off, my tires shooting a rooster tail of pebbles and dust behind me.

# 19

When I arrived at the practice tee, I could already feel myself getting nervous. The anxiety that comes over me when I have an important round to play is like a live wire running up my spine, and the electricity was switched on full blast this morning. Grateful Ted was already there, as usual, sitting under his favorite mulberry tree eating a popsicle that, judging from the bright-red juice dribbling down his beard, I guessed was strawberry flavored.

"Morning Ted. Popsicles for breakfast?"

"My kitchen's being renovated," he said with a smile, obviously joking. God knows where Grateful Ted even lived, if anywhere stable at all. I'd caught him sleeping in my mini-golf castle enough times to know that his living situation was, shall we say, fluid.

"Just make sure you don't get any popsicle gunk on my clubs. I don't want sticky grips when I get out there today."

Sometimes having Grateful Ted as a caddie was like taking care of a toddler, constantly having to tell him to wash his hands and zip up his fly. The last thing I needed was something to throw my game off, or throw me off for that matter. I had to keep my cool today. I took out my driver and dumped half a bucket of balls in the trough as Grateful Ted finished the last of the popsicle. He headed over to the trash, but as he stooped to toss the popsicle stick into the can, he stopped and looked at the stick for a moment.

"Hey, check it out. It's a riddle," he said, his eyes lighting up.

*Jesus Christ, you dippy old hippie. I've got enough riddles to figure out on my own*, I thought, but I kept myself from snapping at him. I didn't want to dampen his enthusiasm this early, so I let him continue.

"Why couldn't the detective solve the mystery of his mustache?" he read off the stick.

"I don't know, Ted," I said, playing along. "Why couldn't the detective solve the mystery of his mustache?"

Ted looked down at the stick and read the answer.

"He couldn't see what was right under his nose!" Grateful Ted howled.

I barely contained my groan. "Brilliant," I said, becoming a bit annoyed. "Who writes these things?"

"I think kids send 'em in," he said, handing me my driver. "Come on, Duffer, it's funny, don't you think?"

"Well, maybe for a kid," I said, tolerating this conversation for another moment, putting my first ball of the day on the practice tee.

"Sometimes it helps to think like a kid," said Grateful Ted. "Keep it simple. Don't overcomplicate things."

"I'm afraid it's a little late for that," I said, now officially sick of this conversation. My fuse was short this morning, a bad sign that I tried to ignore. I set myself over the tee, swung my driver, and sent my ball rocketing off the tee at a sharp right angle, almost pelting an elderly woman walking by on the cart path. It was an ugly shot, the meanest slice I'd hit in years.

We both stood and marveled at the shot, momentarily stunned.

"What the hell was that?" asked Grateful Ted, scratching his head.

"That," I replied, "was garbage."

I hung my head. I could feel the tension in my body beginning to coil itself tighter and tighter around my muscles.

*"Not today,"* I thought, *"please dear Lord don't let me lose my shit today."*

I couldn't start this way. Today had to go well. I tried to shake it off. I put another ball on the tee and stepped up. Halfway through my swing I could feel that I was tight, and I topped the ball, sending it skittering across the grass about a centimeter off the ground, likely scaring away more snakes than St. Patrick himself. I didn't think it was possible to hit a worse drive than the first, but I'd somehow managed. I was two shots into the day's play and already off the rails.

"It's okay," said Grateful Ted, immediately settling into his role as calming influence and coach. "It's good to get a few bad ones out of the way. It's just practice. Save the good ones for the course."

"You know what, Ted," I said through gritted teeth, hanging

on perilously to the last shred of patience in my system already, "why don't you just give me some space, okay?"

He caught my drift immediately and retreated to his mulberry tree. I took a deep breath and tried to refocus myself. I needed to get out of my head.

I teed up a third ball, let my arms and legs go limp, and tried to relax. I closed my eyes, trying to find my focus, when suddenly my phone buzzed in my back pocket. I pulled it out and was surprised to find a text from an unknown number with a 310 area code.

> Mr. McDermott - This is Bill Dwyer. I have urgent business to discuss. Please meet me at the wildlife preserve this afternoon at 3 p.m. I'll be at the clearing at the end of the path.

*Huh?* That was odd, I thought. My mind was immediately flooded with questions. Why did Bill Dwyer want to meet with me? Did he speak with his secretary, or, a much worse scenario, did he know about the break in? It's possible he had information about Don Osborne's murder, but why meet at the wildlife preserve? Besides all that, how did I know this was really even Bill Dwyer texting me? The whole thing could be a setup.

I had no choice but to find out, so I texted back that I'd see him there. I wasn't sure what he had to tell me, but I was glad to follow any path that might lead me away from anything that would implicate Kitty, or me, as the killer.

I put my phone away and settled over the ball once again. This time, my swing was fluid and the contact was solid, sending the ball straight and far. It was amazing what a little bit of distraction could do for my game. As long as I have something to think about other than golf while I'm playing golf, I can do okay. I felt as if I was finally figuring out how to get out of my head, and distraction seemed to be the key. For perhaps the first time in my career, I was glad to have a murder to worry about.

I called Grateful Ted back over and we headed for the clubhouse. I was feeling better about my chances after my minor revelation on the tee, and I decided to keep my focus on absolutely anything but the round of golf ahead of me.

"All right Ted, let's play your little Grateful Dead game," I said as we headed from the practice tees toward the players holding area.

"You're on." He smiled. "Name a date."

Without giving it much thought, I gave him the date that was still floating around in my head since I had spoken to Milt Jackson of the NYPD about the murder of Ethan Schaefer.

"What about September eighteenth, 1987?"

His eyes suddenly came alive, and he looked up at me like a kid who'd just been asked if he wanted to open his birthday presents.

"Oh my God!" he exclaimed, a hand to his mouth. "Nobody ever asks about that show."

"What? Something special about that show?" I asked, puzzled by his reaction.

He looked at me as if I was surely joking, as if everybody knew what was special about that show. However, when I remained perplexed, he finally blurted out the answer.

"*That was the night of the levitating Jerry!*" he cried, his smile so wide I could almost see my reflection in his teeth.

"The night of the levitating Jerry? Didn't Jerry levitate every night for folks like you?"

"No, no, for real this time! He levitated! It was incredible. When they walked on stage that night, Bob Weir asked the crowd to join in and help him 'levitate Garcia.'"

"What the hell does that even mean?" I asked.

"It was just a gag, really. An old parlor trick. They had done it on *Late Night with David Letterman* the night before as a goof, so everyone knew what he was talking about. Bob asked us to focus our minds together and the crowd roared, trying to get Jerry to levitate."

"So it was just a gag?"

"It started out that way. But then, *it really happened*! He levitated! I swear to God I saw it with my own eyes."

When I looked in those eyes it was clear he believed everything he was saying.

"All right, well. I'll just have to take your word for it. So they started by levitating Jerry, but can you name what they played?"

He didn't even hesitate for a moment before launching into the set list from that night.

"They opened with 'Hell in a Bucket,' and I could have sworn they were playing it just for me. It was hot, man, smokin'. Then they cruised through a nice version of 'Sugaree' . . ."

I listened with half an ear as we made our way up the cart path, the sound of his soothing voice pushing out all thoughts of golf disaster and easing the pressure I could feel bearing down on my shoulders like I was carrying an elephant.

"For the second set opener they laid down a monster 'Shake-down Street,'" he continued, "and then segued right into 'Women Are Smarter,' a song with a sentiment I've always agreed with . . ."

At those words, my thoughts turned to Kitty. There was something about her that made me oblivious to the glaring head-light barreling down the tunnel toward me. I should have seen it coming and saved myself, but instead I just stood there and let her run right over me. She was beautiful, sure, that was a factor, but that wasn't what initially drew me to her. What did it for me was how singular she was.

La Siesta is full of beautiful women, but scratch the surface of the cruelty-free makeup on any one of them and you'll often find a personality as dull as dust on a windowsill. Not Kitty. Not even close. Kitty was her own woman. Unlike all of the Stepford Wives that throng to the rich men of La Siesta, she was a fully developed human. She needed more to keep her interested than hair salon appointments and dull country club dinners. You could tell just by watching her walk down the street that she was different, her tight jeans and a black leather motorcycle jacket in direct opposition to the sea of flouncy fake bottle blondes in high-end couture that filled Worthmore Avenue. With her shoulders thrown back and her helmet tucked under her arm, she wasn't looking to anyone else for approval. She wasn't worried about what others thought. She was confidence personified. It was part of what made her so alluring. It also made her dangerous.

That self-assurance made her stand out, but it also kept her isolated. The other women in town were either intimidated by her, dismissive of her, or just plain snarky behind her back. What really seemed to bother them the most, however, was that she didn't care one whit what they thought of her. But with that came loneliness. It's all well and good to stand out from the crowd, but then you're on your own, and that comes with its own kind of pain. She was an outcast—a rich, beautiful, pampered outcast—and she needed to find someone she could relate to, someone who understood what it felt like to not fit in with the locals of La Siesta.

She found me. I had stuck out like a sore thumb from the moment I arrived, and I think she found that appealing. In a small town like this, even a minor change like a new police officer on the force is met with gossip and speculation, and when word got out I was also an aspiring golfer, the socialites had a field day.

"He must play on the *public* course at the edge of town. We certainly haven't seen him *at the club*."

"Of course not. He's a *civil servant*. Where would he find a sponsor to join La Siesta?"

I remember catching this snippet of conversation at Vernetti's one night. When the couple of old gossips saw me come around the corner of the bar, they almost choked on their chicken Caesars, but I just gave them a smile and tip of the cap.

I was used to being different, being talked about behind my back. Even in New York I had been apart from the others on the force. Spending all of my free time traveling around from golf course to golf course trying to gain entry to amateur tournaments didn't leave a whole lot of time to forge close friendships with my colleagues. So I'd learned to be content with my own company, to look within myself for whatever I needed, and that served me well, both as a cop and as a golfer. But as a person, it left me lonesome.

Until Kitty came into my life. Once we found each other, it was like the sky had changed color, and we were the only two who could see it. It made no difference to either of us that our relationship was doomed from any practical standpoint. We weren't practical people. I was a middle-aged man trying to make it onto the PGA Tour, for chrissakes. It doesn't get much more impractical than that.

But we were everything to each other. Despite the extramarital aspect of our affair, we didn't spend our time sneaking around, or, not much anyway. We just waited for fate to bring us together, a weekend when Don was away, a stolen moment in my office at the Pitch N' Putt, the occasional romp on an empty stretch of beach. We had each other, and we knew we would always have each other. That was enough.

When I drifted back to reality, Grateful Ted was cruising into the home stretch of his soliloquy and really getting into it.

". . . and then, the *coup de grâce*. For the encore, they played 'Knockin' on Heaven's Door,' the third and final Dylan tune of the night, bringing an absolutely perfect ending to an evening I will never forget as long as I live."

When I looked over at him, I could see he was still there in his mind, far away from the course, in a much happier place, and I understood for the first time the power of the mind to take us anywhere we needed to go. He went to a Dead concert, and I went to Kitty. We both found a place of peace within ourselves.

We were approaching the players' holding tent, and it was

nearly time to tee off. The anxiety I felt inside gripped me like a straitjacket holding me hostage, but now I felt I knew a way to handle it if I had to. The only other thing that could relieve the tension was to just get out there and play. I told myself that I'd be okay as soon as I teed off, and I tried to convince myself that I believed it, even as an ice-cold bead of sweat started to crawl down my back.

# 20

As I walked out of the clubhouse, the crunch of my golf spikes hitting the cart path sounded like a starting gun in my head. It was time, whether I was ready or not. Grateful Ted was right behind me, wearing his best coveralls that he'd tie-dyed just for the occasion, light purple with white circles that looked like smoke rings. He looked a little ridiculous, sure, but I was glad he did. Screw it. Anybody can be a clone, but Ted had personality. In a game like golf that's infamous for its outrageous clothing, where bright-green pants and plaid hats are not only tolerated but encouraged, I thought it fitting that Ted had his own unique style.

I made my way through the crowd and was surprised to hear my name on the lips of some in the gallery. Catching little snippets of encouragement, "Go get 'em Duffer" and "Atta boy, Duffer," gave me a surge of confidence I badly needed. Enough confidence even to ignore the other comments I heard such as: "My daddy says Duffer's a tubby loser," and "Hey, I think that guy gave me a speeding ticket last year!"

As we passed the leaderboard, I looked up to find my name. It wasn't at the top, far from it, but seeing it made my heart sing. There, ten strokes off the lead, was F. D. McDermott. To some, all the pain and suffering and heartache that went into getting to this point wouldn't be worth the reward, but to me, all that I'd been through in the past didn't matter. My name on that board was worth more to me than any rich man's fortune. It made me proud to think that all these years after the game of golf nearly destroyed my great-grandfather, the family name was back on the leaderboard. My mother was convinced that golf was "madness," but I was equally convinced I knew the cure: victory.

The crowds lining the fairways on Saturday morning were double the size they'd been on Thursday and Friday, and when I took in the sea of people in front of me, it was more than a little overwhelming. I could barely see the fairway in front of me, there were so many people lining the course. I scanned the crowd for any sign of Kitty, hoping that she would bring me good luck as she had on day one, but she was nowhere in sight. However, that's not to say I didn't recognize any of the faces in the crowd—two, to be exact.

The Racquette Brothers, Gordo and Barrie, stood out from the crowd of neatly dressed fans in fleece vests and branded base-ball hats, despite the fact they'd obviously done their level best to blend in. They'd cleaned themselves up for the occasion, wearing loud golf shirts in nauseatingly busy swirls of color, and they'd pulled their mullets back into neat little ponytails, taking the "business up front and party in the back" look and turning it into a greasy slicked back style that was equally anachronistic and out of place. They looked like bit players on an old episode of *Miami Vice*, the kind that get killed on a speedboat in the first scene, but it was the first time it occurred to me that both of them fit the criteria of having a ponytail, and I made a mental note to add that to the list of boxes they ticked.

Then, to my surprise, who should walk up to them from out of the crowd but George Graft. Approaching from behind, he gave Gordo a friendly slap on the back and the two greeted each other like old friends, Barrie handing George a beer as if he'd been expecting him.

*How did George Graft hook up with the two biggest slimeballs in La Siesta?* I thought to myself. My head was filling with questions I didn't have time to ponder as I made my way toward where they were buried in the crowd. They spotted me coming down the cart path, and when we made eye contact they both held their beers aloft in a sort of mocking toast.

"Ho, there, Duffer, make, like, a hole in one, eh?" hollered Gordo, a friendly smile on his face.

"Yeah, right, eh? Or we might have to put a hole in *you!*" added Barrie with a cackle, as they clinked beers and downed a celebratory gulp, a merry band of brothers from the look of it.

They seemed absolutely thrilled to be there, and now that Don was dead, I guessed they felt free to come to La Siesta. It was a pretty bold move if they'd been the ones to dispatch Don, but I wouldn't put it past them. Sometimes the best place to hide was in plain sight, eh?

I continued to the first tee and was suddenly struck with a bolt of anxiety when I realized I had to pass the announcer's booth, a moment I dreaded like a kid dreads the walk to school when he knows the bully's waiting for him. As I came within earshot of the announcers' booth and I recognized Joe Roebuck's deep baritone beaming out to millions of viewers at home, I got a lump in my throat. I just hoped they weren't talking about me.

"Well, Jill," said Joe, as I passed directly in front of the booth, "we've seen a lot of talented golfers tee off here this morning, and now it's time for a little change of pace, as Duffer McDermott makes his way to the tee box."

Ouch. That seemed unnecessary. *What is this guy's problem with me?*

"It's one of the things I love about open tournaments, Joe: you wind up with some unlikely players in the hunt," said Jill Smelt.

"*Very* unlikely!" chimed in Wee Jackie, picking up the insult and driving it home, as they all shared a hearty laugh. Jesus, I was their favorite punching bag this weekend, and it was really starting to piss me off.

"Ha ha, it's true," chortled Joe Roebuck, rolling with the theme, "but I think it's nice to spice things up a little bit. I mean, let's face it. The level of play on the PGA Tour is so top-notch these days, full of superbly conditioned athletes with beautiful swings and perfect accuracy, that I think it's refreshing for the fans to see someone like themselves, just a regular guy out there hacking away, taking ugly swings and grinding out double bogeys, still manage to get himself in contention."

"It's kind of fun to watch. That could be my dad out there. No offense, Dad!" Jill said, and they all erupted in another little laugh.

*No offense, Dad?! What about me, you overpaid chatterbox?!* I was really starting to fume, and that was not a good sign. I had to get away from the TV tower as soon as I could, but the crowd in front of me was backing up and I couldn't move at the moment. I had no choice but to listen to them, my confidence eroding with every insult.

"Aye, the poor ol' chap's got as much shot at the title as a wee cow has of bein' queen!"

They all joined Jackie Argyle for another merry chorus of laughter at my expense. Grateful Ted looked over at me, and it was clear he could sense my anger level rising.

"Don't listen to 'em, Duffer. They don't know what they're talking about," he said, giving me a reassuring pat on the shoulder.

"You're right, Ted. Screw 'em," I said, thankful for his calming influence and determined to let it go. "Hand me my driver, will you?"

He slid the driver out of my bag and handed me the club, grip first, and as soon as it hit my palm and I wrapped my hand around the shaft I felt it, my thumb squishing into a sticky warm substance.

"Damn it, Ted! You got popsicle gunk on the grip!"

I couldn't believe it. The one thing I'd told him specifically not to do. Suddenly, without even realizing what I was doing, I snapped my driver over my knee in a sudden impulse of rage.

Grateful Ted looked down at the broken driver, one half in each of my hands.

"Duffer, what the hell?"

I looked down to see what I'd done. The day hadn't even

started, and I'd already snapped a club over my knee in anger. This was not a good sign. Now I had to play the entire round without a driver, a handicap I could ill afford. The crowd finally began to move and we mercifully headed for the tee box.

Grateful Ted's face immediately went slack, realizing his error, and he practically jumped to grab the club from my hand.

"Sorry, man, sorry. I'll take care of that right away," he apologized, taking the club and replacing it with my three wood. "Here, use this instead."

I let the rage flow out of me. I had no choice. I couldn't play golf in my current state of agitation, so I had no choice but to let it go. I would play without a driver. I'd done it before. I could be mad at Grateful Ted, but that wouldn't help anything. I was the one who'd snapped the club, and I would have to live with it.

I walked on ahead of him toward the tee, praying that my nightmare morning was about to get better but unable to ignore the sinking feeling in my gut.

• ———————— •

By the time we arrived at the tee box, the sun was high in the sky and I could feel it starting to bake my pasty white skin, so I asked Grateful Ted to hand me my sunscreen. When I upturned the bottle and gave it a squeeze, all I got was the disgusting sound of a slightly wet fart; nothing but air came out of the empty bottle.

*Shit.*

"Ted, I don't suppose we have another bottle of sunscreen?"

He made a cursory search of the pockets on the bag, but

we both knew the answer. I wasn't the type of player to come prepared with an extra anything. Hell, I was starting this round without even a driver. This was yet another bad sign. Without sunscreen, my pale Irish skin would fry like bacon on a hot day like today. This day was already shaping up to be a parade route of pain when a surge of applause from the grandstand behind told me that my partner for the day had arrived.

Pete Fox was everyone's favorite player on the tour, an amiable twenty-year veteran of the PGA. He was tall and lean, with a crown of still boyishly blond hair and an easy smile. Pete and I had started out our careers at about the same time, but Pete had qualified for the tour his first year and gone on to a successful golfing career, and I had spent the next twenty years walking a beat instead of walking the fairways of America's top golf courses.

Pete was a model of grace under pressure, a steady rudder in a stormy sea, and I was determined to use him as an example for my own behavior today. I could already feel myself boiling inside, just waiting to erupt, a pressure cooker full of anxiety and nerves and doubt percolating just below the surface. But I couldn't let myself blow. I had to remain calm, not lose my temper, not flame out, and I was glad to have Pete as my partner for the day.

The gallery behind me parted like the Red Sea as Fox arrived with his caddie, a big walrus of a man named Burley who'd been his looper for his entire twenty-year career. Pete smiled when he saw me and greeted me like an old friend.

"Duffer. Good to see you again," he said with a genuine smile, his giant right hand enveloping mine in warm white leather. "Still chasing bad guys?"

"Only on the leaderboard," I said.

He had the grip of a golfer, firm but not overpowering, sensitive, like he was holding a new putter.

"How's the tour treating you, Pete?" I asked.

"Oh, you know how it is. I'd like to win more. But then again, I'd also like to lose less," he said with a chuckle, clapping me on the shoulder. "Best of luck out there, Duffer." He headed over to his caddie and grabbed his driver.

I could see he was being genuine, and I instantly knew why this guy was so popular with players and fans alike. In a game as cutthroat as golf, it's rare for anyone to be friendly and supportive like this. Guys mostly play their own game, and that's fine. Winning is paramount, but it sure feels nice when you get a break from all the psychological warfare and can just play a friendly game of golf. A friendly game with twenty thousand people watching from the gallery and a million more at home, plus the half million dollars at stake, but still, just a game.

The tournament marshal held his paddle aloft, signaling the crowd to be quiet as Pete stepped up to the tee, but before he was able to drive, Charlie Winer, the rules official, noticed something amiss in my bag.

"How many clubs in that bag, McDermott?" he said, a slightly annoyed look on his face.

*Jesus, did he spot the difference just by glancing at my bag?* This guy was tough.

"Relax, Winer. It's thirteen, one less than the limit. I can be under, just not over."

"What happened to your driver?" he asked.

"Things weren't working out between us and I had to let him go."

The crowd seemed to think this was funnier than old Charlie, who scowled and took his position at the side of the tee box. Pete looked back at us, bemused, but ready to go.

"Okay if I tee off now, guys?"

Another chuckle from the crowd and the tournament marshal signaled for quiet once more. Then Pete Fox showed us all why he'd been a major tour contender for the last twenty years with a picture-perfect drive to start the round. His swing was a thing of beauty, an example of perfect form that could have been drawn by Leonardo da Vinci. From then on, the laughter died down.

I managed to keep a grip on myself well enough to squeeze out par on the first three holes, and I was starting to find my groove as I settled over my approach shot on four. I watched my ball soar high into the air, tracing a graceful arc over the small stream that trickled across the fairway before bouncing up to the lip of the green and rolling gently to a spot about thirty feet from the hole. It was a solid shot and was met with a smattering of applause, which always had a calming effect on me. Applause from the gallery of a golf tournament is as comforting as the sound of a summer rain on a rooftop. In moments like this, my mind has to focus so intently that when I'm over the ball I hear nothing but my own heartbeat. But once I hit the ball, the soothing sound of the clapping crowd brings me back to reality like a warm ray of sunlight waking me from a dream.

My ball was geographically close to the cup, but I was mentally a mile away from holing a birdie putt on what should have been a relatively easy par three, one of the few holes on the entire course that shows a player even the slightest hint of mercy. I really needed to start shaving some strokes off my score if I was going to be in any position to win this tournament on Sunday. What I needed was a nice easy putt. What I was looking at was a long, uncertain putt to the far back right corner, a hole placement surely devised by the devil himself to make this otherwise simple hole a pain in my ass.

Pete Fox landed his ball on the green, ten feet in front of mine and in much better position, and I rode the wave of his applause as we walked up the fairway. When we arrived at the green, Pete was greeted like a returning hero, while I was greeted like the guy who happened to be partnered up with the returning hero.

I approached my ball like it was a live grenade, cautiously squatting down near it to have a look.

"What am I looking at here, Ted?" I asked, consulting my golf guru.

"What you're looking at and what you are seeing are two entirely different things, I'm afraid," he said, stroking his beard as if he were a professor, deep in thought.

"How do you mean?" I asked, playing the part of unenlightened pupil.

"This green's like an optical illusion," he explained. "There's more hills and valleys on that supposed flat plane than it seems the laws of physics would allow," he warned me.

"Okay, then how do we defy the laws of physics and hole out a birdie on this one?"

"I know of two ways to defy the laws of physics. One of those ways is illegal, and the other one is flimsy at best."

"What's the flimsy one?"

He smiled over at me. "Hope," was all he said.

"Hope?!" I balked.

"Hope," he repeated, like a mantra.

"This is your read on this green? Just hit the ball and *hope* it goes in?" I barked. *Jesus Christmas*, I thought, *maybe I shouldn't have put all my trust in a bong-hit Buddha.*

"It's the same advice I'd give you on any hole."

"But I mean, aren't there numbers to consult and charts and maps of the green and stuff?"

He just shrugged as I grabbed my putter and headed for the flag stick, grumbling to myself the whole way.

"All these other guys have caddies like NASA scientists," I muttered to myself. "I've got a damn space cadet." I was officially sick of Grateful Ted at the moment.

Arriving at the flag stick and looking back down the barrel of this putt from the other side, I could see what Ted was talking about. What looked from a distance like a nice flat green was actually riven with peaks and valleys, with at least two distinct plateaus between my ball and the hole. It seemed nearly impossible to judge how much speed I would need to get this ball all the way there. Trying to read this green nearly made my eyes cross. It was like something designed by M.C. Escher. Maybe Ted was right: hope was all I had.

I walked back to where my ball sat on the lip of the green, trying not to hang my head at my situation. I desperately needed every birdie I could get, and this should have been an easy one, but it wasn't going down that way, so I just had to make the best of my situation. The crowd went quiet as I leaned over my putt. I knew I had to hit it hard enough to get it there, but if I hit it too firm and it went past the hole, I would be in the sand trap directly behind the green, looking at a possible bogie.

I went for it. Hitting the ball with as much force as I dared, the crowd gasped when they saw how hard I'd hit it.

A voice from the gallery cried out, "*Get in the hole!*"

Somebody *always* yells "Get in the hole!" and God bless 'em. Sometimes I wonder if the PGA plants people in the crowd to yell it just to make sure it gets done.

The ball crested the first rise and seemed to be gaining velocity as it headed down the slope toward the next plateau. It gradually started slowing as it reached the crest, then down again one more time on the downslope. The train was headed into the station pretty damn fast, and I was afraid it was going to find the lip and get rejected.

But no.

PLOP.

Down it fell, disappearing down the drain.

The crowd erupted, and this time it was no soothing patter of summer rain but a great thunderous applause, the air charged like the flash and crack of heat lightning in a sudden electrical storm.

When the crowd noise died down and I had retrieved my ball from the bottom of the cup, always a satisfying feeling, I heard a familiar voice from the crowd.

"Pretty putt, Francis."

I looked behind me and there she was, standing apart from the crowd in her signature straw hat, a wicked smile on her face underneath a pair of sunglasses so big I could see the sky reflected in them. Kitty always stood out in a crowd, but today she appeared to me as the only living person in the world, her beauty blocking out the light from everyone else. When she saw she had my attention, she slid her big black shades down the bridge of her nose and gave me a wink. I barely had time to contemplate the meaning of this when she blew me a kiss, turned around, and walked off toward the clubhouse.

As I watched her go, I was surprised to see a man peel off from the crowd and join her. He was younger than she, handsome and fit. Something about him made me think I'd seen him before. As they headed off toward the clubhouse, he took a hold of her hand, and they walked off hand in hand. When his back was turned to me, I couldn't help but notice one detail about him. He had a ponytail poking out of the back of his baseball hat.

*Who the hell is that guy?* I thought to myself. *And why the hell is she holding his hand?* Christ, that's about all I needed, to add jealousy to the already-toxic mix of emotions coursing through my veins.

# 21

After spotting Kitty, things began to deteriorate rapidly. I bogeyed the fifth hole and double-bogeyed the sixth, and as we rounded the far edge of the course and sidled up to the seventh, I thought I might just leap right off the cliff and into the sea and drown myself, but I held myself together as best I could, swallowing my fear, my pride, and most of my dignity.

By now the sun was blazing like a furnace, and I could feel my pale skin beginning to redden. I wasn't even halfway through the round and I was already burning, the curse of my Irish heritage rearing its ugly head. It felt like there was a child in the sky with a giant magnifying glass concentrating the sun's rays on me like an unsuspecting ant, and I had nowhere to hide.

"Watch out on this one. The shark will eat your balls," said Grateful Ted, gazing down the fairway like a sailor scanning the horizon for any sign of land.

"What's that?" I asked, in no mood for any more cryptic advice.

"They call the sand trap on this hole 'the shark' because it looks like the outline of a hammerhead shark, but I think they call it that because it eats everyone's ball."

From the tee box, only the slightest glimpse of the sand trap was visible, just the lip, but something about it looked ominous. I pulled out my green book and looked at the hole. Sure enough, the green was protected by what looked like the outline of a hammerhead shark wrapped around the green on three sides. If you miss the green on any side you'll be caught in the shark's trap, and if you miss on the back side, your ball will roll downhill into a short rough backed up by a penalty area, a piece of protected wildlife that made it almost impossible for them to put a hole into this part of the property. They managed to squeeze the hole in by keeping the yardage short and designing the dastardly shark to make it more difficult, an endeavor in which they succeeded a bit too well for my taste.

"I don't like the smell of this one," said Grateful Ted, his voice taking on a hint of trepidation as he slid a seven iron out of my bag. He sniffed at the breeze again and a concerned look passed across his face. "Smells a bit fishy," he said, sampling the sea air like a chef testing a broth.

"Fishy? What does that mean?" I asked, already afraid to hear the answer.

"Smells like low tide," he said, sounding like an old sailor. "That can be dangerous on a hole like this."

I sighed in exasperation. "Jesus, I gotta worry about *the tides* now? What in God's good name do the tides have to do with my golf game?"

"Everything is connected. The position of the moon is critical. It pulls everything to it."

"The *moon*? Well, that's just terrific. I don't have enough to worry about. Now I gotta be concerned with the position of the moon!" I was really starting to lose it. "I mean, what's next? Is the rotation of the earth gonna throw my ball into the ocean?!"

Grateful Ted could feel me spinning out and did his best to calm me.

"Duffer," he said, his voice low and soothing like a therapist.

But it was too late, I was already in rant mode.

"It's DUFFY!" I snapped. "Not DUFFER! My name is Francis DUFFY McDermott!"

There was an awkward hush from the crowd. It's not every day they see a PGA player lose his shit. But then, maybe that's why I'm not a PGA player. Not yet anyway. And I was most definitely about to lose my shit. Maybe it was too much at once: investigating a murder, being a suspect in that same murder, trying to stay out of the Racquettes' clutches, trying to win a tournament, and now Kitty walking off hand in hand with some stranger. I was dripping in sweat and I was staring down a sunburn that might put me in the burn ward. I was about to crack. The word *fuck* was perched on my lips and ready to roll out, when I looked over at Charlie Winer, the rules official, and stopped myself.

*No.*

I would not go out this way. I wasn't going to lose this tournament on a disqualification. Throwing away my dream by saying a forbidden word was not how I was going to end my last chance at a golf career. I swallowed it. I let the word sink back into me. I took a deep breath, closed my eyes, and counted to ten. When I opened them everyone was staring at me. Grateful Ted looked concerned.

"You all right there, buddy?' he asked gently, like he was talking to a wounded bird.

"Yes. Sure. Fine, thanks." I snapped out of it. I took a sip of water, shook it off, and took another look at the hole.

I stepped into the box and a hush fell over the gallery, I bent down and placed my ball flat on the turf, no tee for this one, at only a hundred and seventy-five yards, it was almost a chip shot, but this shot was about accuracy, not distance.

At the apex of my backswing, I felt myself swinging just a touch too hard, but it was too late to adjust. I swung through, and the ball leaped into the air off the face of my club, arcing high into the air, too high, but heading on a straight line to the hole. I cringed as I saw how high it was going.

"Sit, sit, sit down . . ." I said, willing the ball not to overshoot the green. To my great relief, it landed just behind the flag stick, completely avoiding the waiting jaws of the shark. A cheer went up from the crowd.

But then, the steep slope of the green, as vicious an angle as I've ever seen on a golf course, a descent straight out of the Swiss Alps, sent my ball running toward the back of the green like an escaped convict. The gallery gasped as they watched my ball roll all the way to the back of the green and off, tumbling down over the rough and beyond, landing in a sandy and scrubby spot just a hair's breadth from the penalty zone.

"Well, at least you didn't get swallowed by the shark," said Grateful Ted, trying to paint a cheerful face on disaster.

I slammed my seven iron back in the bag in frustration and watched as my partner for the day, Pete Fox, taking a lesson from me no doubt, decided to lay up, landing in the mouth of the shark, but still only an easy up and down for a par putt. I, on the other hand, was looking at, well shit, I didn't even know what I was looking at until I got over there.

When I got there, what I was looking at, was, indeed, shit. The ball had rolled to within a few inches of the penalty area, a large area of protected shrubs, the edge of the nesting ground for gnatcatchers. Owing to the delicate nesting area I couldn't step into it. Not even a toe. To make matters worse, in the position my ball lay, it was impossible for me to take my shot without stepping out of bounds, the ball was nestled right up against the sign that warned golfers away, and I would only have a shot at the ball from the left-hand side.

Charlie Winer, the rules official, came over.

"Looks like you'll have to take a drop and a penalty stroke," he said.

I shook my head. "No way. I'm not taking a penalty. My ball's not in the penalty area."

"But there's no way you can make that shot."

I looked him in the eye with a smile. "Not as a right handed golfer. But as a lefty . . ."

I could hear the murmuring in the gallery, a few scoffs and groans and grumbles amounted to a small symphony of doubt. Through the din, I picked up the words *crazy* and *illegal*.

I walked to the other side of the ball. From this angle, as a lefty, I could set my feet and swing at the ball with a clear shot at getting it back on the green. It was unorthodox, but I felt like it could be done. But what club to do it with? All my irons were angled the wrong way. But what about backwards?

I walked over to my bag and looked at my choices. I pulled out the two iron, then flipped it around. Looking at it with a new purpose in mind, I noticed that the back of the club face was basically straight up and down, and the other side was only a few degrees different. It looked nearly identical from one side to the next.

Winer saw what I was contemplating and scoffed.

"You really think you can make this shot with a two iron?"

"No, I think I'm going to make this shot left handed with a backwards two iron," I shot back.

Winer looked at me like I'd insulted his mother. "Backwards?! But this is highly unusual," he protested.

"I'll give you that, but is it illegal?"

Clearly unsure, he quickly pulled out his rule book and started madly searching for the proper ruling. After a few moments he looked up, and from the disappointment on his face I could tell it was legal.

"Go ahead," was all he said, sounding dejected.

Great, now all I had to do was pull off a near impossible shot, left handed, with a backwards club. No problem.

I stepped up to the ball, planting my feet as best I could to angle myself toward the hole without stepping in the restricted area. It was like playing a tough game of Twister, but I found my footing and settled over the ball. Even with the extra room afforded me by hitting left handed, I still only had enough room to take a quick chop at the ball. As the gallery hushed, suppressing their giggles at my ridiculous predicament, I choked up on my club, shortened my backswing, and dropped the head of the backwards two iron almost straight down on top of the ball, squeezing it off the hard ground underneath.

The ball burst off the ground like a kernel of popcorn, clearing the rough and heading directly for the flagstick, which Grateful Ted removed just in time for the ball to land in the dead center of the hole.

SWISH!

The ball never even hit the green, just found the center of the cup like a bird flying home to its nest. The crowd exploded into paroxysms of joy. I ran to the green to see if it could possibly be true, but all I had to do was see the smile on Grateful Ted's face to know I had done the near impossible.

From that point on, the round was a breeze. I played like a man reborn, with confidence surging through my very being like oxygenated blood. I holed par after birdie after par, shedding strokes as I went like a stripper dropping clothes on stage. I was climbing the leaderboard faster than King Kong climbing up the Empire State Building. The only thing missing was my Fay Wray, who'd just sauntered off with some stranger.

But nothing else mattered at that moment. I was in my element. I could feel the contours of the golf course like a Reiki master finding the hot spots of energy on the human body. If there's such a thing as a pure golf zone, I was now in it, strolling the course in a near trance, Grateful Ted whispering advice in my ear and my body turning it into pure golf gold.

I finished the day just five strokes back from the top, an

incredible climb. I felt as if I was watching another, better golfer than myself play the course, and it was only seeing my name on the leaderboard at the end of the day, right in the thick of the best players in the PGA, that made it all begin to seem real. I could actually do this. I was in contention. Only one more day to go, and I could write myself into golf history.

## 22

I was seated in George Graft's home office, a well-appointed study at the back of an enormous white-clapboard house overlooking La Siesta Bay in the tony Shepherd's Isle neighborhood, just north of the country club itself. I took a look at the wall before me and saw a plaque announcing George's membership on the board of the club, as well as photographs of George with various celebrities and politicians, all of whom flocked to La Siesta to play the famed golf course and apparently felt compelled to pose with the club's board of directors.

A table along the side wall was home to a number of trophies and mementos, civic awards from various charities around town, and what looked like gifts from visiting dignitaries: small statues and trinkets; a medal of merit from La Siesta's sister city, Augusta, GA; and one item that caught my eye in particular, a bottle of maple syrup with a French label.

I stood up as George entered, a handsome older gentleman with dyed black hair and a tan as deep a shade of brown as the leather chair behind his desk. He shook my hand in greeting and I noticed he shared the distinctive trait of many of the country club members, one hand whiter than the other from constantly wearing a golf glove.

"Well, if it isn't Duffer McDermott," he said with a smile. "It's a real pleasure to meet you." He pumped my hand so vigorously I thought he was trying to get water to shoot out of my mouth.

"It is?" I said, a bit surprised at this friendly greeting.

"Why, sure, I've got a lot of money riding on you!" he said in a booming, jovial voice that filled the room. "You're gonna win that tournament for me, aren't you?"

"Oh, I see," I said, smiling back, genuinely pleased that he felt I had a chance to win. "Glad someone around here believes in me."

"I couldn't resist. God knows I love a long shot, and there hasn't been a shot quite this long in a dog's age!" He laughed, bursting my bubble.

"Right, of course." I extracted my hand from his tight grip and got down to business. "Well, anyway, George, thanks for seeing me. Your wife's told me a lot about you."

"So I gather," he said, his enthusiasm suddenly muted. "If there's one thing Elaine's good at, it's talking."

"I just wanted to ask a few questions about Don Osborne."

"Don Osborne was an asshole," he said with a shrug. "I hate to put it that way, but it's the truth."

He was certainly not trying to hide his disdain, which I found rather forthright under the circumstances.

"If I hear one more person put it that way, I might just be

inclined to believe it," I replied, getting tired of hearing the same old refrain.

He offered me a seat in front of his desk, and I couldn't help but admire the view from his window, which featured a sweeping panorama of La Siesta Bay. Once again, one boat in the sea of beautiful sailboats, yachts, and really big yachts stood out as unusual, the listing, half-sunken sailboat *Bill's Baby*.

He followed my gaze out the window to the bedraggled boat and let out a sigh.

"I keep telling Dwyer he should just drag that thing out to sea," he said, shaking his head.

"That's Bill Dwyer's boat?"

"It is. Who else would leave a hunk like that floating in the bay? But he's been bull-headed ever since we met."

"That would have been in the Army Rangers? You both served with Don, is that correct?" I asked, thankful for his convenient lead in.

"That's right. We served three years together. Nothing cements a friendship quite like the experience of war. You find your true friends in a foxhole, as they say."

"And yet you say Don Osborne was an asshole. Why?"

"Well, it's complicated. Don and I served together, and then we worked together for many years after that at OSS, and every day was a struggle to overcome his odious personality and get the job done."

"And then one day last week it came to an end. Why was that?"

He stiffened at the question but didn't hesitate to answer. "That was typical Don Osborne bullshit. He accused me of something I had absolutely nothing to do with, and well, I wouldn't stand for a man besmirching my reputation. So I left. It was ten years too late, if you ask me."

"What was the accusation?"

"That I had something to do with a bunch of inventory that went missing. I had nothing at all to do with it and I showed him the proof, but he insisted."

"So that was it? That was the end of your relationship?"

"Pretty much. Of course I couldn't avoid him entirely. We saw each other at the club."

"You remain on the board of the La Siesta Country Club, is that right?"

"Don didn't like it, but yes. I'm in charge of operations for the tournament, and the other members knew that nobody else could get the job done, so when he tried to remove me from the board, the others overruled him."

"So, as director of operations for the tournament, would you be in charge of hiring the company responsible for setting up the infrastructure? The grandstands, scaffolding, stuff like that?"

"That's correct. I take care of all that stuff."

Suddenly, seeing George Graft sharing beers at the tournament with the Racquette brothers made sense, as well as explained how they managed to get the gig setting up the tournament infrastructure despite their acrimonious relationship with Don Osborne. George said he had a lot of money riding on me winning this tournament, and it was well-known that the Racquette brothers ran most of the illegal sports gambling in La Siesta. If I had to make a bet of my own, I'd say George Graft was in to them for a substantial gambling debt. I was starting to get a clearer picture of their relationship, but I also wondered what other arrangements he might have made with them.

I could tell George was becoming uncomfortable with the direction of the questions by the way he started to fidget with the cigar cutter on his desk, so I decided to leave well-enough alone, and wrap up the meeting.

"Anything else I can help you with?" he asked, a touch of anxiety rising in his voice.

"Just one thing. When was the last time you saw Don alive?"

"The night he was shot."

"You were in the ballroom?"

"I was. I was sitting right next to my wife."

●————————————●

The scorching afternoon sun was beating down on the black-top of Highway One as I pushed the gas pedal on my Crown Vic to the floor, hurrying toward the nature preserve at the south end of La Siesta. I was on my way to meet Bill Dwyer—about what, I wasn't sure, but I was hoping he wanted to get something off his chest about Don Osborne. A nature preserve is a funny place to hold a meeting, but it occurred to me that maybe he didn't want anyone to see us together. Other than that, I couldn't imagine what this was all about, but I figured I'd at least hear him out. I was hoping this could lead to the break in the case I'd been wait-ing for. Either that, or I was walking into a trap.

I pulled over on the sandy shoulder and parked next to a few other cars along the edge of the freeway. The nature preserve was spread out in front of me: several wild acres of dunes with winding paths cutting through scrubby chaparral and coastal sage, dotted here and there with large boulders and a few Monterey Cypress trees providing an occasional shady oasis. One look at the spectacular view, and it was easy to see why it was a popular spot for bird watchers and nature lovers, and why local developers had been slobbering over the beachfront property for years. It was a magical place, where the desert meets the ocean. A place where worlds collide.

At the top of the trailhead there was a map of the sanctuary, which showed the outline of walking paths that curved around the property in roughly a figure-eight shape, with the territory outside of the designated pathways strictly off-limits, unless you were a gnatcatcher, or presumably, a gnat. Situated throughout the preserve were several raised duck blinds for bird watchers to view the nesting sites from above. They looked like lifeguard stands, except these were full of nerds with binoculars instead of buff *Baywatch* types.

Today the place was relatively empty, the hot afternoon air baking the soil and keeping most visitors away until the cooler evening hours. I took the path leading to the right, the fine sand squeaking under my sneakers, and headed for the rendezvous point Bill had indicated for our meetup. It looked to be about five hundred yards in, but the path was full of twists and turns, a few taller bushes and short trees obscuring the view, making it difficult for me to orient myself, and by the time I emerged onto the clearing I had to locate the ocean before I could finally get my bearings.

I was admiring the soaring beauty of the place, letting the silence fill me, when I heard someone huffing and panting down the path behind me. I turned to see Bill Dwyer, sweat staining his shirt in ever widening circles under his arms as he strained to crest the rise. He was wearing a suit, or half a suit anyway, his blue slacks now brown at the cuffs with dust from the path and his tie hanging down around his neck like a noose. He was holding his hand in front of his face in a vain attempt to keep the sun at bay, but it was futile, the sun scorching his bald head flaming red as he came scrambling up the sandy hill toward me. He reached the clearing and folded himself in half at the waist to catch his breath.

"It's murder out here," he huffed.

"Yeah, but what a beautiful death," I said, gesturing to the breathtaking view.

When he stood up I could see he agreed with me. He sighed as he straightened up and filled his lungs with sea air.

"I have to agree. It's always been one of my favorite spots in all of La Siesta."

"Is that why you wanted to meet me out here, the natural beauty?" I asked, fishing for his motive behind the meeting.

He gave me an odd look. "What are you talking about? You set up this meeting."

"No, I didn't. You sent me a text." I pulled out my phone and showed him the message.

"That's not my phone number," he replied, and I got a sinking feeling about this whole business. "I got a text from you asking to meet here," he countered, showing me his phone, which displayed a text from the same 310 number.

"Well, somebody wanted us to get together," I said with growing unease.

"I assumed you contacted me because Kitty informed you she'd hired me as your attorney," he said.

"Wait, what? She hired you to represent *me*?" I couldn't hide my surprise. "Why would she do that?"

"I assume because you and she were together at the time of the murder. She told me everything. She's afraid the cops will come after her, and she wants both of you on the same team."

I stopped short of telling him that, in reality, Kitty and I were together right before the murder, but at the actual time the shot was fired, I didn't know exactly where Kitty was. The fact that she'd hired Bill to protect me could signal that she cared for me, or that she was worried I'd blow her cover, and she figured the best way to keep me from crumbling was to protect me with a high-powered lawyer before I ever got the chance. This whole thing was getting twisted in a way I hadn't anticipated. Suddenly this case had more wrinkles than an old man's nut sack.

"Well, I appreciate the gesture. And I know you're one hell of a lawyer, but I'm not on anyone's team. That's why I play golf. It's an individual sport."

"Fine by me. Frankly, I think the whole thing stinks, and the less I have to do with it, the better. I only took her on as a client out of loyalty to Don."

"I was under the impression you and Don were on the outs. I heard about your fight on the golf course the morning he was murdered."

"Oh, that was nothing," he said with a dismissive wave of

the hand. "Don and I argued all the time. I'm not sure if you've heard, but Don Osborne was an asshole."

"I might have caught some whispers to that effect." I sighed, which made him chuckle. "So what were you two fighting about that morning?"

"You're looking at it," he said, making a sweeping gesture at the coastline in front of us.

"The wildlife sanctuary? What about it?"

"I didn't want to see it become another high-end development for millionaires," he said.

"Wait. What? You didn't?" I couldn't believe what I was hearing, but the impish grin he gave me indicated he was telling the truth. "But you and Don spent the last twenty years fighting in court to try to get its designation as a nature preserve revoked."

"Well, yes and no," he said, a guilty smile curling his lips, like a kid who's been caught with his hand in the cookie jar.

"What do you mean? I've seen the court cases. There's dozens of them. And appeals, and injunctions and lawsuits against the government and all the rest. All initiated by you."

"All initiated by Don, you mean," he said, making a point of the distinction.

"But you were his lawyer for all of it."

"And I did what my client asked me to do. But . . ."

"But what?"

"But, I guess I didn't always do my job to the fullest of my abilities."

"What are you saying?"

"I'm saying that Don wanted to turn this into another luxury golf community. But that doesn't mean I wanted to."

"So what does that mean?"

"It means that when it came time to argue Don's case before the court, I may have left out some things."

"What things?"

"Environmental reports."

"Environmental reports that said what?"

"That said the gnatcatcher is no longer endangered. That they no longer need this as a nesting ground."

"In other words, that this piece of land no longer needs to be a nature preserve protected by the government?"

"Exactly. I buried the reports and when the judge gives his ruling on Monday, we're going to lose that case."

I couldn't believe it. The whole time Don Osborne was fighting to turn this land into another real-estate deal, his own lawyer was secretly working against his interests.

"But why?"

"Just look at it. I mean, come on. That view alone is priceless."

We both looked out at the sweeping coastline, a jagged rocky shore that ran south for miles before it curled out to sea, the view uninterrupted by any houses or manmade structures. Just then, a giant wave crashed against the rocks and sent a jet of sea-foam cascading into the air, an explosion of white foam, like a storm cloud getting punctured by the rocks.

"Out here, land, sea, and air become one," Bill continued, gazing at the beauty before him like a true believer. "Raw, wild, untamed Mother Earth. Out here, there's no separation between humans and nature. We are only humans *in* nature, just one more creature in the ecosystem. At some point we have to let nature be nature. We don't have to divide it up among just a very lucky few."

"You're right, Bill. But frankly, I'm surprised you feel that way," I said, looking at him in a whole new light.

"I grew up around here. I remember when there was barely anything but beach between here and San Diego. I used to spend all my time on these beaches, and I don't want to see it disappear for other kids, just because a few rich folks want another McMansion."

"So this had nothing to do with the gnatcatchers? It's not about the birds at all, it's about the kids."

"Well," he shrugged, "the birds can stay too, I guess." He smiled and gave me a chuckle.

"So what happened when Don found out you fudged the data?" I asked.

"He blew up at me."

"So that's what the fight on the course was about? The day you didn't finish your round."

"That was it. He was so mad he threatened to kill me."

"Did you believe he would do it?"

"Not really. Don was all bluster."

I tried to take all this in, as I mentally crossed Bill Dwyer off my list of suspects.

"So who do you think killed Don?"

"Well, I can't be sure of course. But I have an idea. You see—"

Just then a shot rang out.

The bullet whizzed by our heads so close I could feel its heat on my cheek. The bullet ricocheted off the rocks behind us, causing a spark that set fire to some dry grass in the dunes. A small puff of smoke curled up from the brush. I looked up and saw the barrel of a rifle poking out of a birdwatching stand about five hundred yards from us, just before the second shot rang out and hit Bill Dwyer in the temple.

He fell dead at my feet.

Before I could register what was going on, the dunes around us burst into flames. I looked back at the birdwatching stand to see who had taken the shot, but the smoke billowing from the dry grass made it impossible to see anyone who might have been running away.

I looked at Bill, the bullet wound to his temple leaking blood onto the dusty ground and a spray of brain matter on the bush behind him. I knew there was nothing I could do for him. The fire was growing all around me, the heat starting to singe my exposed skin, so I left Bill's body and ran back down the path toward my car, already calling 911 on the phone to report the fire. I decided I didn't need to report the dead body in the fire, not just yet. Once they found him, I would have some explaining to do, but right now I was the last one to see a dead man in a secluded spot where his remains were found in the aftermath of a suspicious wildfire.

I would need a second to get my story straight.

# 23

hopped in my Crown Vic and tore ass out onto the highway, hoping to get the hell away from the conflagration as fast as I could, when I was suddenly forced to slow down to a crawl by a tiny little electric car puttering along up the highway at the speed of a tipsy turtle. I could tell from the Bob Marley bumper sticker that I was going to have to pass this hippie if I was ever going to get the hell out of there, but the highway at this juncture was one lane in each direction, so it wouldn't be easy.

I pushed the gas pedal down and started to make my move, but when I came abreast of the driver's side window, I looked over and was shocked to see who it was I was passing, none other than Shiloh Greene, the egg wrangler from the Wildlife Preservation Society. What the hell was he doing here? I was so startled to see him that I didn't even spot the fire engine barreling down the highway in the opposite lane. I slammed on the brakes just in time to let it pass and swerved to control my vehicle, keeping it right behind Shiloh Greene. Could this be the sniper who just killed

Bill? He certainly appeared to be fleeing the scene of the crime, if that's what you call it when your getaway vehicle tops out at forty-five miles an hour.

I decided to follow him, and after an agonizingly slow drive up the highway, he pulled into the parking lot of a nondescript office building at the edge of La Siesta, a two-story commercial office building that could have easily doubled as a cheap motel, with a peeling paint job and an outdoor stairwell leading to a walkway along the second floor. He parked in the lot and popped the trunk of his Tiny Toons car, and to my surprise he pulled out what looked like a rifle case. I couldn't believe it. If he was the one who'd killed Bill Dwyer just now, there was a damn good chance he was also Don Osborne's killer. I took a deep breath. Maybe this was it. I'd had to escape a fire to find it, but I may have just stumbled upon my solution.

Of course, I would have to be careful. Even though he looked like a harmless hippie, if he had two bodies to his name already, I wasn't eager to become number three. I watched as he went up to an office on the second floor, ducked inside quickly, and pulled the shades. I didn't want to give him any time to get rid of evidence or get his story straight, so I grabbed a dark-blue windbreaker out of my backseat, the cheap one-ply plastic kind only worn by cops and Little League coaches. I was hoping it made me look enough like a cop as I left my car in the lot, bounded up the stairs behind him and pounded on the door.

"Mr. Greene?! Open up!" I yelled, the authority in my voice belying the fact that I had none. I stopped short of identifying myself as a cop, but I wanted him to think I just might be.

He was nervous and sweaty when he opened the door, obviously rattled. The room smelled like a freshly smoked joint, doubtless sparked in an attempt to calm down from whatever trauma he'd just been through, or perhaps, caused.

"Yeah? What is it?" he asked through the crack in the door.

"May I come in? I have a few questions to ask you." I held my green book in one hand and a golf pencil in the other, looking for all the world like an officer intent on jotting down some notes, but I was careful not to identify myself. I let his brain fill in the blanks, which he seemed to do, opening the door wide for me to step into the room.

He was a wiry little weasel of a man with long brown hair pulled back in a ponytail and a real fist-magnet of a face. Something about him just begged to be punched in the nose. Despite his obvious middle age, he was dressed like the captain of a college Hacky Sack team: hiking shorts, Birkenstock sandals, and a tie-dyed t-shirt reading EARTH DAY IS EVERY DAY. He peered at me through thick Coke-bottle glasses, blinking in the sunlight, the look on his face a condescending scowl of self-righteousness.

"Cannabis is legal in California, cop!" he squealed.

"Relax, Harry Pothead, I'm not here about the weed." I was already sick of this guy, but I liked that he'd swallowed my cop routine.

"Then what do you want?" he shot back, a little too quickly for my taste.

"I saw you leaving the wildlife sanctuary just now. What were you doing there?" I asked, easily slipping back into my old interrogation voice. The second I mentioned the sanctuary, his eyes got wide.

"I, I work there," he stammered, clearly unnerved.

"Oh, yeah? You always take a rifle to work?"

He walked over and picked up the rifle bag leaning against the wall. "Yeah, I do."

"And why is that?"

"It's for animals. It's a tranquilizer gun."

He opened the bag and slipped the rifle out, and sure enough it was equipped to shoot darts, not bullets.

"I use it in case any coyotes try to steal the gnatcatcher eggs. I want to stop them, but not kill them."

I took this in. It seemed to make sense. I tried another tactic.

"You sure seemed to be in a hurry to get away from the sanctuary just now," I said, as he squirmed and fidgeted. "You didn't happen to see anything unusual while you were doing your daily egg count or whatever?" I pressed.

He shook his head.

"You sure? Listen, if you get out ahead of this thing I can make it go easy with the DA. I'm in good with her," I lied, never having met the DA in my life.

He looked down at his lap, shaking his head once again, defiant, but I could tell he wouldn't hold out forever. He was hiding something, and I was determined to get it out of him.

"This might be your last chance before the chief gets here. Confess now and there's a chance I can smooth things over for you come sentencing."

Something about the word *sentencing* made him buckle.

"Okay, okay, man. I admit it! I'm guilty!" he cried, breaking down. "I did it!" He hung his head, tears starting to flow.

"So you admit to killing Bill Dwyer? And Don Osborne, too?" I pounced, surprised he cracked so easily.

He suddenly opened his eyes and looked up, surprised. "What? No, I didn't kill anybody, man," he protested, wiping tears from his cheeks.

"But you just said you admitted it. You said you were guilty."

"I was talking about the fire, man."

"What?"

"I started the fire at the wildlife sanctuary! Oh man, I'm such an idiot."

"What are you talking about?" I asked, as confused as he'd been just a moment ago.

"I was just trying to light a joint, but I guess an ember must have blown away into the brush. Oh, jeez, what the heck was I thinking?!" he cried. He clutched his head in a sudden seizure of self-loathing.

I shook my head. I should have known better than to think this guy could have murdered anyone. "Don't beat yourself up. It wasn't you," I said.

"What?"

"It wasn't you," I assured him. "Someone else started the fire."

"They did? Oh, thank God, man."

Relief washed over him like a wave of patchouli oil.

"Who was it?"

"That's what I'd like to find out."

# 24

I was standing outside of Shiloh Greene's office, leaning on the rail and taking in another showstopper Southern California sunset as I contemplated what to do next. I knew what I *should* do—talk to Kitty—but I still wasn't sure if I was ready to face up to the reality that she may have killed Don. I wanted this thing to end, but I didn't want it to end at Kitty's doorstep. As I stood there prevaricating, an older gentleman in a threadbare tracksuit came out of the office next door and lit a cigarette.

"Hell of a view," he said by way of a greeting.

"Sure is," I agreed, "just goes to show you that even the shit-holes in La Siesta come with a beautiful view."

"You got that right."

"Nobody owns the sunset," I said wistfully, thinking myself poetic.

"I wasn't talking about the sunset," he said, dragging on his cigarette.

"Then, what . . ." I asked, not following and suddenly feeling stupid.

"The hottie on the Ducati." He gestured with his cigarette, directing my gaze downward from the horizon.

I looked down to the highway and there she was, stopped at a red light, one leg thrown over the sleek silver frame of a Ducati Panigale. She wore a black leather racing suit that clung to her sculpted figure like a second skin, and a pair of heavy black-leather motorcycle boots adorned with tiny silver chains on the heel, a flash of metal winking in the sun. Even with a helmet obscuring her face I knew there was only one person it could be.

Kitty.

To my surprise, she looked up and waved at me.

*What was she doing here?* I wondered. *Had she followed me?*

I had no time to waste and bolted from the balcony, bounding down the stairs two at a time and racing to get to my Crown Vic before she raced off up the highway. There was no way I could make it in time, and I saw the light change as I was just about to reach my car.

The instant the light flashed green, she twisted the throttle and rocketed off the line with a squeal from her back tire, shooting up the coast highway like a roman candle and leaving only the smell of burning rubber behind. Seconds later I peeled out of the parking lot after her, my bald back tires leaving a cloud of smoke and a long black smear on the tarmac before finally gripping the road and propelling me forward, desperately chasing the one woman in La Siesta I didn't want to talk to.

I was lucky there was little traffic at this time of day, and I caught up to her pretty quickly, although I realized before long that she appeared to want me to catch up to her. She turned around several times as we wound our way up the coast, as if she was making sure I was following her, even slowing down to let me keep up at times. Finally, at the next light, I pulled into line a few cars behind her, and she turned around and gave me a thumbs-up.

*She did want me to follow her,* I thought, but when the light changed she gunned her engine, shooting off once again, taunting me.

*What kind of game was she playing? Where was she taking me?* I wondered, my mind racing like the hulking V8 engine of my old sedan as it struggled to keep up with her nimble Italian sport bike.

I tailed her as closely as I could on the straightaways, but she lost me time and again on the curves, seemingly at will. She toyed with me, disappearing around corners, blending in and out of traffic, in command of the machine between her legs like it was an extension of her body. She hugged the curves of the road tighter than her riding suit hugged her own, leaning into each switchback like a pro, laying the bike down on its side, her knee hovering inches from the pavement, then straightening back up again and disappearing in a haze.

As we came closer to La Siesta proper, I caught up just in time to see her take a right-hand turn at La Siesta Terrace and head toward town. Things slowed down once we got on surface streets, but not by much. She weaved her way through the immaculately maintained resort-town streets at speeds that would be considered unsafe by even the most hardened of Hells Angels, scandalizing the wealthy widows out walking their dogs as the jarring sound of her high-performance engine cut through the neighborhood peace like a chainsaw.

We flew through the center of town, past the glittering early evening revelers on Worthmore Avenue emerging from their afternoon siestas for the golden hour, when the sunset provided the most flattering light for taking Instagram photos. The sidewalks along the wide avenue were steadily filling with the cocktail crowd, a parade of rich and beautiful people strolling, chatting, and photographing their fabulous lives for everyone to envy. After all, what was the point of being a have if you couldn't flaunt it in front of the have-nots?

Kitty didn't show any signs of letting up as she led me on a meandering high-speed tour of the town. We raced past The Cloisters, a leafy enclave of "smaller" homes, some of them only six or seven bedrooms, then through the Diamond Head District, where the homes got bigger and the lawns got longer, before turning into the Garden District, where the houses were no longer visible from the street, which is how you know they're gigantic. Finally she led me into Shepard's Idle, the wealthiest and most exclusive of all the neighborhoods in La Siesta. Here the real estate made the jump from mere houses to estates, and as I followed her through the neighborhood, we didn't pass houses so much as front gates. Finally, we arrived at the crown jewel of the neighborhood, indeed of La Siesta itself, the Osborne Estate.

*She was leading me home? Why? Who leads someone on a high-speed chase to their own house?*

As we approached the wrought-iron gate, she signaled the

guard with a wave of her hand. The gates swung open, and I followed her up the long winding driveway to the house.

She parked the Ducati in front of a large barn painted forest green that was situated to the left of the house, which turned out to be an enormous garage with room for fourteen cars. She climbed off the bike and walked over to where I'd parked the Crown Vic, which was still shuddering and kicking from exertion.

She took off her helmet and greeted me with a wide smile, her hair mussed up in a sexy tussle. Suddenly the idea that she may be a murderer didn't seem to matter so much anymore; my lower brain was immediately taking over for my upper brain.

"You look surprised. Didn't you know it was me?" she said, playfully stripping off her leather riding gloves.

"Who the hell else could it be?" I replied, trying to swallow the lust that was rising in my throat and threatening to cut off the oxygen to my brain.

She threw her head back and let out a laugh, exposing her long slender neck, then fixed me with a mischievous look, like she knew something I didn't. I had no idea what to say. I was struck dumb by her.

"Why did you bring me here?" I finally managed to mutter.

"Because I wanted to fuck you, silly."

———————

We never made it out of the garage, getting only as far as a Bentley convertible before tumbling in a knot onto the backseat. When it was over, I sat up and looked around, amazed to find

myself in a private museum of automotive treasures, the aftermath of our dalliance a trail of clothing along the otherwise-pris-
tine garage floor. For a garage, the place was immaculate, cleaner
and better organized than a laboratory. All the tools were neatly
hanging on the walls underneath individual labels, and, despite
the fact that the room was full of engines and auto parts, not a
spot of oil or fleck of dirt could be seen on the ground. The cars
were all freshly washed and waxed, gleaming like jewels under the
soft lights. It was like some sort of heaven for anal retentive auto
mechanics.

"Jesus Christ. Who has this many cars besides Jay Leno?" I
asked, groping around for my pants.

"What can I say? Don loved to collect things. Houses, cars,
people," she said with a shrug. She pulled a pack of cigarettes out
of the burl wood center console and lit one with a silver lighter
engraved with the letters *KO*.

I pulled on my pants and took a stroll down the row of high-
end automobiles, which included a neon-green Lamborghini, an
old Ford Model-T, and the Rolls Royce Silver Cloud I'd seen Kitty
arrive at the club in the other day.

"What's with the golf cart?" I asked, nodding at the incongru-
ous vehicle at the end of the line. "Seems a little slow compared
to the others."

"Oh, that was Don's favorite."

"Really? Of all these cars his favorite was a golf cart? Why?"

"It has a Ferrari engine."

"It has a what?!" I yipped.

"That reaction is exactly why Don loved it." She laughed.

"You mean this thing actually has a Ferrari engine under the hood?"

"Sure does. Specially made for Don himself."

I ran my hand along it in disbelief. From the outside it looked just like an ordinary golf cart: plain white plastic bench seats and a storage space in the back for golf clubs, but when she popped the hood I could see she wasn't kidding. Sitting in the front of this otherwise-ordinary-looking golf cart was a gas-powered V-12 engine that looked like something you'd see racing on the streets of Monte Carlo rather than on the fairways of a country club golf course.

"Do you have the keys?" I joked.

"Don't need keys. This thing comes with a launch button."

"A launch button? Holy shit, that sounds serious."

"Oh, it's deadly fucking serious."

There was an awkward pause. She looked at me, holding my gaze, her eyes telling me she knew I'd followed her here for more than just sex. She broke the tension by pulling me out of the door of the garage.

We made our way through the grounds, toward a wide flag-stone patio laid out on the edge of a cliff overlooking the ocean. The sun was gone and the moon was on the rise as we stood looking out over the cliff, the sound of the waves crashing on the rocks below at once soothing and menacing, peaceful but dangerous, a bit like La Siesta itself.

"You're not thinking of sacrificing me to the sea are you?" I asked, only half joking.

"I would never do anything to hurt you, Francis, you know

that, right?" she said, purposely using my real name to soften me up, I suspected.

She took my face in her hands and looked me in the eye. I was searching for sincerity but wasn't sure what I was finding. I didn't trust myself anymore. I was afraid that she'd blinded me to the truth, that she just had me seeing what she wanted me to see.

"I don't know anything for sure. Not anymore," I said.

"Well, then what do you want to know? Ask me anything and I'll tell you the truth." Her words were coming out in a rush. "I swear, I had nothing to do with this. You can ask me all the questions you want. I've already answered them all for the chief, but if you want me to do it all again, I will. Please, you've got to believe me when I tell you I had nothing to do with any of this."

"Okay, for starters you can tell me why you hired Bill Dwyer to represent me."

"I did that for your own protection. I happen to know your alibi is shit," she said with a coy smile.

"You sure it wasn't your own alibi you were worried about?"

"But, Duffer," she said, gently stroking my cheek, "you're my alibi."

I pulled away. "I may be your alibi for the time we spent in the sand trap, but when the shots were fired, I can't be sure where you were," I said, looking her dead in the eye.

"You really think I could have done this, don't you?"

"That's not an answer, Kitty."

"Fine. You want an answer, I'll give it to you. I was in the clubhouse. I snuck around back just like I said I would, just like

I told the police I was. I was right where they found me, in the ladies locker room freshening up."

She had me by the shoulders, looking into my eyes, but I broke the embrace and turned away. I couldn't let my feelings for her distract me from my mission to find out the truth.

"Okay, fine. Now how about another answer. Where were you coming from just now?"

"What? What do you mean?"

"Did you not understand the question, Kitty? Where were you coming from just now when I caught up with you on your bike?"

"I was taking a ride up the coast."

"So nobody can verify your whereabouts?"

"I suppose not. I wasn't giving anyone a ride on the back of my bike if that's what you mean. Why?"

"Because Bill Dwyer was just killed by a sniper."

She looked genuinely shocked at the news.

"What? But that's . . ." She grappled for what to say. "Where?"

"At the wildlife sanctuary, which happens to be the same direction you were coming from."

She thought for a moment. "Is that what all the sirens were about? I saw the cop cars and fire trucks, but I thought it was just a brush fire."

"It was, but before that it was the scene of a murder."

"But how do you know about it? I mean, if the cops are still there this must have just happened."

"I was standing next to him when he was shot."

"My god. Thank God you weren't killed."

"I thought so, too. But it seems the killer didn't want to kill me, just Bill."

She looked at me then, and I could tell she got my implication.

"Duffer, you couldn't possibly think I would do this?"

So it was back to Duffer—no more Francis from here on out, I supposed.

"I don't know what to believe anymore, Kitty," I said, a trace of indignation seeping into my voice.

"But Duffer, why would I kill my own lawyer?"

"He was your lawyer, but he was also Don's lawyer and one of Don's best friends and closest confidants. Lawyers know a lot about their clients' lives. Maybe Bill knew too much."

"Frankly, I don't know what Bill knew, and I don't care. I had nothing to do with his death. Or Don's either."

"Both of those shots were fired by an expert marksman, which you just happen to be."

"I also happen to be telling the truth, not that it seems to matter much to you," she shot back.

"Why didn't you tell me you were a trained sniper?" I asked, still not convinced.

"I'm a trained *athlete*, Duffer, not a sniper. A sniper shoots people, an athlete shoots at a target."

"What about me? Was I your target?"

"Duffer, do you really think I would set this whole thing up just to end up with a terrible alibi like being a hundred feet away from the scene of the crime with my lover?"

The word *lover* stabbed me in the gut. I was reeling, from information overload and from desire. My desire to find the killer weighed against my desire to believe Kitty. It was getting to be too much. I looked out at the angry black ocean churning below and tried to get a hold of myself.

"I don't know. Maybe you're trying to pin this whole thing on me," I finally said.

"Is that what you think? Okay, let's just say, hypothetically, I did kill Don. What about Ethan Schaefer? Huh? Did I kill him from a rooftop when I was seven years old?"

"Ah ha! So you know about Ethan Schaefer's murder!" I exclaimed, pouncing—on what I wasn't quite sure.

"Of course I do!" she shot back. "He was a good friend of my husband, who was murdered under very peculiar circumstances. The subject came up! So what does that prove?"

"That proves you knew about it," I said, grasping for a line of reasoning. "So maybe . . . maybe you staged Don's murder to look like Ethan Schaefer's murder to throw the police off your scent."

"My *scent*? What the hell is my scent?"

"Well, if I'm not mistaken, it's lilac and citrus shampoo, but don't distract me!" I was flustered, trying to keep it together. "Who was that guy you were with at the club? The one I saw you kiss?"

"That was my brother!"

"Your brother? You mean your alibi for your first husband's murder?"

"He's not my *alibi*, he's my brother, goddamn it!"

"I've never seen him hanging around before. What's he doing here all of a sudden?"

"He came because my husband died! Is that so strange?!" She looked up at me, her green eyes filled with disbelief.

"So he just shows up whenever your husbands die? That's a pretty convenient coincidence. Just like I suppose it's a coincidence that your first husband also died by gunshot?"

"*I told you the truth!*" she raged, suddenly losing all composure. "He was shot by drug dealers."

"So you say."

"Goddamn right, I say! Listen, Duffer, I've had just about enough of this. I'm not a killer. The only thing I've ever shot in my life is a target. Why won't you believe me?"

"Because every time I ask you a question, you hit a bullseye. It's too perfect. And in my experience, when something's too perfect, it's an illusion."

She breathed a heavy sigh, her tone downshifting from anger to melancholy. "I thought we were perfect," she said, looking into my eyes for any hint of love that remained. But what she must have seen was doubt. "God, do you really believe I could do this, Duffer?"

I could see in her eyes that she knew I truly suspected her of murder, that I thought that she was indeed capable of killing her husband, and no matter what the truth turned out to be, there was no coming back from that look. At that moment I knew our relationship was over, that whatever we had was gone.

"You swear to me, on our love, that you didn't kill Don?"

She stood up, suddenly angry. "I didn't kill *anyone*, Duffer! Not my first husband. Not my second husband. *Nobody!*"

I wanted desperately to believe her, but what I wanted and what I needed were two different things and I had to keep digging.

"What about the will?" I plunged onward. "Why didn't you tell anyone your real name was Katherine Osborne?"

"Nobody ever asked! But Don knew my real name. For Christ's sake, it's on my marriage license!"

"So Don knew your real name was Katherine Osborne?"

"Of course, he knew. He's known it since the night we met. We both thought it was funny, a coincidence, a sign perhaps that we were meant to be together. It was one of our little things that we laughed about."

"If he knew you and his daughter had the same name, then why leave the will ambiguous?"

"He was going to change the will. He had an appointment with Bill Dwyer to take care of it, but—"

"But what? He never got around to it?"

"No, he never did. Someone shot him."

I was stumped. I didn't know what to believe anymore. She could tell I was still unconvinced.

"Fine," she said with a sigh, "you want proof I'm telling the truth about the will?"

"It's nothing personal, but in my line of work, proof is always good."

"What line of work is that? *Golf?*" She scoffed, her newfound contempt for me beginning to show. "Fine. You want some proof I'm not full of shit, come with me."

# 25

I was stumped, my head reeling with possibilities, as Kitty led me from the terrace through a set of French doors into a large wood-paneled den. The fireplace was roaring and the bear-skin rug looked like it was about to wake up from hibernation.

She walked over to an antique roll-top desk in the corner of the den, opened a drawer, pulled out an envelope, and handed it to me.

"What's this?" I asked, curious.

"Don's speech. The speech he was planning to give at the club the night he was shot," she replied. "It was among Don's personal possessions when the police brought them by this afternoon."

"The speech he never gave?" I opened the envelope and removed three pages of handwritten notes, folded like a letter. "What does this have to do with—"

"Just read it. You'll see."

I looked down at the speech. At the top of the page was the title, *Golf Doesn't Give a Damn Who You Are.*

"Read it out loud. It was a good speech. It deserves to be heard."

She poured us each a tumbler of Scotch, handed me one, and settled into the silk-upholstered couch to listen.

*Good evening everyone, and welcome to the tenth annual La Siesta Open. I'm Don Osborne, president of the La Siesta Country Club, and I love the game of golf.*

*(hold for applause)*

*I love golf, because golf doesn't give a damn who you are. No matter your station in life, the game of golf is the great equalizer. You can be a billionaire, a captain of industry, or a bum, and golf doesn't care one whit. Golf is impassive. Golf is a rock. Golf just does not give a damn. You might have just closed the biggest deal of your life in the boardroom, and that might get you plenty of kudos and slaps on the back in the clubhouse, but it doesn't count for a thing out on that putting green. There's no amount of money in the world that will help you sink a thirty-foot putt to save par. The sand trap doesn't care if you're a CEO, a king, or a commoner.*

*That's why I chose to make this tournament an open tournament. Golf doesn't care who you are, and neither do I. Unless of course you're applying for a club membership, but that's another matter.*

*(pause for laughter)*

*This weekend, golf will decide who's the champion. And golf doesn't give a damn who it is.*

*Golf is a beautiful game. Golf has taught me a lot of lessons over the years, but one of the most profound is to appreciate nature. To play a round of eighteen holes is to be fully engaged with the environment we live in, to be aware of every tree and every shrub, to appreciate the size and slope of every hill and valley, to take note of the angle of the sun, the speed and direction of the wind, and even the amount of dew on the grass. Before I took up the sport, I didn't fully understand the environment, and my connection to it, but golf has taught me to see the beauty in our natural world.*

*The only other time in my life I've ever been more aware of my environment, and the only other place in my life where I've been so inspired by the actions of other men than on the golf course, is in the field of combat. As many of you know, I spent three years of my life fighting in the jungles of Vietnam. The only people who ever gave a damn who I was out there were my fellow soldiers. The men I care about most in this world are the men I fought with, the men who saved my life countless times, and the men whose lives I saved.*

*Sadly, there were many good men who didn't make it back alive, and more importantly, there are some who are still out there. They may still be in POW camps, or they may lay in unmarked graves in the jungle, but they're out there. We haven't always done right by them, and it tears me up to think about it.*

*I've lived a long life, and I've made a lot of money, and when I'm no longer here I want my money to do some good. I want to dedicate it to finding them, alive or dead, and bringing them home. That's why tonight I'm proud to announce that I'm giving the entire bulk of my fortune to the search for missing POW/MIA soldiers.*

*(hold for applause)*

*To those brave men I say this:*

*Golf doesn't give a damn who you are . . . but I do. If you're out there, alive or dead, by God, we'll find you!*

*Good night, and to all the golfers, good luck.*

I folded the speech and handed it back to Kitty.

"So you see? I wasn't going to inherit a dime," she said, with a hint of righteous indignation.

"That's a hell of a speech, and I get it. He was going to change his will, leave everything to the search for missing veterans," I said, washing down this new information with a swallow of Scotch.

"I told you I had nothing to do with it."

"There's just one thing. He never actually got a chance to change the will."

"So?"

"Well, if you still get the money, then you still have the motive. In fact, Don getting killed right before making the announcement could actually make you look *more* guilty. What bigger motivation could there be than to kill Don before he cut you out of his will?"

She slumped back into the couch. "But Duffer, I swear, on our love, I didn't do it. You've got to believe me."

For some reason, against my better judgment, I did.

# 26

As I left the Osborne estate, my head was in a fog, the result of the combination of Scotch, exhaustion, and doubt. Every time I thought I had a way to clear Kitty, it just became more and more likely that she'd done it, and for whatever reason—love, loyalty, or perhaps a refusal to believe my own logic—I still didn't want to believe she'd done it.

Instead of dwelling on the increasing inevitability of my conclusion, I decided to follow up on the lead Katherine Osborne never had a chance to investigate and turned my Crown Vic in the direction of the pawn shop on the outskirts of La Siesta. I wanted to see if they had any records of who tried to pawn Ethan Schaefer's Medal of Honor, maybe some surveillance video, anything that might lead me to the conclusion that someone else besides Kitty killed Don.

You might not think a town as wealthy as La Siesta would be home to something as lowbrow as a pawn shop, but the thing about these mega-rich people is that quite a few of them are mega-full-of-shit, their supposed fortunes largely smoke and mirrors. The truth is a lot of these people needed quick cash to support their outrageous lifestyles, and when the bills came due, sometimes they looked down at their watch and realized it was time to hock the Rolex.

I was glad to find them still open, and the clerk, a middle-aged guy with a buzz cut, was busy with a customer when I walked in so I took a look around to see if I might be able to find the medal on display. It's illegal to sell a Medal of Honor, but my years as a police detective had taught me that pawn shops were full of stolen items, everything from guns to guitars to grandma's ashes as long as the urn was worth something. I perused the display cases while the clerk was occupied. The amount and variety of items for sale was staggering; flat-screen TVs, bicycles, jewelry, cell phones, video game consoles, even an old jukebox. There was an old felt-lined box full of coins from around the world, with examples from places as far away as Luxembourg, Argentina, and Vietnam, but no medals of any sort.

Finally the clerk was free, his customer walking away with a strange mix of regret and joy on his face, without his drum set but with enough money for a big bag of weed.

"I'm looking for a Medal of Honor," I said, approaching the counter and getting right to the point.

"You a cop?" he replied with a hint of annoyance, "because I already told that lady on the phone that I don't know anything about the medal. I wasn't working when it happened."

"So you knew it was illegal to sell a Medal of Honor?" I asked, surprised to find him one step ahead of me.

"I *did* know that. And I never would have bought it myself. But my kid was working that day, and he's only sixteen, he didn't know. He thought it was cool, so he bought it. It was a mistake, and I reported it as soon as I came in the next day. I don't need any trouble, believe me. Besides, my dad was in the service, did two tours in 'Nam. I would never disrespect our boys like that."

"So you never saw the person who sold it?"

"Sorry, no. Like I said, I wasn't here. Whoever it was filled out some paperwork, but the name was a fake, Ron McKernan. Cops came up with nothing when they ran it."

"Any idea what the person who sold it looked like? Any surveillance footage?"

"The cameras are strictly ornamental, I'm afraid," he said, pointing out two ancient cameras that looked like they'd been installed in the eighties. "Been broken for years, but they work just as well as the real thing for deterring crime. As long as people think they work, that's good enough."

"What about your son? Think he remembers anything about the seller?" I asked, hopeful.

"Well, you can talk to him, but, see . . ." he said, trailing off, suddenly looking a bit embarrassed.

"See, what?"

"I love him, but let's just say he might not be the sharpest pencil in the drawer," he explained in a hushed voice, before turning and bellowing into the back room. "Magnum!" he yelled through the beaded curtain, "get out here!"

"Magnum?" I asked, a smile crossing my face. "You named your kid Magnum? Like the gun?"

"Hell, no. Magnum like the P.I!" he said, his chest swelling with pride.

"Shit, that's awesome," I said. "I love *Magnum, P.I.*"

"Me too, brother. Best show ever. That dude was the shit. Hell of a mustache too. My wife didn't like the idea of naming the boy after a TV show, but I won her over," he said, before filling his lungs and bellowing again. "Magnum!" he yelled. Then, in a low voice turned to me and added, "I'm his daddy and all, but between you and me, I don't think the boy has what it takes to follow in the footsteps of his namesake."

Magnum entered through the beaded curtain, a sloppy, over-weight kid in a black Ozzy t-shirt and baggy pants, his eyes glued to the portable video game player in his hand.

"What?" he moaned. "I'm about to level up!"

"Put that game down and answer some questions for this man."

"But dad, I already talked to the police," he whined.

"And now you're going to talk to this gentleman," his father said sternly. "Don't argue with me."

Magnum groaned and reluctantly paused his game.

"Could you tell me what the man who sold you the Medal of Honor looked like?" I asked, hopeful I could extract some sort of memory from this kid's brain.

He shrugged. "I don't know. Just some dude," he said, help-fully.

"Could you be any more specific?"

"He was like, old."

"Okay, he was old," I said, trying to engage him. "How old was he?

"Like, hella old."

His dad leaned in. "Keep in mind, to him, anyone older than Billie Eilish is old."

"Anything else you remember?" I pressed, hoping to squeeze something out of this kid, but he shook his head.

"I was mostly looking at the medal. It was super cool. Never seen one of those before. Not a real one. It had this awesome eagle on the front with these like super sharp talons and . . .

*Great*, I thought, *he can describe the medal in detail, but the person who sold it to him is nothing but an old blur.*

After a few more questions and non-answers, I realized I was getting nowhere with young Magnum and gave up.

27

After all that, I was back to square one. I decided the best thing to do was circle around to the beginning, to the photo hanging in Don's Osborne's locker at the club. I had a feeling something in that photo would lead me to the true killer. I just wasn't sure what or how.

I was hoping the club would be mostly cleared out, and I was pleasantly surprised to find the locker room more or less deserted, just a few tired and distracted tournament employees cleaning up and getting ready for one more day tomorrow, the biggest day of the tournament, the final round.

I found Don Osborne's locker among the rows and was reaching into my pocket for a pick to work on the lock when I noticed the lock was gone. I opened the locker and everything looked the same, right down to the stench of his noxious-smelling cologne. My eye was immediately drawn to a bottle of aloe vera, and I praised the lord for the sweet relief about to come for my horrific sunburn. I peeled off my shirt and slathered myself with the cool green jelly, a brief moment of succor before continuing my quest. Once I lowered the temperature of my skin to a reasonable level, I turned to the picture hanging on the door of Don's old army buddies. I looked past the younger versions of Don, Bill, and Ethan Schaefer, hoping to make something more out of the face obscured by the crease, when I suddenly heard a familiar gravelly voice behind me.

"Looking for this?"

I turned around to find Chief Garrett standing at the end of the aisle holding an AR-15 sniper rifle in his hand. He was flanked by several members of the La Siesta Police Department, including Lopez, who looked a little too concerned for my liking.

"What? No, I was just looking for aloe vera," I vamped. "I figured a rich guy like Don would have the good stuff."

"Put a sock in it, Duffer. You can't charm your way out of this one. Especially now that I've found this," he said, gesturing with the rifle. He took a step closer and banged his shin on the bench in front of him, cursing under his breath as he reached out to get his bearings.

"How's the old depth perception, Chief? Still giving you fits?" I asked, unable to contain my inner wiseass. "You know, maybe if you got a set of blinders, like a horse . . ."

There was a quiet chuckle from the others, which he quickly shut down with an angry wave of his hand.

"Joke all you want, dipshit, but this is the murder weapon that was used to kill Don Osborne. Same make as the bullet in the wall. We're just waiting for ballistics to confirm it's an exact match."

"Where the hell did you get that?"

"From Don's locker, hidden in his golf bag. Right where you left it, I assume," he said with a twinkle in his eye.

I couldn't believe what was happening. *Was he serious?* A brief moment of eye contact with Lopez told me that he was.

"Me? Why would you think I shot Don?"

"Well, for starters, what about the bruise on your right shoulder? Looks to be from the recoil of a gun."

Huh?

I looked down and sure enough, there was a bruise on my right shoulder from the baseball shot at me by the Racquette brothers.

"That? That's not what it looks like. I, well, shit, I don't have time to explain it, but surely that's not enough to—"

"Surely not," he agreed, his smile telling me he had an ace up his sleeve. "We got an anonymous tip that the murder weapon was here. Fortunate timing for us, or else you might have gotten here before us and successfully disposed of the evidence."

"I wasn't trying to dispose of any evidence, Chief. I was just . . . wait, you said you got a tip? Where did it come from?"

"We got a text message telling us exactly where it was. It came from an unregistered burner phone. But the tip isn't the point. The point is that it led us to the evidence, which you clearly returned here to dispose of. Why else would you be looking in Don Osborne's locker?"

"I returned because I'm actually trying to solve this case, not wandering around La Siesta acting on *assumptions*," I said sharply, desperately trying to defend myself from these insane accusations.

"Well, these *assumptions* led me right to the murder weapon!"

he gloated. "And now here you are trying to get rid of the evidence. So I'd say my *assumptions* are doing a pretty good job on this case after all."

"You know what they say about assumptions, don't you?" I was ready to let him have it, but to my surprise, this time he was ready and beat me to the rhetorical punch.

"Yeah, I know all about assumptions, and this time they make an ass out of *you*, not *me*."

This got a laugh from the officers except Lopez. Garrett leaned in close now, having gone for the kill and moving in to twist the knife.

"Why don't you just give it up, Duffer? I've always known you were no good." His contempt for me burned from his one good eye.

"I was good enough to hit you dead in the eye while you were on a moving target three hundred yards off shore," I quipped, but my heart wasn't in it. I could feel myself sinking, and my cocksure attitude with it.

"I'm not talking about *golf*, you nitwit! I'm talking about *life*!" he cried, a maniacal laugh escaping his lips.

"Same thing," I muttered under my breath,

"You're no good at *life* and you never will be. So you took the easy road to success, like so many cowards before you. Your own life was a complete mess, so you decided to kill a man and take over his."

"Chief, I told you. I didn't kill anyone." I tried to reason with him, but his argument had momentum now and he rolled right over me.

"You saw another man with what you wanted: money, power, fame, a beautiful woman . . . He had what you could never have, and you knew you could never get it on your own, so you took it. You took his life. Just like you took his wife."

"Chief . . ."

"It's over, Duffer. Don't try to wisecrack your way out of this. I've finally got you dead to rights."

"Dead to rights?!" I cried, suddenly standing up, realizing I had better fight back or this was going to end badly. "What proof do you have?!"

He held up the rifle. "We have the murder weapon!" he bellowed, triumph ringing in his voice.

"You have nothing that connects me to that rifle other than your assumptions!" I yelled, the two of us now nose to nose.

He stopped dead. "No connection, you say?" he asked, a look of smug self-assurance on his face. "Other than your fingerprint?!"

"What?! Bullshit! That's impossible!" I yelled.

He let out a soft chuckle.

"Oh, Duffer. You poor dumb jock. You should have spent less time on your golf swing and more time planning this murder."

"I told you, I didn't murder anyone," I barked, but my protestations were beginning to sound hollow, even to me.

"You see, old boy, my *assumptions* led me to believe that you were the killer, so based on those *assumptions*, I dusted the gun for prints on the spot, and then, following my *assumptions*, once again I compared that print to the prints in your employee file from the La Siesta Police Department. And guess what? They were a one-hundred-percent match!"

"Chief, this is nuts. This is a setup. There's no way . . ." I trailed off, stunned.

I sat down on the bench, the wind suddenly knocked out of me. I didn't even have the heart to mess with Garrett anymore. I was out of jokes. This time, I was truly scared.

"Garrett, I'm going to tell you this only once. I had absolutely nothing to do with Don Osborne's death," I said, as straightforward as I'd ever been with him in my life.

"Okay then, if that's true, why don't you tell me where you were when Don Osborne was killed?"

*Oh boy, here we go*, I thought. *Time to produce the world's worst alibi.*

"You know where I was, chief. I told you the night of the murder. I was here, at the country club," I admitted, not wanting to give him anything more specific.

"Oh ho!" he exclaimed, far too happy to be reminded of this little detail. "And just exactly *where* at the country club where you at the time of the fatal shot?" he followed up, his one good eye lighting up in anticipation of my answer. It was truly an unnerving feeling to have that one beady little eyeball on me.

"I was on the eighteenth hole . . ." I said, mumbling half into my chest.

"What's that? I couldn't hear you," he said, a smile growing in his face as he had me increasingly backed into a corner.

"I was in the sand trap of the eighteenth hole."

"Oh, I see, the sand trap of the eighteenth hole. Just a few yards from the sniper's roost, then?"

I nodded.

"Anyone in that sand trap with you, Duffer?" A smile was growing on his face.

"I think you know who it was."

"Oh, I do, I do, but I want to hear it from the horse's mouth."

"Well, if you want to hear it from your mother, then why don't you dial her up!" I spat, unable to endure the smug look on Garrett's face.

"Now, now, Duffer. Let's not get snippy. It's unbecoming of an officer, or a golfer, or whatever the hell you are."

"What I am sure as hell *not* is a murderer!" I hollered, but he just shook his head.

"Now tell me, Duffer, who were you with in that sand trap just moments before old Don Osborne was assassinated?"

"Kitty Osborne," I replied, defeat creeping into my voice.

"So your alibi for this murder is that you were a few yards away at the time of the shooting, with the wife of the murder victim, who just happens to be a trained sniper, with whom you were having an adulterous affair, and who stood to gain a sizable fortune upon her husband's death?"

"Well, when you put it that way, Chief, it makes me sound guilty," I quipped. Just because I couldn't joke my way out of it, didn't mean I couldn't joke.

This got a slight chuckle from the cops surrounding Chief Garrett, but not from Lopez. His look of concern hadn't faded.

"Wait a minute, Chief. If Kitty was the sniper, then what are my prints doing on the gun?"

"Simple. You brought her the weapon. After all, she couldn't arrive at the gala with a sniper rifle in her hand. So you met her on the eighteenth hole, as you've already admitted, and provided her with the weapon. Then, when it was over, you disposed of the rifle in Don's locker, leaving your print on the gun in the process."

"That's a hell of a theory, Chief, but it isn't true."

"We'll see what's true when ballistics and fingerprints all come back," he continued, not letting me up for air. "Now let's talk about Katherine Osborne."

"I don't know anything about Katherine Osborne's disappearance."

"But you went to see her the night she disappeared?"

"That's true. I wanted to learn more about her relationship with her father. I was working the case, something you might have thought about doing instead of just acting on your assumptions," I said, a little of my contempt coming through in my tone.

"Let's not make this about me, Duffer. This is all about you. You were the last person to see Katherine Osborne alive."

"Alive? Are you implying she's no longer alive?"

"Why don't you tell me?"

"What? I don't know! I had nothing to do with it."

"Okay, so it's just a coincidence that she disappeared right before your girlfriend revealed her little trick with the will?"

"I swear, I didn't know anything about the will, or Kitty's real name."

"Okay, fine. Let's forget about Katherine Osborne for a second," he said, changing tack. "When was the last time you saw Bill Dwyer?"

"Bill Dwyer?" I swallowed. *Shit*, I was surprised they'd found the body this fast. I could feel myself sinking deeper into this giant stinking pile of incriminating circumstantial evidence.

"Well . . ."

"I'll tell you," said Garrett, helpfully coming to my aid. "It was at the wildlife sanctuary, just before you put a bullet in his head and set a brush fire to cover your tracks."

"That wasn't me!" I yelled, jumping to my feet. "I mean, I admit I met Bill at the wildlife sanctuary. He asked me to meet him there. But I didn't kill him, I swear, and I didn't start the fire."

"Then who did?" he yelled, right up in my face.

"I don't know!" I insisted, holding what little ground I had. "As far as I know the sniper did. The bullet that missed Bill must have caused a spark in the dry grass or something. Besides, this is Southern California for chrissakes, half of it's on fire at any given moment!"

"Yuk it up all you want, Duffer, but this doesn't look good. You started that fire on purpose to cover up your crime. That alone could get you put away. You're just lucky the fire department got there before it could burn more than a small patch of scrub."

"Face it, Garrett, you've got jack squat," I said, pulling my spirit up for one last fight. "Everything you just laid out is circumstantial. My relationship with Kitty, my visit to Katherine Osborne's office, my meet up with Bill at the wildlife sanctuary. None of it will stand up in court. You've got no hard evidence. "

"What, you mean like your fingerprints on this gun?"

"I have no idea how those got there! You can't do this! You can't pin this on me!"

"Oh, yes, my friend, I can. We're just waiting for the ballistics reports back from the lab to match the gun with the bullet that killed Don Osborne."

He took a step closer and reached for his handcuffs, which took several tries as they were attached to his right hip and he couldn't see them.

"Stand up and turn around, Duffer, you're under arrest."

"For what?" I protested. "You have no proof! You said yourself the ballistics report hasn't come back. You don't even know for sure that's the murder weapon!"

"You're right." He grinned, enjoying this moment a little too much for my taste. "That's why you're under arrest for trespassing."

"Trespassing? Where? What are you talking about?"

"Osborne Storage Solutions. When you visited Katherine, you never signed in to the building."

"*I never signed in?* Are you crazy? You're arresting me for not signing in to a building?!"

"That's trespassing, and it's enough to hold you on until the rest of this puzzle falls into place."

"That's what you're arresting me for?!"

"Until the ballistics comes back, and then we add murder, kidnapping, and arson. Turn around, you're under arrest."

"Under arrest? You can't do this!" I shouted. "I have golf to play!"

Lopez finally snapped, yelling at me.

"Jesus Christ, Duffer! Can't you stop thinking about goddamn *golf* for one second?! This is serious!"

The chief spun me around and clasped my hands behind my back.

"But I just have one more round to play!" I cried. "Chief, you can't do this!"

"Oh, but I can, and I'm going to enjoy it so much," he said, snapping the cuffs closed around my wrist.

"You can arrest me tomorrow, and I won't even care!" I begged. "I promise! I'll even admit to the whole thing if you just let me play this last eighteen holes!"

"Duffer, from here on out the only hole you should be worried about is your own."

# SUNDAY

## 28

The only thing I knew for sure when I awoke Sunday morning was that I'd been framed. I hadn't murdered anyone, hadn't kidnapped anyone, hadn't done anything wrong. And yet there I was, rotting in a jail cell in the La Siesta Police Department for a crime I didn't commit. Well, technically I was in jail for a crime I *did* commit, trespassing, but that was a bullshit charge and everyone knew it, even the chief. What he really wanted me for was the murder of Don Osborne, and anything else he could manage to pin on me.

What really had me upset, however, was that I was going to miss playing the biggest round of golf in my life. One more round of eighteen holes and I could actually fulfill my dream of winning a PGA Tournament, and here I was, lying on a metal cot, staring at the ceiling. I still couldn't figure out how my fingerprint got on the gun in Don's locker. It's possible even the chief himself put it there just to frame me. At this point anything was possible. My suspicion was stronger than ever that all this was somehow tied to the picture in Don's locker, to the military in some way, or the war in Vietnam, but I hadn't gotten the chance to examine the picture in any more detail before Chief Garrett had shown up and arrested me.

I went over the list of suspects in my head one more time. Now that he was dead, I could rule out Bill Dwyer. However, the fact that he was also shot by a sniper confirmed for me that there was very likely a connection between the two killings in La Siesta and the murder of Ethan Schaefer in New York City.

Shiloh Greene had proven to be a dead end, no pun intended, and the pawn shop yielded nothing about the identity of the person who sold the Medal of Honor, only a fake name.

Mr. Lo had access and motive, and the sprinkler head I found in the sniper's roost tied him, loosely, to the crime scene. He had a volatile temper, a house full of guns, and a grudge against the U.S. Military. However, I couldn't figure out why he would work for the country club for so long, right under Don and Bill's nose, without pulling the trigger sooner. If his objective was to get revenge on Don, why mow mile after mile of fairways before finishing the job?

The Racquette brothers had plenty of reason to get rid of Don, but somehow, it just seemed too neat. They had something going on with George Graft, but I wasn't sure exactly what. What I did know was that he'd given them access to the club by hiring them to set up the tournament infrastructure, which they'd used to set up a scaffold utilized by the sniper. However, I suspected the Racquette brothers would know better than anyone that if something happened to Don they'd automatically become suspects.

They were criminals, but they knew they were criminals, and they knew everyone else knew it too.

Then, of course, there was Kitty. I couldn't help but think that she had just enough time, after leaving me in the sand trap, to climb up that tower and make the shot. But was that really possible? I still wasn't entirely convinced Kitty was innocent, and the anonymous phone call tipping off the chief to the whereabouts of the gun could easily have come from her. She also would have had access to my fingerprints. They were all over her ass, for one. If I was on the hook for the murder, that could possibly get her off the hook, which was a pretty good motive for setting me up. Or maybe she just wanted to drag me down with her. Anything was possible. The more time I spent with Kitty, it seemed the less I felt I knew her.

I sat up, the long metal shelf bolted to the wall that served as my bed for the night getting in a few last licks on my spine as I swung my feet over the side. I was sunburned head to toe and my whole body felt like one big blister. I could practically hear my skin crackling as I stood up and tried to stretch the soreness out of my limbs.

There was only one cop in the bullpen, which was right outside the bars of my cell. I thanked my sweet Irish luck it was Lopez.

"Morning, sunshine," he said without looking my way, his eyes glued to a flat-screen TV hanging on the wall across the room, which I noticed was tuned to the Golf Channel.

"What are you doing here this early?" I asked with a yawn. "I thought you usually didn't get in until after lunch," I said, reviving an old joke of ours.

"Just checking the scores from yesterday's round at La Siesta," he replied without turning around.

"Oh, yeah, how's the leaderboard look?" I asked, suddenly wide-awake.

Finally, he spun around in his desk chair and looked over at me, a sardonic smile on his face. "Oh, you know, the usual suspects," he said.

Somehow, he didn't seem terribly surprised at my predicament. I guess we'd been friends long enough that he could see something like this was coming, perhaps inevitable. My penchant for taking chances had gotten me in trouble before, and I was acutely aware that it was a liability I carried with me. But taking chances is also the only way I've ever accomplished anything, either in life, or on the golf course. It's helped me solve cases and helped me win tournaments. Without a little recklessness every now and again, all the practice and preparation can turn you into a robot. That's true if you're a cop trying to solve a case, or a golfer trying to beat a golf course. So I took chances, lots of 'em. And I've won a few and lost maybe more than a few, but it was clear to me now that taking a chance with Don Osborne's wife may have just been a step too far.

I stood up slowly and walked over to the bars, the creaking from my bones louder than ever after a night spent on a metal slab.

"I didn't do it, you know," I said with as much sincerity as I could muster at this early hour.

"I know," he replied, a hint of sympathy in his tone, but not much more than a hint. "But you *did* manage to get yourself into this mess. Or at least, your dick did."

"Well, I guess I'll cop to that, but now that I'm in it, how the hell do I get out?"

"Brother," he said with a heavy sigh, "I have no idea."

A moment of silence fell between us. This was serious.

"Think my dick can get me out of it?" I joked, gallows humor being the last resort of a condemned man.

He laughed, breaking the tension, but leaving us staring at the same ugly mess. "Jesus, Duffer, you really got yourself stuck in a bunker this time," he said, evoking that moment when a parent goes from angry to "disappointed" with their child.

"But I didn't do anything!" I said again, probably pointlessly. "And the worst part is I'm going to miss the last round of La Siesta Open!"

"For the last time, Duffer, that is *not* the worst thing about this situation!" he snapped, standing up from his desk and walking over to the cell. "The worst part is that you might end up in prison!"

"Well, if I can't play golf, I might as well be in prison," I replied.

"You really are insane, you know that?" he said, exasperation creeping into his voice. "Hell, maybe you did do it. I don't even know anymore."

"You really think I killed Don Osborne?"

"You were fucking his wife."

"Yeah, sure, okay, I admit that. But I did that plenty while he was alive. I didn't need him dead to have an affair with Kitty."

He sat down heavily on the edge of his desk.

"Do you think I kidnapped Katherine Osborne?" I asked.

"I don't know what to think, Duffer. You were in the building. And it sure is convenient for Kitty now that she's gone."

"But Don was about to change the will! I saw the speech!"

"Oh, well, then I guess we can put a bow on that and call it settled," he said sarcastically. "Duffer, the man was killed the night before he changed his will to cut her out. Do you really think that makes her, or you, look *less guilty*?"

"Well, I guess if you put it that way . . ."

"That's the way *it is*. Katherine Osborne is missing, making Kitty the sole heir, and Kitty can swear up and down that she knew nothing and did nothing. But I've got to tell you, Duffer, this whole thing stinks like the docks at low tide."

Once again, I was at a loss. He was right. Every time I tried to talk my way to a different conclusion, it always circled back to make Kitty, or me, look guilty. I slumped against the cell door, leaning my forehead on the cold metal bars.

"I didn't kidnap Katherine Osborne," was all I could bring myself to say. I felt defeated. Then, I looked past Lopez at the television on the wall, and my whole world flipped upside down.

"And I can prove it!" I suddenly shouted, pointing at the TV behind him.

"What?" he scoffed. "How the hell can you prove that?"

"Turn up the TV!" I shouted, pointing over his shoulder at the flat-screen behind him.

He turned around and saw what I had just seen, a half-naked woman walking out of the ocean on the thirteenth hole at the La Siesta Country Club.

He grabbed the remote and hit the volume.

*"This is Jill Smelt at the La Siesta Country Club, where a woman has just walked out of the ocean on the thirteenth hole!"*

As the woman, wearing only a torn button-down shirt, staggered half dead toward the shore, both Lopez and I immediately recognized her.

Jill ran into the waves to help her out of the surf.

*"Miss! Are you all right? Can you tell me your name?"*

The shivering woman stumbled out of the waves and into Jill Smelt's arms. She looked directly into the camera and stammered, her teeth chattering with cold.

*"K-K-Katherine Osborne."*

Lopez turned to me, disbelief draining the color from his face.

"You've got to be shitting me," he mumbled. He turned back the television, transfixed by the surreal scene playing out on the beach.

"I told you I had nothing to do with it!" I cheered, relief flooding my body like new blood. "She can clear me! You have to get down there and get her statement."

"Duffer, she just crawled out of the ocean."

"So get to the hospital or wherever they take her! Don't you see? She can make the trespassing charges go away and get me out of here. She'll prove I had nothing to do with any of this!"

He stood frozen for a moment, then finally turned to me. "You are one lucky son of a bitch," he said shaking his head as he grabbed his keys and headed out the door.

"If you get me out of here soon, I can still make my tee time!" I yelled after him.

# 29

An hour later I was tearing down La Siesta Boulevard toward the country club in the back of Lopez's cruiser, flying through the streets and swerving around traffic with lights and sirens blaring. There was entirely too much to think about—the murders, the tournament, Kitty—so I just shut down my brain and tried to get my head together. My whole life was on the line today, but I couldn't let it get to me. I couldn't snap under the pressure.

Lopez had given me the lowdown as he processed me out of jail. Katherine Osborne had been rushed to St. Andrews hospital where she was able to give a brief statement before succumbing to exhaustion and being whisked away into the ER. She was unable to identify her attacker. Someone had grabbed her from behind and knocked her out with some kind of ether-soaked rag.

Sometime later, she'd woken up on a boat and eventually she was able to free herself and swim to shore. She confirmed that I was a welcome guest at the OSS offices and therefore the trespassing charges against me were dropped. Garrett threw a fit, of course, but there was nothing he could do about it until he had the ballistics to prove the rifle in Don's locker was the murder weapon.

I was free, for now. But if the ballistics came back on that gun with my prints, I'd be back in the soup before the end of the day. I didn't want to go back to jail. What I wanted to do, more than anything else in the world, was play golf.

We raced up the driveway of the La Siesta Country Club, the flood of fans on their way to the tournament parting like the red sea for Lopez's light show. He screeched to a stop in front of the clubhouse, and I jumped out of the car at a full galop and sprinted into the locker room, where Grateful Ted was waiting for me.

"Duffer! I didn't think you were going to make it," he said, looking surprised to see me as he grabbed my clubs from the locker.

"I never miss a tee time," I said, and it was true. In all my years of playing, no matter what was going on in my life, busy with work, sick as a dog, or too hungover to wobble straight, I'd never missed a tee time. Some things were sacred, like Sunday Mass, Southern California sunsets, and the curves of a woman's body.

I was happy to be back in the locker room one more time, even if it was to be my last. The last twenty-four hours had somehow taught me to appreciate this moment all the more. Everything looked as it did that first day, the wood paneling polished to a golden shine, the giant pile of fluffy white towels, the steam from the showers wafting down the aisles, even the lingering smell of old Don Osborne's noxious cologne was sweet to me. This is where I belonged.

I was especially glad to see Grateful Ted's friendly face there to greet me, with his tie-dyed coveralls, long white beard, and hair down to his ass. If magical caddies really exist, he was surely one of them. I honestly didn't know where I'd be without him. I clapped him on the shoulder, my compadre.

"Ted, old buddy. I'm going to need everything in my bag to help me win today, including the guy carrying it."

"I'm here for you, man. Always have been," he said, looking me in the eye and showing me his inner strength. The bond between us forged on the golf course over these last few years was as deep as any I'd had with another human since moving to La Siesta, even Kitty. At moments like this, I was truly grateful to have a caddie like Ted to lean on.

I sat down to put on my spikes and try to clear my head for just one last peaceful moment before walking out there. There were over twenty thousand fans waiting for me to tee off. This was the toughest course I'd ever played, against the strongest field of golfers in the PGA. If I was going to walk away with this thing, I had to play insanely good golf. This round was a monster I had to slay. This was my white whale. I had to find my center. I needed something to distract me from everything that was going on in my head, so I called on Grateful Ted to do what he did best.

"Okay, Ted, I think it's time to play your little game. Why don't you recite a set list for me. Any Grateful Dead show you want."

"Any show I want?" he said, his eyes lighting up at the chance to perform his parlor trick.

"You pick it, bud."

He thought for a moment. "How about June seventeenth, 1972, at the Hollywood Bowl."

"Right up the road. Okay, sounds good. Why that one?"

He looked down at me as I sat at the bench and I could see he was suddenly a bit misty eyed.

"It was Pigpen's last show, man," he said, half choked up.

"All right, twenty bucks if you can name the whole thing without a mistake."

"You're on, boss," he said, his eyes lighting up.

"And don't skip any songs because I'll be checking up on you," I said with a wink.

"They opened that night with a Chuck Berry classic," he began, "an ode to sweet lady California herself, 'Promised Land' . . ."

From there he was off and running, the song titles tumbling from his mouth as if they were the names of his children, allowing me the chance to drift off to the soothing sound of his babble and find some peace within my thoughts.

Today was the final day of the tournament. I was hoping it wouldn't also be the final day of my life as a free man. I wouldn't do well in prison, and as a former cop I'd recognize far too many faces when I got there. Besides, I was fairly certain I would lose my mind without the game of golf. I could just see myself twenty years from now as a crazy old prisoner with a pet rat sitting on my shoulder, putting golf balls made of dried fruit into the shower drain with a broom.

*No thanks.*

Besides, who would take care of my dog, Nicklaus? I couldn't let that happen. But first things first. I had to make it through the round. If I could manage to pull off a miracle, I could win the damn thing outright and automatically qualify for my tour card. But it wasn't strictly an all-or-nothing proposition. All I had to do was not get disqualified. If I finished at all, at this point, with where I stood on the leaderboard, I would finish in the money. I would be able to pay off the Racquette brothers, save the Pitch N' Putt, and hell, maybe have enough left over to pay a good lawyer to get me out of this mess. I closed my eyes as I listened to Grateful Ted wind up his disquisition.

". . . then they sailed into a *ripping* rendition of 'Going Down the Road Feelin' Bad,' before finally ending, twenty-five songs later, with another classic, this one by the immortal Buddy Holly, bringing back 'Not Fade Away' for a reprise. The crowd took it home from there."

Then he closed his eyes as if in prayer and began to tap a beat out on his chest.

*Thump thump thump, thump-thump.* "You know our love will not fade away," he chanted in a soft voice.

*Thump thump thump, thump-thump.* "You know our love will not fade away."

It was like an incantation. His recitation of the set list had emptied me like a vessel, and now his chant filled me like a spirit. I opened my eyes. I was ready to take on this golf course. I was ready to take on any golfer with a bag of clubs. I was ready to take on the world.

I stood up.

"Ted, here we go."

He opened his eyes and looked up into mine. I saw peace there.

"Play like your life depends on it," he said, hoisting my bag on his shoulder.

"Oh, I will," I replied, heading for the locker room door. "Because it does."

As I walked towards the door he stopped me.

"Just one more thing..."

He reached behind him and pulled out a driver. In the frenzy of everything that had happened, I'd completely forgotten about my broken driver. But Grateful Ted had remembered. It didn't look like much, just an old relic with chipped paint on the head and a worn grip, but it was lot better than being short a key club.

"I thought you could use this. It's from my own personal bag."

I was truly touched. A good caddie is a hard thing to find in this life. The same goes for a good friend. Grateful Ted had proved himself to be both.

———•———

On my way out of the clubhouse, I checked the leaderboard hanging in the hallway outside the locker room as I hurried past. I was thrilled to see my name right near the top, just under the leader, five strokes behind, but my heart sunk when I saw the name at the very top of the board: none other than my old nemesis, Danny Master.

*Christ. Why did it have to be that insufferable towel snapper?* I thought.

Not only that, but since we were at the front of the pack, we were paired together in the last group of the day. Now I'd have to suffer through eighteen holes of dick jokes and juvenile put-downs if I was going to win this tournament. I was in no mood to deal with Danny Master's shit today. I had too much riding on this round. I had to remind myself that guys like Danny like to play head games. It's one of the ways they beat you before you even step up to the first tee, employing psychological warfare to mess with your most important piece of equipment, your mind. Golf is a game played in your head as much as with your hands, and if a guy can get in your head, he can really affect what you do with those hands. That's what was behind all the dirty jokes and put-downs. Well, that, and a deep insecurity and a need to be loved, probably.

But I couldn't let him burrow into my brain if I was to have any chance today. I was almost clear of the locker room when I rounded the corner and ran smack into him.

"Well, if it isn't Sherlock Homo!" he cried, charming as ever, a huge grin on his face.

You could feel a collective cringe race through the locker room as other golfers distanced themselves from Danny Master as quickly as possible.

"Solve any mysteries today, Inspector?" he asked with a derisive snort.

"Just one. The mystery of why you're such an asshole. Turns out your mother did it," I said, prepared to meet fire with fire.

"Hey, you leave my mother out of this!" he squawked.

"Just like your father did when he was banging every house-wife on Long Island?"

He smiled and shook his head, sizing me up. He seemed surprised to have someone not roll over and take his shit for once.

"Well, well, look who's feeling feisty today. I like that. What's gotten into you Duffer?"

"My name is *Francis. Francis Duffy McDermott.* And from this day forward, you and everyone else will remember it, believe me."

"Don't worry, *Francis,* this will be fun"—he paused, a self-satisfied look on his face—"for me," he laughed. "Besides, I haven't had the pleasure of beating you since I was kid."

"If only your dick could say the same," I shot back.

He was winding up to pitch his rejoinder when I stopped him.

"Listen, Danny, I don't have time for your sh—" I stopped myself, remembering the club rules, "for your *nonsense* today. I have golf to play. So don't try to rattle me, throw me off my game, or whatever mind games you're trying to play. Now, we can spend all day insulting each other like kids, or we can settle this like real men, on the links. Right here. Right now."

He grinned, cocksure as ever. He stepped in close so that we were nose to nose. "Bring it, *Francis.*"

## 30

hurried out of the clubhouse and past the TV tower one last time, trying to sneak by as fast as I could, but I knew it was pointless. Before I got halfway down the cart path, Joe Roebuck had me in his sights, a cameraman trailing just behind him.

"Well, if it isn't the king of the long shots, Duffer McDermott. Think we can get an interview for all your fans on the Golf Channel?" he asked, a smug smirk etched on his annoyingly handsome mug.

"You guys have been bagging on me since the start of the tournament. Why would I help you?" I balked.

"Hey, I can't help it if you make good TV."

"Is that all you care about, good TV?"

"I'm just doing my job, Duffer."

"It's *Duffy*!" I snapped. "Francis *DUFFY* McDermott. Okay, fine, you want good TV, turn on that camera. I'll give you the damn interview."

I could still feel the sting of all the crappy things he and the others had said about me on the Golf Channel. That I had "*no chance.*" That I had "*a swing like a broken robot.*" My every instinct was to strangle the son of a bitch, but I knew I had to keep my cool. Still, that didn't mean I couldn't have a little fun with him.

The cameraman lined up his shot and the red light went on.

"Good afternoon, golf fans. Joe Roebuck here with Francis *Duffy* McDermott, who's had a, well, let's say, *unbelievable* tournament here on the links at La Siesta, coming out of nowhere to make the cut on a rain-soaked, windswept Friday and then surviving what was a truly miraculous round on Saturday to somehow, some way, still find himself with a spot on the leaderboard. All this despite never having played in a PGA Tournament before. In fact, I'm willing to bet you've never even heard his name before this weekend."

"We get it, Joe. I'm a dark horse." I smiled into the camera, biting my tongue as Joe pressed on.

"Dark horse? My friend, you are Black Beauty! I mean, let's be honest, before today they wouldn't even let you mow the fairways at a place like this!"

I had to give it to the guy. I thought he didn't have the guts to say these kinds of insults to my face, but he seemed to be enjoying it.

"But now you're in contention," he continued. "How does it feel?"

"It feels good, Joe. It's been a long time coming."

"I'll say. Until yesterday you were a complete nobody."

It took all my patience and restraint, which is in short supply even on a regular day, not to react, but punching an announcer on national television would probably not help my golf career, so I held it together.

"So how does a duffer such as yourself turn it around to make the cut at La Siesta?" he said with a smirk, pleased with himself for sneaking in a little jab. "Tell us your story."

*Duffer? Did he really just do that again? Okay, fuck this guy*, I thought. *I'm going to make things awkward.* If I couldn't punch the man, I could at least make his job as difficult as possible.

"Well, Joe, I guess it all started with a love of tiny pencils," I said, turning and looking sincerely into the camera.

"Tiny pencils?" he said, puzzled.

"That's right, Joe. That's what got me interested in golf, the pencils. You see, as a child I suffered from a deadly fear of pencil erasers, so when I first saw a golf pencil, that beautiful little yellow half nubbin with no eraser, well, I knew this was the game for me."

He didn't know what to say, and that was exactly my intention. He let the answer go and started in again.

"Did you play golf as a child?"

"No, Joe. As a child I played polo."

"Polo?" he asked, his expression moving from confused to flummoxed.

"That's right, polo. Until one day my polo pony died right in the middle of a match, and, well, I just held on to the mallet and continued hitting the ball. That's when I learned I'm as good at hitting balls on foot as I am mounted up on a horse, and I've been a golf man ever since."

Joe didn't know what to say. I could see the panic flash across his eyes. *What the fuck is this guy talking about?* But he had no choice but to continue.

"So your, your, um, polo pony died?" he followed weakly, trailing off.

"Sure did, Joe. Had a coronary right out from under me. Sad thing that. I miss old Buttercup. But now I ride golf carts instead of horses and that suits me fine."

"Well, there are no golf carts allowed in PGA tournaments," he said with a bit of a chuckle, hoping, praying for this interview to get back on track.

"Damn shame, too," I continued, letting the bullshit really begin to flow. "I think driving a golf cart should count as a part of the game. Make speed a factor. Maybe make it a race, you know? We all start at once and whoever finishes eighteen holes first is the winner. Really give the fans something to cheer about. Hell, I bet I could take any one of these chumps out here in a speed golf race."

He looked aghast, stricken. He didn't know what the fuck I was talking about and neither did I, but just watching him flounder was worth it. For a man who was always in control, who got to sit back and judge while others tried to perform their job, it was fun to turn the tables and mess with his game for once.

"You can't be serious."

"Heck yes, I'm serious! Bring a little NASCAR action to the links. What do you think?"

"I think you're insane."

"And I think you wouldn't know a good golfer if he beat you over the head with a nine iron," I said, suddenly turning to him. He looked into my eyes and saw that I was dead serious. He was taken aback, but at that moment, he finally realized I had been fucking with him. "I heard what you said about me, Joe. That I have *a swing like a broken robot*. That I have no chance of winning," I said pointedly.

He looked stricken. He wasn't used to being challenged, certainly not on the air. Most golfers wouldn't dare. But I'm not most golfers. And I needed him to know that.

"Well, it's just that the odds . . ."

"Screw the odds. Odds only mean something to bean counters like you. I'm a golfer. I play the course, not the odds," I said turning to leave. "I look forward to answering more of your questions after I win this tournament."

As I turned to walk away, he tried to get in a parting shot.

"Big words from a man who has yet to prove himself."

"Go sit on a sprinkler."

I left him there stunned, staring dead eyed into the camera, as I walked down the cart path toward the first tee. I could hear Grateful Ted laughing as Joe cut the camera and stormed off.

# 31

The tournament marshal signaled for quiet, and I stepped up to the first tee. As I settled over the ball, I willed myself to be calm. I reminded myself that this was my destiny. Ever since my great-grandfather John J. McDermott stepped up to the tee at the US Open in 1911 and became the first American golfer to win it, the family's fate had been sealed. We were golfers, like it or not. There was no choice. It was just who I was. Whether it was a blessing or a curse was yet to be determined, but "the madness" had brought me here, and I was counting on "the madness" to put me over the top. It was my birthright to play in this tournament, but it was up to me to win.

I sprung out of the gate like a racehorse, picking up birdies on two and three while otherwise making steady par through the first six holes. Danny matched my birdies, but a bogey on four showed a crack in his facade. He recovered with a par on five but I narrowed the gap by holding steady on six while an errant tee shot into the trees left him with a double bogey, leaving him badly rattled. I had picked up three strokes and was making up ground on him. His lead was down to two strokes.

There's something supremely satisfying about watching a smug son of a bitch like Danny Master get his comeuppance. This phenomenally talented jerk-off had cruised through life with a swing like Freddie Couples, Brad Pitt's looks, and more good fortune than a Chinese cookie factory. He lived a gilded life, with no appreciation for how good he had it, and I hated him for it. While everyone else had to work for every single stroke, he strolled the fairways at his leisure, his ability to make shots innate, the act effortless, every swing seemingly guided by an invisible hand. He putted like the hole was a magnet and the ball was made of metal.

But today was different. Today Danny Master looked human. I was cruising now, and he could feel it. I kept my eye on the leaderboard, and I could see the rest of the field was struggling, the course living up to its reputation for chewing up and spitting out even the hardiest of professionals. The greens were firm and fast, the hole positions hellish, and the sand traps felt like the trenches of World War One, leaving the only option to stand below the lip, lob a grenade, and pray.

One by one, the other golfers were falling apart. Lleyton Vanderfinch flamed out on thirteen, hitting his ball into the ocean three times in a row and falling completely off the leaderboard, while steady-as-a-rock Pete Fox was racking up enough bogeys to melt even his icy composure. Buong Ho Park was out there hacking away, but had no more luck trying to crack this course than the others, fading from contention with every stroke. Only one man could keep up with me that day, Danny Master, and he hung onto his lead like he was gripping the window ledge of a tall building.

Grateful Ted was in sync with me every step of the way, reading the greens like a blind pastor with a braille bible, his very soul at one with the course. I don't know if he was receiving messages directly from Mother Earth, the ghost of Jerry Garcia, or if he was my spirit guide leading me on a path to glory. I sublimated all conscious thought, listened to what he said, and simply swung my clubs. The ball was popping cleanly off my irons on the fairways, landing softly on even the fastest greens, and flying far clear of the bunkers. The trees wanted nothing to do with me, and the rough couldn't bury my ball deep enough to stymie the march I was on.

The gallery following us swelled as the day went on, and it became clear it was a two-man contest. Dimple-heads converged from all over the course to get a glimpse of the action. I was climbing up the leaderboard and breathing down Danny Master's neck. I slashed another stroke off my score on eight, and when we came to the turn on nine, I looked up at the grandstand and there, in the box seats, was Kitty.

I came crashing back to earth. The reality of my situation off the course had intruded on my fantasy round and burst the surreal bubble I was living in on the course. The sudden realization that I was in deep, deep trouble once this was all over hit me like a bus. What did it matter if I won the tournament if I was going to celebrate my victory in prison? What was the point of playing at all if my life was essentially over?

I watched as Kitty got in her Ferrari-powered golf cart and drove off toward the clubhouse, and for all the world I wanted nothing more than to get into the seat next to her and just drive off into the sunset. To hell with everything else. Maybe none of this was worth it: the PGA, La Siesta, Don Osborne's murder. Maybe none of it made any difference at all. I could just find some tiny town somewhere in the middle of nowhere, become a club pro, and live a leisurely life.

But then I heard my name crackling through the PA system once more.

"Now teeing off on hole number ten, Francis Duffy McDermott."

A chill went through me. I looked up at the leaderboard and saw my name sitting one spot from the top, and I knew I couldn't stop now, couldn't stop ever. I had to finish what I started. I had to win the tournament, solve this murder, or both.

I held steady for the next seven holes, matching Danny Master par for par, so that by the time we were through seventeen holes we were dead even. This was it. I was so close to winning that trophy I was already polishing it in my mind. Only one more hole to go.

●————————————●

"Ooh, popsicles."

We had just arrived on the tee at eighteen. If I could shave one more stroke off my score I could win one of the most renowned tournaments on the PGA Tour and change my life forever.

And my caddie wanted a popsicle.

"Are you serious, Ted? You want a popsicle?" I couldn't believe it. "*Now?*"

"I haven't eaten all day, boss. And there's a TV timeout anyway until they get back from commercial."

"I'm about to tee off on eighteen!"

"Not for a few minutes. Please? It's just right there."

I could see the concession stand just over on the other side of the cart path, and I really didn't have the patience to argue with him about it.

"All right fine. But make it quick."

"Um," he stood there for a moment.

"What now?"

"Well, it's just that, I don't have any money and, well, you owe me twenty bucks from the set list earlier."

I sighed, dug out twenty bucks, and he hurried off.

The tournament marshal had us just standing around and waiting, so I pulled out my phone to distract myself. I had learned over the last few days that I play better when I'm distracted, so I decided to take my mind off the magnitude of the hole I was about to play and check up on Ted's Grateful Dead parlor trick. Who knows, maybe he was full of shit. Could anybody really have all those set lists just living in their head?

I called up setlist.fm on my phone and ran a check, and sure enough, there it was, June 17, 1972, they played the Hollywood Bowl, opening with "Promised Land" just like he'd said.

I scrolled down to the bottom, and sure enough, the last song was a reprise of Buddy Holly's "Not Fade Away."

Then, just below the set list, was an asterisk.

*Final show with Ron "Pigpen" McKernan before his passing on 8 March 1973.*

Something jogged in my memory. Ron McKernan? Wasn't that the fake name given at the pawn shop?

A flash went through me. I looked over at Grateful Ted, who was calmly waiting in line for his popsicle.

I suddenly had an idea.

Still on setlist.fm I searched September 18, 1987, and up popped the set list from the Grateful Dead's show that night. When I saw the venue my heart sank.

Madison Square Garden, New York City.

Grateful Ted was in New York City on the night of Ethan Schaefer's murder? That had to be a coincidence, right?

I looked again at Grateful Ted, but this time I focused on his long white hair, halfway down his ass and plenty long enough to put in a ponytail. I'd never really considered that before. What's more, as my caddie for the tournament, he would have had knowledge of the grounds and access to places others wouldn't. We'd already played the qualifier on Monday, giving him plenty of time to scope the place out.

I didn't like where this was leading me, but I had to follow the thread. I thought back to the pawn shop. What else had they given me besides the name Ron McKernan? Then it hit me. The coin collection on the counter had coins from all over the world. One of them was a weird-looking coin with a wavy edge that looked just like the coin Grateful Ted had marked my ball with on Thursday. I decided to Google the word *dong*.

*BIG MISTAKE.*

However, after quickly scrolling past a series of adult websites, I came upon a Wikipedia page for dong and read the description: *A Vietnamese coin that came into usage after the end of the Vietnam War.*

Vietnam? Had Grateful Ted been in Vietnam? He'd never said anything about it. Thinking back, he did mention that he wasn't around for that Grateful Dead show at Princeton University in 1971.

But that didn't mean . . . It's just . . . there was no way I was going to believe it.

Grateful Ted came back, happily noshing on a strawberry popsicle. It made me think of the popsicle smudge on my three wood the day before, a splotch of sticky sugary gunk would be a great way to lift a fingerprint.

But no, it couldn't be. I must have been losing my mind. I was seeing things that weren't there. There was no way my caddie could possibly . . .

The tournament marshal suddenly signaled for quiet. It was time to tee off.

I tried to put the thought out of my mind. I had one more hole to play. One more goddamn hole. My life, my career, my future, all came down to this one hole.

Besides, it was impossible, I convinced myself. What I was thinking?

I bared down on my driver and struck the ball cleanly, hitting a solid shot down the center of the fairway. The driver Grateful Ted had given me as a replacement after I hastily snapped mine in anger yesterday was a finely tuned instrument, and was quickly becoming my favorite club in the bag. Danny Master followed with a strong drive of his own, giving everyone one last look at his perfect swing, besting me by twenty yards or so but finding the rough.

As we walked up the eighteenth fairway at the La Siesta Country Club, I could feel the surge of energy coming off the fans. It was a sensation I knew I'd never forget. The roar from the crowd washed over me like an ocean wave. It was like a powerful aphrodisiac, pulling me inextricably toward my fate.

We both took one more shot to get onto the green, my ball landing softly on the lip of the green and getting a bit of help from the downward slope to roll within ten feet of the hole. The crowd roared its approval. Danny Master chopped an eight iron out of the rough to land on the back fringe of the green and followed roughly the same line, his ball stopping about ten feet short of mine.

When we arrived on the green at eighteen, the crowd surrounding us appeared endless. It seemed like every man, woman and child in La Siesta wanted to see us putt. Even the seagulls hovering overhead were waiting to see how this played out.

In the stands, I could see the Racquette Brothers hoisting beers with Mr. Lo, the atmosphere festive, everyone laughing and drinking and, no doubt, betting on the outcome. It made me smile to see so many people happy. *This is what it's all about*, I thought to myself. The fans. This *is* entertainment, after all. Every weekend, the PGA puts on a golf show, and no matter who wins or who comes in last place, the fans always win. Even though I desperately wanted to win, I was happy in this moment that no matter the outcome, I had done the job of a professional golfer. I had given the fans one hell of a show. It was time to close it out.

Lining the far edge of the green was Chief Garrett and a coterie of La Siesta's finest, including Lopez, who was alone among the bunch rooting for me, at least judging from the scowl etched across the chief's face.

I scanned the grandstand for Kitty and was disappointed to not see her, but then I spotted her in a roped-off VIP section just off the green, her Ferrari-powered golf cart parked on the cart path behind her. She saw me and blew me a kiss, then turned to the person next to her, who, much to my great chagrin, was none other than John Stamos.

*John Stamos?!* Are you kidding me? I've got to make this putt with everyone in the world watching, *plus John Fucking Stamos*? It was my nightmare come true. Talk about pressure. And also . . . *was he hitting on her?*

I tried to put it all out of my head and concentrate on my putt.

Danny Master's ball was away, so I asked Grateful Ted to mark my ball.

He walked over, picked up my ball, and replaced it with a ball marker. A glint of sunlight hit the edge of the tiny object, a small brass disk with a serrated edge, and I suddenly realized what it was: the gear from a sprinkler head, the same type as the one I'd found in the sniper's roost. When I saw the marker, my heart sank and my brain turned itself off.

"OH, SHIT!" I yelped.

There was a collective gasp from the crowd.

Before I realized I'd even said it, the referee Charlie Winer raised his hand and flagged my infraction.

"Curse word!"

*Huh?* I looked up, stunned. Everyone was silent, staring at me, a collective "*What the hell*" on everyone's face.

I looked over at Kitty but unfortunately made eye contact with John Stamos instead, who looked horrified, as if he'd just seen a dirty movie starring the Olsen twins. I saw him mouth the question on everyone's mind.

*"Why?"*

Why had I done that?

Then I looked over at Grateful Ted. He knew. The look in his eyes told me he knew I'd finally figured it out.

"Duffer McDermott you are hereby disqualified from the La Siesta Open!" shouted the referee.

And just like that, it was all over. I was out of the tournament, out of the money, and out of luck. My dream of earning a PGA Tour card was as dead as Don Osborne. And to top it all off, my caddie was the goddamn killer.

The crowd around me was going nuts, exploding, losing their minds at the inexplicable event they'd just witnessed, a man throwing away a half-million-dollar purse by saying a bad word. It was a pitch-black nightmare playing out in the bright Southern California sunshine.

The tournament marshal finally got the crowd under control long enough for Danny to tap in his putt to make his win official.

But I didn't have time to dwell on the horror. I knew what I had to do. I may not have been an active-duty officer anymore, but I still had a duty to justice.

I turned back to the hole where Grateful Ted stood holding the flagstick.

"Shall we take a ride downtown, Ted?" I asked gently.

He looked up at me, and instead of guilt or regret, I was surprised to see a smile on his face, almost as if he knew all along I'd get him eventually.

"What gave me away?"

"Your old pal Pigpen."

He dropped the flagstick and waded through the surging crowd toward me. I was glad he seemed to be coming quietly, until he suddenly wasn't. As he got over to where I was standing on the far edge of the green, he reached out his hand, and I thought he was going to shake my hand, but instead he sidestepped me and yanked a nine iron out my bag.

Suddenly, Grateful Ted made a break for it, bolting toward Kitty's nearby golf cart. He cleared a path through the crowd by swinging my nine iron at anyone who came near, and jumped behind the wheel of the souped-up golf cart.

He pushed the launch button and a look of surprise flashed in his eyes as the powerful engine roared to life, the lion hiding under the hood waking from its slumber. He stomped on the gas, and the cart flew off down the eighteenth fairway leaving a trail of skid marks in the grass.

"You've got to go after him!" yelled Kitty.

But I knew it was too late. That engine was too fast. I'd never catch him. There was only one thing to do.

I grabbed my driver.

"Clear a path!" I yelled as I stuck a tee into the turf and balanced a ball on top.

Grateful Ted was about a hundred and fifty yards ahead of me and moving away fast. I had to pray that all my practice trying to hit a moving target would pay off.

I lined up my drive and swung. The ball shot off the tee like a rope, straight on target. Grateful Ted never knew what hit him.

But it wasn't the ball.

Oh, the ball found its target all right, the tailpipe of that Ferrari engine. With the exhaust plugged up the engine seized and the cart instantly came to a dead stop. Grateful Ted, however, continued on his current trajectory, as the laws of physics insist, and went flying over the hood of the cart, landing in a sand trap with a thud.

A cheer went up from the crowd. They had no idea what they had just witnessed, but they loved it.

Lopez ran down the fairway and cuffed Grateful Ted in the sand trap where he lay.

I walked down the fairway to where Lopez had Grateful Ted in cuffs.

By the time Chief Garrett had waddled his way down the fairway to the sand trap, Grateful Ted knew he was beaten and was ready to confess.

"Here's your murderer, Chief," I said, holding Grateful Ted by the elbow. "He's also the person who planted my prints on the rifle and tipped you off. He'll clear my name, won't you, Ted?"

"It's true. I killed them," he spat. "But they had it coming!"

The chief was furious, not only that I'd solved the murders and not him, but mostly I think he was livid that he wouldn't get to see me rot in prison.

"How can you be sure?" he stammered. "This man's clearly

deranged, he could be making the whole thing up," he protested, grasping at straws.

"Let me ask you, Chief, what phone number did the anonymous tip come from?" I asked.

"Um, I don't know. It was a 310 number, I don't know it offhand."

I took out my phone and showed him the text I had received setting up the meeting at the wildlife sanctuary, supposedly sent from Bill Dwyer.

"Was it this?"

He reluctantly nodded. "That looks like it."

"These both came from you, didn't they, Ted? You arranged the meeting between Bill and I. Then you shot him in the head, just like you shot Don Osborne, and if my theory holds, Ethan Schaefer back in New York City. Then you tried to pin the murders on me by planting my prints on the gun, which you got from the sticky popsicle gunk you left on my grip."

The sinister smile on Grateful Ted's face confirmed it. He was clearly proud of himself.

Suddenly, he looked like a different person, or maybe I just saw him in a whole new way. He wasn't the peaceful, mystical caddie, but an angry and bitter man, broken by a war he didn't start, but for him would never end.

"It's true. I did them all."

The chief stormed off in a huff, muttering something about needing French fries.

"Mind if I bring him in, for old times' sake?" I asked Lopez.

"Sure, just don't let him go like you did the last time," he said with a smile.

It was just then that it occurred to me this was all my fault. If I had just given Grateful Ted a ride out of town like I was supposed to when he first showed up, none of this would have ever happened.

*Whoops.*

## 32

I put Grateful Ted in the back of my Crown Vic and drove him to the station. Despite all that he had done, I wanted to say goodbye.

"When I found you that first day wandering around town, you didn't just drift in here by accident, did you?" I asked, eager to finally get the truth. "You came looking for Don."

"When you picked me up for vagrancy, I thought the jig was up, but then . . ."

"But then I let you go."

I winced just thinking about it. My desire to win at golf had once again outweighed my better judgment and gotten me in trouble. Shit, if you think about it, my love of golf got two people killed and endangered a third. But I preferred not to think about it that way. Grateful Ted was clearly a disturbed individual. He would have probably found a way to kill them anyway, right?

*Right?*

"Why'd you do it, Ted?

"They left me there! They knew I was still out there and they left me there to rot!"

"Left you where? Vietnam?"

"Five long years, man. Five years in the jungle, and they did nothing."

"You were a POW? I'm sorry to hear that, old friend," I said, the compassion in my voice genuine. "How did it happen?"

"We were out in the shit. I was on point, the farthest out in the group, scouting for VC when we got ambushed. Suddenly I was surrounded, and just as quickly, the rest of the Rangers were gone. They just split. Never even looked back."

"So you were captured?"

He nodded. "They got me and Schaefer."

"But I thought Ethan Schaefer got released after two years. Why were you in for five?"

"Because those stinking bastards left me there! The VC took Ethan to a different camp, and after two years, a rescue delegation from the Rangers came back for him. But they just left me where I was. Ethan knew I was there and he did nothing. That's the worst of all. He and I were in the same position, but even when he got his freedom, he never came back for me. He just saved his own skin and went the hell home. I spent another three years in a cage because he was too selfish to help me like the others had helped him. It was like a double betrayal."

I could feel the bitterness in his words, the harsh feelings that could never be quashed.

"The sons of bitches got what they deserved," he muttered, finally trailing off.

And that's when I finally saw it. The rage that had been bubbling just below the surface for years. It was there in his eyes. Where before I had only ever registered a blank stare, now I saw a burning hot flame of anger, a raging desire to kill, a need for revenge, for blood. He wasn't the zen creature I had known, but a calculating ball of anger bent on destroying those who'd hurt him.

Suddenly it all made sense. This didn't have anything to do with money, or Kitty, or the country club. This was about revenge.

"So when you eventually got out, you came back to the States and took your revenge."

"It took me a while, but I got the bastards. One thing the Viet Cong taught me was victory doesn't always have to be quick. If you can wait out your enemy, you can achieve your goals."

"You had a long time to think about it. It must have been hell."

"You'll never understand that kind of pain, man. Not in this lifetime. Five years in a cage. The only contact I had with the outside world came through a radio the guards had in their lookout tower. It only got one station, a pirate radio broadcast out of Lao Cai run by an army vet named Cosmic Charlie that played nothing but Grateful Dead concert bootlegs twenty-four hours a day."

"So that's where you picked it up? Memorizing all the set lists?"

"It was all I had, man. That music kept me alive in the jungle. I had nothing else but a bowl of rice a day to look forward to. Everyday he'd play a different show from a different town back home, and wherever they were that day, that's where I went in my mind. If they were in Buffalo, New York, I went with them, and if they played the Fillmore West in San Francisco, I saw myself there. Through those bootlegs and the music of Grateful Dead, I travelled around America without ever leaving the jungle. Even though my body was trapped in a cage, in my mind I was back home at a Dead show with a beer in my hand, a joint in my mouth, and a sexy hippie chick dancing by my side."

He was far away now, his mind drifting back through the hazy memories, both real and imagined.

"It was magical. Like teleportation. And not only could I travel America with them, but I could also travel back through time, so if it was listening to a show from July of 1966, then I was transported back to a hot summer day in 1966 with them, back to a time before I ever even thought about the army, or war, or . . . hell." He trailed off, the haunted look returning to his face.

"But you eventually did get rescued. That must have offered some solace."

"When I finally got free and came back to the states, I went on tour and followed the Dead everywhere they went."

"Even to New York City. Like you did on the night of September eighteenth, 1987?"

"The night of the levitating Jerry!" He beamed, looking up at me.

"The night of the levitating Jerry. Which also happens to be the night Ethan Schaefer was mysteriously shot, some say by a trained sniper from the building across the street."

"A guy'd have to be a hell of a sniper to make that shot," he said with more than a hint of pride.

"He sure would. Ethan Schaefer was shot around dusk, plenty of time to get to Madison Square Garden and see a show.

"And what a show that was," he said, not bothering to deny anything.

"So. Ted, if you were bent on getting revenge on the soldiers who left you behind in Vietnam, why take so long to come after Don and Bill?"

"I hadn't planned on getting revenge on anyone. Killing Ethan was just a fluke. I had long since worked out my rage and found peace following the Grateful Dead around on tour, or so I thought. But then I was in New York for the Madison Square Garden shows and I happened to see him walk past the school bus I was living in. All of a sudden all my rage came flooding back. This was the *motherfucker* who left me there. He was the reason I was locked in a cage in the jungle for three more years than necessary. I was so overwhelmed, I didn't know what to do. I was boiling inside, so I jumped out of the bus and went after him. I followed him to some fancy apartment building, and as he was walking in, he said something to the doorman about "there's some boxes being delivered, send those up to the penthouse," and so I figured that's where he lived. Then, I looked across the street and saw the building under construction and suddenly, bingo, I had an idea."

"Where'd you get the gun?"

"I already had it. I travelled with it everywhere I went."

"You followed the Grateful Dead on tour with a sniper rifle?"

"I travel everywhere with it. Ever since the war."

"Where did you keep it? I mean, you said you were living on a school bus."

"In my golf bag, of course. When you're living on a bus with a bunch of hippies, nobody's going to bother with your golf clubs. I still played, and I caddied everywhere we went, everywhere the band went. It's how I made money. When the others were selling psychedelic mushrooms and tie-dye t-shirts in the parking lot, I would go to the local golf course and make some quick bread as a caddie. Everybody's got to have a gig on tour. Some sell grilled cheese. I'm a looper."

"So you committed a murder and then went back to Madison Square Garden and took in a show?"

"Well, *shit*," he laughed, "*there was no reason to miss the show, man!*" he said, shaking his head as if I were the crazy one for suggesting it.

Somehow I could understand it. He was obsessed with the Grateful Dead like I was obsessed with golf. We both followed our obsession around the country trying to get something from it. Peace. Glory. Revenge. Whatever it is we're chasing from moment to moment.

"And so after that you just went back on tour?"

"Until Jerry died, then I went back to being a looper full-time. I decided to travel the country and caddie at all the best courses—"

"That led you to La Siesta," I finished the thought for him.

He looked at me and smiled. "It really is a spectacular course."

"When did you spot Don?" I asked.

"Oh, you couldn't miss Don. He was the biggest asshole in town!"

"You sure didn't miss him at the opening night gala."

He looked pleased, like a boy with a trophy. "No, I sure didn't," he said.

"And you pulled me into this. Why?"

"You pulled yourself in. I didn't know you were going to have the world's worst alibi, and I didn't put you in that sand trap with Don's wife. But once you were set up anyway, I just played it as it lay."

I couldn't argue with his logic. As usual, I had done as much damage to myself as anyone else. I let my obsession get the better of me, just like Grateful Ted. I drove him through the plush, manicured streets of the world's wealthiest town one last time, a final look at freedom before he went back into a cage for the rest of his life. It seems unfair, so much pain and misery heaped on one man, but then life is cruel. If you don't agree, you've never tried to land a ball on the thirteenth green at La Siesta.

# MONDAY

# 33

On Monday morning I sat in my Crown Vic outside the church where Don Osborne's funeral was being held, watching the few mourners file in through the carved marble portico that had been donated by Don himself. It was telling that, for all his wealth and power, for all the people who'd lined up daily to kiss his ring at the La Siesta Country Club, when it came down to it, Don Osborne had very few true friends. I guess that's what happens when you're an asshole.

As the last of the mourners trickled in, a long black limousine pulled up to the curb, and out stepped Kitty, wearing a tight black dress and a lace veil covering her face. I was thankful I couldn't see those green eyes, unsure what my reaction would have been if I was exposed to her full radiant beauty one more time. My whole body was filled with regret, not for what I had done with another man's wife, but for what could have been. Kitty had nothing to do with Don's murder, and we could have been happy together if things had gone differently, but my actions had driven us apart, and the damage was done. I was resigned to add it to a long list of missed opportunities, but then another figure, dressed in a black Armani suit emerged from the back of the limo. John Stamos.

*Are you kidding me?!*

Well, now I was just pissed. He took her hand and escorted her into the church, and I watched the credits roll on our life together.

I let out a sigh and went back to the morning paper that sat on my lap. The news of Don's death had finally leaked to the press, conveniently after the end of the tournament, and the headline read DON OSBORNE DEAD in bold black letters, with the sub-headline underneath: "La Siesta Millionaire Murdered in Cold Blood."

Alongside the story was a picture of Grateful Ted, which identified him as Theodore Wilson, ex-Army Ranger turned professional golf caddie. The face that had been hidden behind the crease in Don's photo now looked out at me in stark black and white, older but not much wiser than the kid who'd been shipped off to war fifty years earlier. He looked weary, and I could only hope that the pain and anger that had tormented him throughout his adult life was at an end. I had genuine affection for Grateful Ted, despite what he had done, and I'd always be grateful. He'd taught me that to win I need to learn to get out of my head, to find a tiny bit of distraction to clear my thoughts and allow my body to do what I'd been training it to do my whole life: play golf.

Under the fold was a story about the Racquette brothers being charged with grand theft, Katherine Osborne having managed to connect them to the cache of stolen AR-15 sniper rifles that had gone missing from an OSS storage warehouse. Gordo and Barrie had been the ones responsible for Katherine Osborne's kidnapping, stashing her on Bill Dwyer's half-sunken old boat in the hopes that they could convince her to stay quiet about what she knew. Unfortunately for them, she'd woken up and swum to shore while they were gone. When asked why they hadn't simply killed her to keep her quiet, Barrie was indignant.

"We may be violent criminals, but we don't just go around shooting people, eh? We're not *American*."

There was a photo of them being led to jail in handcuffs along with George Graft, who'd been working with the brothers to pay off gambling debts going back several years. I was relieved I wouldn't have to worry about paying back the money I owed them, at least not until they got out in a few years.

After all was said and done, I found myself still a mere mortal. I had blown my shot at a PGA Tour card, and with it my dream of a brand-new life as a professional golfer. For the first time in forever, I had nothing to do. The Southern California sun was shining down, the ocean sparkling like the jewels inside the window of Tiffany's, and the beautiful people of La Siesta were out and about enjoying their life of pampered privilege, so I decided to join them.

I drove to the Pitch N' Putt; picked up my faithful companion, Nicklaus, and took him out for a long walk at the wildlife sanctuary. It was truly the most beautiful spot in all of La Siesta, a place that couldn't be bought or sold, a place for everyone to enjoy, whether they were filthy rich or dirt poor.

For the moment, it felt like my life was over. I was starting from scratch, walking up to the first tee on a whole new course.

But I would be back. I would never give up on my dream of playing in the PGA. I had proven, at least to myself, that I could play with the big boys. No matter what horrible things happened to me in this life, I knew one thing would always be there for me: golf.

But I was going to need a new caddie.

# Acknowledgments

My sincere thanks to the many people who contributed to the creation of this book; Abigail Lechthaler, Josh Danson, Melanie Haynes, Derek Pratt, Molly Schmenke, Peter Kalmbach, Christopher Peter, William Peter, Rachel Kowal, Rafael Andres, Jenny Kelly, and Jesse Hassenger. Special thanks to Ward Carey, Elizabeth Doyle Carey, and Carrie Doyle for their invaluable advice.

And a very special thanks to Sue Carpenter, without whom this book would not exist.

**CORNELIUS PETER** is a comedian, actor and writer based in Los Angeles. His television credits include *Silicon Valley, How I Met Your Mother, Atypical,* and *Fresh Off the Boat. The Big Snooze* is his first novel.

Made in United States
North Haven, CT
21 June 2022

20469264R00211